D0160503

THE BUTTERFLY CLUES

THE
BUTTERFLY
CLUES

KATE
ELLISON

EGMONT
NEW YORK
USA

This story takes place in Cleveland, but its neighborhoods, landmarks, and characters are entirely of the author's own invention.

EGMONT

We bring stories to life

First published by Egmont USA, 2012
443 Park Avenue South, Suite 806
New York, NY 10016

1 3 5 7 9 8 6 4 2

www.egmontusa.com

Library of Congress Cataloging-in-Publication Data

Ellison, Kate.
The butterfly clues / Kate Ellison.
p. cm.
Summary: Having experienced compulsive behavior all her life, Lo's
symptoms are getting her into trouble when she witnesses a murder
while wandering dangerous quarters of Cleveland, Ohio, collecting
things that do not belong to her, obsessing about her brother's death.
ISBN 978-1-60684-263-8 (hardcover) — ISBN 978-1-60684-268-3 (ebook)
[1. Obsessive-compulsive disorder—Fiction. 2. Emotional problems—Fiction.
3. Death—Fiction. 4. Murder—Fiction. 5. Cleveland (Ohio)—Fiction.
6. Mystery and detective stories.] I. Title.
PZ7.E476485But 2012
[Fic]—dc23
2011024549

Printed in the United States of America

CPSIA tracking label information:
Printed in December 2011 at Berryville Graphics, Berryville, Virginia

For Pauly: an apology—
for all those years
I messed up your
baseball hats.

CHAPTER 1

I spot her out of the corner of my eye and freeze. It always happens like this.

My body goes tingly.

Blood thrums in my ears: a low buzz like a faraway swarm of insects, and every cell in my body screams: *save her save her save her.*

There's nothing I can do but obey.

She is perched on top of a tacky altar on the porch of an old house: a marble angel nestled among an otherwise decaying tangle of plastic creatures. Three smooth-shelled blue birds, three squirrels, three raccoons.

Nine altogether—a perfect number.

The cold air feels thick and heavy, like the Pendleton blankets Dad used to bring back from business trips. It smells like them, too—a good wool smell.

I peer through the window, checking for signs of life inside the house. It looks clear from where I stand. Just my own face reflected in the dusty glass—huge gray-green eyes, flat dark hair—distorted by the warped windowpane, unfamiliar.

I look around and, seeing no one, reach for the angel. The seconds between the reaching and the holding are fast and warm; they vibrate like tiny earthquakes. The whole world falls away, goes quiet, as I move closer, and closer, and closer. Inches. Centimeters. Millimeters. The moment we finally touch is slow, holy, thunderous, the single moment when everything makes sense. The angel safely in my possession, I sprint away toward the part of the sky where the sun has already begun to set, straight into the deep blue, the new weight in my vest pocket jostling with each step.

She's mine now. And I'm hers. And we are each other's.

*   *   *   *

A few houses up the block, I see something change through the panes of a darkened window: a half-stained curtain, settling like it's just been lifted and then quickly dropped.

I clutch at the figurine in my jacket. Has someone seen me?

Now I hear footsteps down the block, and something *feels* different—like the air behind my back is vibrating. Someone is close to me, watching. I can tell.

I turn to confront the footsteps, hands curled into fists, but it's nothing. No one's there. I can hear the angel's thoughts inside my pocket. *You're safe, Lo.*

But this street—the whole neighborhood—is giving me the

creeps. The strange, knotty feeling is spreading into my fingers. I'm not even sure exactly where I am. After school, I've been picking bus lines at random, finding new places to explore.

Mostly I go to other parts of the suburbs, find the high school or the baseball hat store at the mall or a restaurant my brother might have liked. Usually, I end up at some divey pizza place: gaunt, stringy-haired teenagers hanging out of every booth. I order a Coke, maybe, and then I just sit there, listening, waiting for them to mention his name: Oren.

They never have. Not yet.

Lately, though, I've been going farther. I've been finding the city bus lines, getting off at the third stop in, or the ninth, or the twelfth, because these are the numbers that mean I will be safe. These are the numbers that make things right. These are the numbers that will lead me closer to him, to where he's been, to where parts of him might still exist, somehow.

And, today, now, just what I wanted: a sad, strange part of Cleveland, a part of the city I've never seen before.

An abandoned playground sits in the center of the block. Two swings dangle from long metal chains; one of them moves back and forth, just slightly, like someone has recently been swinging on it. But it's got to be nearing eight o'clock on a Thursday night: too late and too cold for playing outside. The gnarled faces of the hobbyhorses, planted jaggedly into the concrete, stare back at me with cold, rusted eyes.

I have a sudden memory: I am on a swing. My brother, Oren, is behind me, pushing me higher, too high. I am laughing—and screaming, too, the full-throat, kid kind of scream, because the sky was getting so close—I'd never been that close to the sky before.

Now, watching the empty swing set, the knotty feeling spreads into my throat.

I stuff my hands back in my pockets and quickly cross the road.

I'm nearing the bus stop—I know it isn't far, it can't be. But as I round another corner onto Lourraine Street, I suddenly hear a *whoop-whoop* sound. Sirens, drawing closer. My stomach flips. Someone must have seen me take the marble angel. I duck into the alleyway beside an ugly yellow house, noticing that the concrete front lawn and driveway are covered in painted daisies as I try to flatten myself into the shadows. Across the street, a black sedan hunkers, engine buzzing and whirring. *Is someone inside?*

There's a window set into the wall just above me, and I'm filled with an almost insuppressible urge to look through it. *Tap tap tap tap tap tap tap tap tap:* nine times, twice—right hand on right thigh, then left on left.

The sirens keep wailing, even closer now.

As I'm shifting in the darkness, I think I hear a shout, followed by a heavy *thump*. Almost immediately, I'm not sure whether I've only imagined it. My brain is tricky sometimes.

Left hand on right thigh. Nine times before I'm allowed to look.

BANG.

Loud, deafening chaos: shattering glass, exploding outward like water from a burst pipe. My body curls itself into a ball. I hit the pavement, skinning my knees, pressing my head between my thighs. A heavy *thump thump thump* pulses through my body; a whooshing feeling; skin on fire.

I look up. In the wall right across from me, just a few feet away, something has lodged itself into the brick that wasn't there before.

I squint.

Bullet.

*   *   *   *

The word flutters through my head. A bullet. Which means gun. Which means—shit oh shit holy shit—I almost just *died.*

I sink back against the side of the house, choking. Panting. My right hand goes instinctively into my vest pocket, gripping the angel. My left hand is bleeding. I hadn't even noticed. I put it to my mouth, trying to soothe it. A tiny shard of glass comes out and cuts my tongue. I spit the glass onto the pavement. Blood in my mouth, metallic.

I've got to get out of here. I have to *move.*

BANG. A second time. My legs lift me from the glass-covered alleyway and torpedo me through the streets. I run breathless, panicked. The darkness is thickening around me and most of the streetlamps are cracked and lightless. I almost trip on a homeless man with gray, clouded-over eyes, swaying and moaning and muttering something incoherent to me as I pass; I don't stop or turn or pause. I have to keep running. I can still hear sirens somewhere, behind me now. There are tears streaking my face, and I guess they must be mine.

When I just can't run any farther, I crouch behind a group of trash cans to catch my breath. Four trash cans. Two more would make them six, a better, cleaner number. Four looks cold; four looks incomplete. Four means no good. The air smells like frost and rotting fish. My cut hand throbs. It suddenly strikes me that whoever fired that shot might have seen me, peering into the window and then bolting madly away. . . .

And then I hear it: a dragging sound, very close. He's here. He's come for me.

I tap the trash can softly nine times with my left foot. Nine times safe. Nine times safe. And then I have to tap six; six times safe. After two nines, there has to be a six. This is the ultimate sequence of protection. I don't know why; it just is. It has been since I was six and convinced there was a monster in my closet. Nine, nine, six meant the monster went away. I slide my wounded hand into my left vest pocket and cup the objects I've been carrying with me—two Micron 005 pens, five bobby pins. Inside my shoe: one slowly disintegrating piece of paper that I never leave home without. And now, in my hand, the angel.

The footsteps stop just beyond the Dumpsters. I can hardly breathe. He's taking his time, screwing with me. I imagine him: a foot-dragger; a tall, lonely man with a gun.

I draw my legs up to my chest, bite my teeth into my knee to keep from screaming. *If anyone out there exists and can hear me— please don't let me die like this.*

Maybe someone *does* hear me, because there's no tall, dragging man with a gun—only a small, thin girl in a coat that looks borrowed from a giant. She's staggering by, hauling a sack of onions. I start blubbering loudly from behind the trash cans. *I'm going to live.* I didn't even know how badly I'd wanted to.

The girl can't be more than eleven or twelve years old, with shiny brown eyes and limp hair. She cocks her head when she notices me, then squishes up her eyebrows and says, "You staying here?" She points to the alleyway behind the trash cans. "Don't worry. I been there. Don't cry. It gets better."

She thinks I'm a runaway. "No, I—I'm not sleeping here; I'm trying to get back to Lakewood." I can barely get out words. I'm still shaking.

The little girl puts the onions down, moves her limp hair to the other shoulder. "Oh, Lakewood." She sniffs at the air, thinks for a moment. "You get robbed, Miss?" She's still assessing me with those shining eyes. Her question takes me by surprise.

I just shake my head, trying to dab my face with my sleeve.

"So, then," she says, shifting her weight, a little sassy now, "why *are* you crying?"

"I'm not," I say. I try to swallow back my sniffling. "Do you . . . do you know how I can get home from here?"

The girl looks me over. I count eight buttons on her coat; eight makes me feel weird, makes my skin prickle. Two fours. Two less than ten. Off-kilter. Dirty. The year I turned eight I wouldn't let Mom put eight candles on the birthday cake. Eight candles would have made it inedible.

"There's a bus a few blocks down, on East 117th," she finally says. "You can walk with me. I'm going that way anyway."

We walk together the few blocks to the bus. I keep looking

over my shoulder, expecting someone to leap out at us. Expecting more bullets, more shattering glass.

The little girl tells me she helps out in her mom's diner, that's why she has the onions, except the mom isn't her real mom because she ran away from home when she was nine. I tell her I'm adopted and have never met my real family but have been searching for them for years, everywhere and anywhere I can, in dark alleyways and behind trash cans. I tell her I'll search for them forever if I have to.

I don't know why I lie; my words rush out, uncontrollable. And after all, who knows? Maybe it's true. Maybe there's an entirely new, healthy family waiting for me somewhere, waiting to fold me up in their arms and make things all right again. Maybe my other-brother version of Oren's there, too—waiting.

The little girl tells me good luck, and I say thank you too many times. I wait for the 96 Line alone, watching her struggle away, hauling her onions one-handed through the dark.

The bus arrives after a few long, shaky minutes. I tap my hand against my thigh three times before entering, utter, "Banana," under my breath so that I can enter, so that it's all right.

In third grade, during the six-month period we lived in Kankakee, Illinois—our house a concrete box between rows of neck-high cornstalks—Shelby-Michelle Packer noticed me tapping patterns into each leg when I was called on to give an answer to a math question. I couldn't answer until I'd tapped the right number of times (that day it was six, on each side, but the answer still wouldn't come to me.) I felt everyone's eyes on me as Shelby announced, to the whole class, "Lo, you're *bananas*."

As soon as she said the word, out of nowhere, the answer arrived; it was *fourteen ducks*. I don't remember the question, but *banana* was a sign; it made things right.

The bus is almost empty. I finally exhale. My face hovers in the bus window: puffy eyes, ghost-pale skin. I look away. I suck some more on the dark gash in my palm and newly dried blood flakes onto my lips. There's a woman with stringy blondish hair in back holding a howling baby. She's staring out the window, not trying to soothe the kid at all. The baby howls as I watch the streets change outside my window, the world of small dark houses and cracked streets becoming the world of planned, tree-lined cul-de-sacs and stone houses and lots of glowing streetlamps. I pull the cord and exit the bus; the baby continues to howl in my head.

*   *   *   *

At home, everything's dark. A low TV murmur comes from my parents' room upstairs. Dad's still at work, I'm sure. Mom doesn't greet me, but I don't expect her to. I pass Oren's bed-room door, closed now forever, and creep upstairs to my attic room undisturbed, surveying everything, sprawled like a wide, warm, glittering lake before me. I think this is the first time I've really breathed all day. I remove the smooth angel figurine from my vest pocket and press her to my cheek.

Stepping across my room, I place her into a small hollow beside a nest of other perfect, smooth, glassy figures—between other marble men and women, and at a safe distance from the stone horses and wolves and bears.

I hum a little—I'm not sure what the song is—finally starting to feel better. The bullet never happened. I pretend that I dreamed it: the sound, the shattering glass. But my hand, still caked in blood, throbs.

I yank my dark hair on top of my head, enter the bathroom to brush my teeth and stare at myself in the mirror for a few seconds, at the smears of dirt and blood on my cheeks and chin. Then I wash my face three times. Finally, I rub cream that smells like oranges into my skin, pushing back my grungy bangs and running my finger along the tiny scar over my left eye. Can't tell which is worse—the scar or the bangs. I push them to the left, and then to the right, and then back again before letting them fall to rest over my forehead. I look like a badly groomed poodle.

Back in my room, I step out of my clothes, throw on a warm, soft T-shirt that reaches halfway to my knees. Oren's old shirt. Then I sigh and fall into bed, finally. Relieved. Clean. Whole. My angel hums with me as we fall together, tumbling into sleep.

But my dreams are full of holes dug deep into the earth, patchy grass, a grave. Oren's grave. Oren's funeral. People in a row, blank faces, everyone silent except for Mom, who is sobbing, while Dad tries to hold her up. The sun disappears. The earth goes sodden beneath our feet. Rain. Rain. Rain. I glance at the top of his casket: the marble angel sits on top. Except now the angel is gone and it's Oren. Oren's green eyes, staring back at me. His tall, lean body. That mole, right at the center of his forehead. He's sitting on top of his own grave, whistling. Suddenly, he says, *I lost my Tigers hat, Lo. Help me find it.* I start backing away, the rain blurring Oren's face. *Lope, I need you,* he says, more urgently now. But now the rain is choking me and I can't see Oren anymore, I can only hear his voice, desperate, fading: *I lost my hat. You've gotta help me, Lo.*

Even after I can no longer see him, his voice echoes, screams through my head: *Lo, I need you. Lo, don't leave me.*

Why did you leave me?

CHAPTER 2

"Rachel Stern and Mikey K. *totally* did it at Sarah's party."

"No *way*. Zach made that up. Are you seriously going to believe Zach?"

"He may be a pothead, but he's totally reliable. They had major full-on sex. Rachel told me *details*."

"Seriously? Like what?"

I put my head in my hands and groan. Ordinarily, overhearing Keri Ram and Laura Peters' whispered gossip might pique my curiosity—a window of insight, cracked open just slightly, to a world of friends and hook-ups that I know nothing about—but, today, it's painful. Unbearable. The whole school day's been this way. Every scrape of a metal chair against the linoleum floors reminds me of that gunshot last night. I'm full of jitters—empty, racing nerves.

I steal the pencil we were given to do more pointless practice SAT exercises, just to feel some kind of relief. I grip it in my good hand throughout class, throughout the rest of the day, hoping for calm. It doesn't help much.

Everything seems even more surreal than it usually does, in every school (besides Carver High) I've ever been to (twelve), in any town I've ever lived in (eleven). Each class designed to prepare us for tests that indicate nothing but how well you memorize useless, pointless facts. Each day a new chance to remember how small you are, how meaningless, how little you matter to most people. Every school a fresh reminder: no one wants to get to know the new kid, especially if the new kid is a weirdo who spends every second of every day trying not to seem like a total spaz in front of her teachers and classmates. Every suppressed sequence of hand-raising, every muted *tap tap tap, banana* is my painful effort to seem normal. And still, it never works.

After last period, I head to my locker—locker ninety-nine, a locker too perfect to leave, despite the fact that it's broken and has never actually *locked*—and shove my AP US history and calculus books inside, on top of a pile of nubby sweaters and scraps of paper. Then I notice a pencil—taped to the inside of the locker door and a note beneath it that reads:

So you won't have to steal one next time —Jeremy.

P.S. Need a study partner?

His cell number's written at the bottom of the note in black ink.

It must be from Jeremy Theroux, the boy in my SAT prep class. He wears the same faded green Neil Young T-shirt and gray skinny jeans almost every day. I don't know much about Jeremy Theroux; only that he is on the track team but seems to hangout more with the band geeks than the jocks. His hair is crazy, wildfire red.

I look around the hallway. Everyone is busy loading and unloading their bags, grabbing their homework, making plans. I didn't realize he had seen me swipe the pencil. I didn't think anyone really saw *anything* I did, barring incidents of incredible embarrassment, like the time I put my shirt on inside-out after gym and walked around with deodorant streaks on my boobs for the rest of the day.

I keep the pencil taped to the locker but peel the note carefully off from beneath it, folding it six times, until it's very small, before sticking it in my pocket. I feel for it every few seconds on my way out of school, pushing through the septic green hallways, dodging a small circle of varsity soccer players. Kevin DiGiulio is pulling off his sweatshirt at his locker; while he wrangles it up over his head, I catch a glimpse of his bare torso as I pass. He's got a dark little patch of hair in the middle of his chest and a thin line of it that snakes below his belly button and into his jeans.

I wonder for a second if Jeremy has chest hair; but then an image of it—a patch, thick and ropey and fire-red, like an external heart—gives me a queasy feeling, and I try to think of a peaceful ocean instead. That's what Mrs. Freed, the guidance counselor, told me to do when I'm feeling overwhelmed in the middle of class or a test, though it sometimes makes things even worse because I'll start to picture terrible things bobbing between the waves, like Oren's body, or just his disembodied head.

Finally, I *tap tap tap, banana*, push through the heavy dark blue exit doors of George Washington Carver High, and gulp in the frozen air. It stings my lungs, but I like it—the thousand tiny, precise needles entering all at once. On my walk home, I feel several more times for the tiny square of Jeremy's note with my fingers, to make sure it hasn't fallen out.

*   *   *   *

Here's the thing: I don't choose to take things. I have to. I've always had to do certain things, since the day I turned seven and began to insist that I wanted to stay six. I didn't know why, but seven felt off, somehow, made me feel like the world was tilting too much to one side. It wasn't so bad at first. Just little things—like the way food looked on my plate, or needing to eat peas before chicken, or needing to put the left shoe on before the right. I started taking little things—a toothbrush or a candy bar from the grocery store, discarded ticket stubs from the movie theater, stickers from the kids at school.

But since Oren disappeared it has gotten worse. A lot worse. Now, when the *urge* comes on, it's like this superhuman force that grips my body and won't let go until I have the thing I've spotted, the thing I need. And it's not the taking or the stealing that I crave, it's the having and the keeping. Forever. With me. Safe.

I figure when you've moved around from town to ugly town your whole life it's only natural to crave beautiful things. When we move, it's always somewhere cracked at the center, somewhere with enough depression and failure for my dad to fix and profit from. In the city consulting business, he says, it's the forgotten cities that need him most: Detroit, Baltimore, Cleveland, where-ugly-ever, USA.

When we moved to Cleveland, it was only supposed to be for

six months, a year tops. But we've been here three years now, and I need my treasures more than I ever have before, just to wake up in the morning. I need to know that beauty exists, to possess it, to surround myself with it, to be encircled by its warmth.

I need it just to breathe, sometimes. Definitely to get through a whole dragging, lonely day of high school.

*   *   *   *

Mom is standing in her bedroom doorway when I get home, barefoot on the beige-carpeted stairs. Her almost-black hair, like mine, hangs limp around her pale face, strands of gray I hadn't noticed before standing out, silver and wild. The large, framed painting on the wall beside her door—ocean, big red sky, inch of dusty shore—reflects muted colors against the pale of her face; the rest of the hallway stretches on, blank, slightly scuffed, to Oren's room. She's wearing blue velour sweatpants, so big on her now-gaunt frame that they fall from her hip bones, and a faded pink tank top with coffee stains skid-marked down its front. Her eyes are half shut, as usual, like she's just sleepwalking. Delivering her a glass of water a few weeks ago, I saw her nightstand drawer open, full of half-empty bottles of pills: Anafranil, Elavil, Paxil, Zoloft, Lunesta, Ambien. I wonder if she even distinguishes between them anymore, or just dumps them all into her palm at once, eating them like popcorn.

"Mom," I say, touching my lips to her cold cheek, "you're up. That's good." She smells like coffee and medicine and, underneath that, something else. Something familiar and

Mom-like—her old lavender soap-smell, maybe—but faint, stale.

"Did you hear about the girl who was killed?" she asks me abruptly. Her lips twitch slightly. "Last night. House on Lourraine Street. East side of the city. She was shot, Lo." Mom leans against the wall. Her eyes are overcast, a wintery mix, freezing; before Oren disappeared they were sunny, clear skies, seventy-five degrees. "Someone just came right in, put a gun to the girl's head." She clicks her tongue, continues in her razor-edged monotone: "All the reporters are saying the crime rate's at a twenty-year high. Drugs they think. Bad things. They say it's getting worse over there."

Lourraine Street—that's where I was yesterday. My heart begins to race; I imagine Mom can hear it thumping away beneath my T-shirt. I zip my gray hoodie up to my chin, just in case, and stuff my cut hand into my pocket, tap against my leg. Nine, nine, six.

"You know the area, Lo?" she presses. "They call it Neverland. The city of lost children. Lots of kids hanging out in abandoned buildings like a bunch of burn-outs." She takes my chin in her hands, eyes blazing. "You don't go there, do you, Penelope? With your friends from school? Do you?" Her breath smells like ciga-rettes. She started smoking them again a few months ago, out of the window in her room.

I pull away from her. She looks very, very old.

"Mom," I say softly, my throat burning, "I don't go to Neverland, okay? I've never even heard of it before."

"Well, good. That's all I wanted to know." And then, just like that, she goes blank again; she retreats into her room and shuts the door.

I have to fight myself from calling out: *By the way, Mom, I'd
actually have to have friends to be able to go anywhere with them.*
She doesn't know anything about my life—that the loneliness is a
constant, that I've learned how to deal with it in my own way, that
I've learned to live without her.

I've learned to live without anyone.

*   *   *   *

It doesn't take long to find the article about the murdered girl
online.

There is a row of pictures spearing the center of the article:
Lourraine Street. The weird yellow house with the daisies. The
murdered girl's house.

My breath catches in my throat; my whole body goes cold. The
noise I heard—the bangs—the bullet. I was right there. Fifteen feet
away. Less maybe. I was there when a girl was shot; the shot that
ended her life, the shot that almost ended my life, too.

I swallow hard.

Jesus. I was *steps* away from a killer. I can't stop replaying
the events in my head—the bangs. The piece of metal wedged in
the wall in front of me, glinting under the streetlamps. I could
have done something. I could have helped. But I didn't.

The girl's name was Sapphire. Just Sapphire; that's all anyone
knew. Nineteen years old and a stripper. She danced at a club
in Neverland called Tens. In every picture she wears thick gray
eye shadow and too much blush. She has angry eyes, and her lips
are a bruised blue-purple color—a lipstick that somehow looks

completely right on her. She looks way older than nineteen—all
that makeup, I guess.

The journalist describes the murder in detail. She was
assaulted, raped, and then shot: carpet soaked in blood, skull cleft,
naked limbs twisted, rearranged. Another stripper, a friend from
Tens, lists things that were taken. Small things. Cheap things. An
old wooden clock, a collection of brass bangles, a silver chain with
a rusted horse pendant, a butterfly figurine, three small paintings
of ravens.

Everyone interviewed is sad but not surprised. So, one more
girl dies, one more drug-addled stripper.

That's just the way it goes.

But it's not enough—not for me. I want more. I need more.

New search: Neverland; Sapphire; murder. Pages of results,
most of them different links to the article I just read in the *Plain
Dealer*. And then, something new, bolded and caps-locked,
catches my attention: B. HORNET'S NEVERLAND CRIME BLOG. My
throat squeezes shut.

Click.

The page loads and it looks like something Martha Stewart
might have designed to advertise a new line of wallpaper: pastel
purples and blues; a border of blooming hyacinth, daffodil,
bluebell; cartoon hornets with enormous stingers perched in the
center of each flower, smiling. A headline in creamy pink reads:
"Everything You Ever Wanted to Know About Homicide, Suicide,
and Other Newsworthy Violent Occurrences, But Were Afraid to
Ask." Scanning the screen, I see it in the top left corner: Neverland
Murders. There's a buzzing between my ears, a strong, savage heat.

Click.

A new page comes up, bordered in the same creepy pastel flowers, but this time it's quilted in a background of gruesome thumbprint photos. A list of bolded names runs like a twisted spine through the center of the screen. "Sapphire: age 19, murdered at home; Lourraine Street" is right at the top. My heart flips. Still just Sapphire. No last name. A blinking banner beside it reads: NEW ADDITION!!! like it's an advertisement for a vacuum cleaner or dishwashing detergent.

Click.

First: a hand-drawn street map called: Neverland and Environs. Below it, more photographs, all obviously taken from the outside, and rendered partially obscure by the stippling of light over the window: her ransacked apartment, things torn up and strewn across the floor, a smattering of blood against the bedroom wall. The pictures are grainy, pixilated, as though snapped with a cell phone.

I picture her sitting in front of a mirror, applying her layers of makeup in that light blue room like she's icing a wedding cake, sliding her bruised-purple lips back and forth against each other. I imagine a surf of blood rising up to her ankles, to her knees, to her neck—everything in her room bobbing in that blood like buoys on a rising tide.

*   *   *   *

Trying to relax before bed, I move the copper elephants closer to the soft-bellied jester dolls and the soft-bellied jester dolls closer to the wooden dollhouse rocking chairs. Their placement is giving me a nervous feeling in my stomach right now, and I've got to make them right again.

Normally, doing this makes me calm, but for some reason, I can't focus and don't feel better. Something's not right; everything in my room looks wrong, rearranged, Twisted.

Cleft. Naked.

I can't make it right.

CHAPTER 3

I wake to a window pattern of light streaming through my blinds, roll over in bed and stretch. Saturday has its own special taste: like the blackberries Mom and I would pick every week during the short three months we lived in Kuna, Idaho, when I was ten. I remember how flushed with pride we'd felt as we hugged the brimming baskets of fruit to our chests, eating blackberries by the fistful, all day long.

Saturday is Flea Market Day, holiest of days.

Then I feel the throbbing in my hand. The cut. The glass. The bang. It was real.

I throw on my army pants, rolling down the giant waist, and my green thermal hoodie, which is loose enough, like most of my clothes, to cover my boobs. I'm still not used to them. I may never be. They arrived around the third week of ninth grade without consulting me—first the right one and then the left, which proceeded to grow some more to meet the right and then surpass it.

I'm pretty sure they're engaged in some kind of constant competition.

I check my shoe for the folded piece of paper I keep there—safer than a pocket, where things might fall out. Still there. I step into my shoes, then scrutinize myself in the collection of antique mirrors (nine) above my dresser. My bangs look stupid in each and every one. I push them back from my forehead and let them fall. Three times. "Penelope Marin," I say out loud to my reflection, in my best scary cop voice, "step *away* from the mirrors. I repeat: get your wallet from the nightstand and step *away* from the mirrors."

My costume ring with the big yellow daisy on it is calling out to me like the yellow house two days ago, and I know I have to wear it, and it feels good on my finger, and I'm ready.

According to B. Hornet's map, Neverland and Environs, the Cleveland Flea is technically within the borders of the Neverland neighborhood, but somehow it's an oasis, a safe haven. It spans blocks: it is its own magical city. There are vendors at the flea six days a week, but Saturday is my day. The right day. The only day of the week with three perfect syllables.

I allow myself to visit only nine stalls per Saturday so that the pleasure of the market's newness remains never ending. By the time I've gone through the hundreds of stalls, after weeks of patient and selective meandering, most of the vendors will have changed, and I can do it all over again. That way, Saturday will always and forever mean waking up hopeful.

As I approach, the sounds of the flea are in beautiful, cacophonous bloom. I *tap tap tap, banana* before I enter the market, three times. Nine taps, three bananas in total. Good. Very good.

People are milling about—hundreds of them, holding hands and touching things and living their lives, and I blend into the crowd. Normal.

I pass a table stacked with antique glasses frames and pocket watches from the twenties: frames jeweled at the corners, tortoise-colored, glossy. Just as I'm about to approach the booth and run my fingers over all the glittering, beautiful, old things—my fingers are practically salivating they're so excited—Keri Ram darts toward me from the next booth.

My hand flies immediately to my bangs; I wish I knew how dumb on a scale of one-to-ten they looked right now. By the feel of it, I'd say eight. I hate eight.

"Hey, girl!" she says, acting excited to see me, which is weird because I see her every day in calculus, and she's never, ever been excited to see me there. My chest feels suddenly tight and I realize that I don't know what to say. I could say *hi* when I'm really supposed to say *hey*. She could report back to her friends at school on Monday about how much of a dork I really am because I still say words like *hi*.

When I finally force myself to speak, all that comes out is an awkward little "Hey," almost a growl.

Her mouth turns slightly sideways, her eyes creasing like she's trying to figure out what exactly I just said. I've been in at least a dozen classes with Keri since I moved to Cleveland at the end of eighth grade, when I was fourteen, but we've never really spoken before. She hasn't always been in the popular group, but she is now, and I don't know if I've ever seen her anywhere without a train of at least three other people following behind. She's on student government and in SADD and mock trial and the field hockey team and probably twenty more organizations I'll only know about when the yearbook comes out and I flip through the glossy spread of everyone else's faces.

There'd been a rumor going around since ninth grade that she was a lesbian—I think it's because she's got kind of broad shoulders and a deep voice—but then last year a different rumor started circulating that she'd lost her virginity to some twenty-eight-year-old musician she'd met at a hotel pool in Chicago, on a family vacation, and that rumor kind of swallowed the other. I'm pretty sure kids at school don't know anything about me, nor do they care; I doubt most of them even know my name. I'm a ghost to them—not even worthy of rumors. If they know about Oren—and I don't really see how they *couldn't* know about Oren—they don't know he was my brother. I doubt they noticed when I was out of school for a whole month last year.

Keri says, "This place is kind of weird, right?" She smiles at me, flashing perfect, blindingly white teeth. "Camille made me come here with her. She's trying to find a gift for her grandmother or something." She doesn't even give me time to respond before moving her big smudgeless leather purse to the crook of her left elbow and continuing: "So, I *completely* spaced out in Keller's class on Friday, not that that's so hard to do or anything. I mean, I know I'm usually right on top of everything, but, seriously, does Mr. Keller actually expect us to be able to focus on *derivatives* right before the weekend?" She shakes her head, giving me a knowing glance, like I *must* understand how hard it is to pay attention to school on a Friday—what with all of the parties and drinking and hotel-pool sex I'm planning for the weekend.

"Yeah," I say. "Right." I nod my head vigorously. Too vigorously. I force myself still, move my bangs to the left, stare at the toes of my scuffed-up Chucks. The good Saturday feeling is draining away. Keri-freaking-Ram has destroyed it with her shiny hair and scar-less forehead and straight-bridged nose and cheerful little paisley-printed dress.

"I know. I mean, it's really *easy*, and it's boring on top of that." Keri adds the *really easy* part to remind me how smart and impressive and strong a leader she'll be once I help vote her into next year's senior class presidency in May (*Only two months away! Never too early to start thinking about new leadership!*)—I'm sure of it. I glance back up at her; she flips her hair over her right shoulder, bites her lip. "So, did you manage to write down the homework or anything? As much as I hate math, gotta get that A or my 'rents will slaughter me, you know?" She looks at me expectantly.

"We. Actually—we didn't have any. I mean, not really nothing, but nothing *really*."

Keri looks confused. "Wait—so, we don't have homework, or we do?"

She's got three small pimples sprouting up on her chin; I can see them under her concealer. I stare at them as I respond. "Well, Mr. Keller said we should just, um, just look over chapter twelve some more if we didn't feel good about limits, or whatever."

Keri smiles and her pimples grow farther apart. "Oh. Awesome."

She straightens the hem of her dress, heaves a happy sigh. "I guess Keller's not all that evil when it comes down to it."

She looks over her shoulder as she hears Camille, calling to her from a nearby booth. When she turns back to me, she looks relieved, like she's glad to have an excuse to be rid of me. "Well, looks like Camille found her grandma *something* worth buying here. . . . Thanks for the good news about the homework, girl."

"Lo," I say to her as she's turning to leave.

She stops, turns around, and looks at me strangely. "What?"

"My name's Lo," I say, and I feel a blush heating my cheeks.

She squints at me with a look of pity. "I know what your name is. We're in, like, four classes together." She shakes her head and frowns a little before galloping over to Camille through the crowd like they haven't seen each other in years.

I see Camille squint hard in my direction and point as soon as Keri reaches her. Keri bats Camille's hand down, whispering something into her ear that makes them both shake their heads as they join the stream of people moving toward the exit.

I keep walking, waiting for the bad feelings to drain away, hoping my tapping and counting goes unnoticed by the hoards of people milling, shopping, smiling.

There's a booth filled with old instruments just a few feet ahead that calms me instantly: brassy tubas and ornate French horns, dangling from the top of the booth like flanks of glossy raw meat. They're all too big to take home and too expensive to buy, but their beauty and the idea of their heaviness makes me wish I could have one just to cradle for a while. The weight of them comforts me; they're solid. They won't evaporate into thin air.

I'm staring up at the glinting instruments, when a boy in a bear-eared hat—at least I think it's a boy, since all I get a really good look at are the bear ears—zooms past, tornado-like. Our shoulders meet for a long second before he knocks me backward, directly into the table behind me. I nearly tip the whole table over trying to steady myself. All sorts of random junk—jewelry and old lamps and brooches and statuettes and silverware and pins and buttons and bow ties—tumbles to the ground.

"Sorry," I say quickly, stooping to lift the fallen things from the ground. I don't even care who the mysterious bear-guy was that slammed me—I'm too focused on the treasure I've fallen into, the opportunity to look, to rearrange and separate and order.

"That's all right, sweetheart," the vendor says, scooting around from behind the table to come help me. "Not too organized around here."

I raise a delicate silver watch from where it landed, diagonally splayed beneath two different colored salad forks. I sway it left to right to watch the glinting sun play against its face.

The vendor sees me holding the watch and looks startled. "Oh," he barks out. "That one's not for sale." He's got one of those sticker nametags on. It says *Hello, My Name Is Mario* in messy red script.

"But—" I start to say. He leans forward and practically rips the watch out of my hand. Filled suddenly with a hot, rising anger that I can't resist, I blurt out: "You shouldn't put things out that you don't want people to buy, you know. It's not fair."

"Sorry, don't know how that one got in there," Mario says, grinning at me.

He squats, reaches under the card table, and scoops up the rest of the fallen objects, then dumps them back on the tangle of stuff piled on his table. Mario's hair is a shock of Manic Panic red, a color I see dripping down the foreheads of most of the punk kids in gym class as they sweat. But he's way too old for high school— forty, at least, sporting an over-size Jimi Hendrix tie-dyed T-shirt and faded jeans, skin leathery full of lines.

"Everything else is for sale, though," he says. "Go ahead and pick something out. Pretty girl like you; I'll give you a discount."

"I'm just looking," I say automatically. I debate leaving the booth entirely but the things—the beautiful things—are calling out to me. I continue picking up the fallen items, lifting, finally, a clot of jewelry from the center of the table, sorting through the dislocated tangle of necklaces, earrings, and pins. Mario eyes me the way salesmen do, sussing out how best to swindle me.

Tangled with the rest of the jewelry is a necklace that seems oddly familiar: rusted silver chain, horse pendant dangling heavy from a wire ring. I turn it back to front, examining its every detail, searching for something that I can't quite identify—a fact, an image—lodged in an unyielding corner of my brain.

"If you like that one, I've got some other stuff you might like, too." Mario turns to a plastic bag behind him and begins extract-ing things from it, directs me to a semi-cleared corner of the table, plunks the items down one by one.

"Should have put these out when I first set up," he says, "but they're all real new, and I just plain forgot." He claps his palm to his forehead, exaggerated, smiling: a clown, a con artist. .

Everything he lays out is so beautiful it makes me shiver—

a crescent moon pin made of dark satiny silver, a bird ring in silhouette, some bangles in sparkly night-sky purples and blues. The thing that I love the most, though, is a jeweled figurine in the shape of a butterfly—it's luminous and glittery and sad-looking.

But all at once the fact is loosened from some dark corner of my brain. Butterfly figurine. Rusted silver chain, horse pendant. Both were things pilfered from the murdered girl's house. Sapphire.

My hands and feet go hot. The articles I read online didn't mention anything about most of the other darkly glittering things Mario shows me, but somehow, without knowing how I know, I'm positive that everything he has just spread before me belonged to her. Objects can tell us a lot, if we're willing to listen. These are screaming.

It's him; he's the one who killed her. He's the one who fired the shot that nearly grazed my cheek. He must be. And he's too stupid not to sell her things just days later. My breath is coming in short gasps, but I manage to ask: "Hey, um—" Pause. Inhale. I can't look him in the eye. "Where'd you get this stuff? It's really great."

"Which stuff? Got tons of stuff here. Comes from all over."

"These things." I gesture toward Sapphire's objects.

"Can't say for sure. Get things all the time, can barely keep track anymore." He laughs, a little nervous guffaw.

Now I do look at him, his darting eyes and gross cherry-colored hair. "You told me a second ago these things just came in." I point to the plastic bag; he narrows his eyes. "And, now, you're telling me you can't remember where they came from?"

He's avoiding my gaze. "Where I get my stuff is none of your business." He shifts a little from foot to foot.

"A girl was murdered," I say, trying not to choke on my own words. "I recognize some of this stuff from the news. So . . ." My head is full of fluttering; I can't believe the words coming out of my mouth.

His eyes narrow. He's sharper than he looks. He reaches out as if to touch me, and I draw back quickly. Instead, he runs his hands through his greasy hair.

"Okay, listen. Now, listen up." His voice is low, filled with urgency. "I found all this stuff in a bag in a Dumpster outside of the Westwood Center. That's where I find lots of things I sell. All right?" He pulls out a pack of Marlboros and lights one, taking a long drag, exhaling loudly. "That's all I know. Swear to Christ. That's it."

Something about the tone of his voice makes me want to believe him—a gentleness, a genuineness. But if he is telling the truth—he did find all of Sapphire's things tossed in a Dumpster outside of Westwood—then why was Sapphire murdered? Why would some out-of-his-mind junkie risk killing somebody for a few hundred dollars worth of things, only to immediately throw those things away?

It doesn't make sense.

Mario continues speaking, keen to my hesitation, stubbing out his cigarette. He leans toward me. "Look, you're not gonna call the cops or nothing, are you? 'Cause I don't know what you need me to do to prove it to you, but I'll do it. I don't know nothing about this shit. It's just coincidence. Just bad goddamn luck." His knuckles are sidled against the edge of his display table, growing whiter and whiter. "This is my bread and butter, you know? It's how come I'm not homeless today, right?"

He lights up a new cigarette, taking quick, greedy puffs this time.

"I'm not going to say anything to the police," I say, and can see him relax. "It's none of my business, like you said." He doesn't realize that I'd do pretty much anything to avoid a confrontation with the police myself. Not after Officer Clevinger dragged me into his squad car a month after Oren died, when my brain was the static of a TV screen and my limbs did things of their own accord, like swipe the little elephant figurine from the Tibetan store at Tower City. I didn't even remember taking it, only afterward, curling against the cold glass window of the squad car, trying to disappear as his hot breath fogged my ear and he sneered: *Get it together.* I tried to explain, blubbering, *I didn't know, I'm so sorry, didn't realize what I'd done.* He just stared at me, like I was an unbelievable idiot. *One more incident like this, and you're on your way to juvie. Then you'll realize.*

Mario reaches for the butterfly figurine still glittering on the table, mid-afternoon sunlight casting shapes in marigold across everything. He hands it to me. "For you," he says. "Thank you. Thanks for being cool."

I nod but say nothing, and that's that. Our unspoken contract. As he turns around, searching for something in a bag on the ground, the *urge* rips through me, fierce, insatiable. My arm shoots forward to the table, and I pull the horse pendent necklace into my fist and walk quickly, sharply away. Clutching tightly to the butterfly in one hand and the necklace in the other, I move through the market, passing tables of food and tables of fabric and trim and creatures made of wood and glass and metal and baseball memorabilia and faded T-shirts and old headdresses of satin and lace, but all I can really think about is her. Sapphire.

Something about her is burning little holes into my heart. I wonder if what draws me to the butterfly is what drew her to it, too: not just its dark, pooling glow but the way its wings are folded back like it has just landed—and not a grand, proud landing but a solemn, lonely one, a head-bowed one, a middle-of-the-night leaving-of-somewhere-or-someone landing.

I wonder whether someone, somewhere, misses her. There's got to be someone, even if no one was there to claim her as a loved one, even if there were only strippers at Tens to speak not of her, but of her things. Now my brain is doing a gushing kind of thing, in tandem with my heart, and I can't stop the thoughts, landing like the heavy kind of snow that sticks and forms thick cold walls around everything.

I wonder if Oren thought he was missed, as he eased down the gradual slope of his slipping away from us, from everything, into nothing.

I clasp the necklace on to my neck, the small, cold horse resting against my sternum, and squeeze the butterfly in my palm. Nine, nine, six. Again. Nine, nine, six. Once more. Nine, nine, six.

What happens to people when no one mourns for them? When no one cares what they were feeling when they died—whether it felt like a million points of light or endless mouths singing arias or whether it felt like nothing, like a wave raising itself to the stars and pulling the world back with it, into the vastness of everything that goes on and on and on.

I have pieces of Sapphire now, pieces she left behind. And somehow, they make me feel I have a responsibility to her, too: to her life, to her death.

We're born alone, and all die alone, too. I read that somewhere, in some book. After Oren died I used to lie awake and think about that: think about the universe sucking up hope for us, soul by soul, until we're so dry we all starve, all at once, and the sky takes our bones and crushes them into mulch and starts over again. So goes the cycle. So go the millions and billions of things we can't ever begin to control. But it can't be that way. It just can't.

Even though I've only stopped at four stalls instead of nine— the pain of four pulling at every one of my cells—I leave the flea market, stumbling out onto the sidewalk in a kind of daze, feeling caught between worlds, dizzy. *Hey, Sapphire—can you hear me? Wherever you are, I hope you're okay.*

I grip the butterfly hard, three times more. *Are you okay?*

I look up at the sky. There is no answer from above—no answer from anywhere—other than a light drizzle that begins to fall.

Or maybe that is the answer.

CHAPTER 4

That night I dream that blue-black snowflakes are falling from the sky, settling like ash. I'm with Oren. I'm always with Oren in my dreams now; we're walking beside a wide, cold lake. The trees are missing their leaves. Then, just as I reach some kind of conclusion in a point I'm trying to make, I turn, and he's gone, and I understand that the lake has swallowed him.

And in the dream I'm not perplexed at this having happened, only angry with myself for not having held on to his hand just a little tighter.

The ash falls on my head and my hands are covered in it. The dream-lake that swallows my dream-brother is full of it, and he is full of it now, too. His dream eyes. His dream tongue. His dream throat.

*   *   *   *

Sapphire's butterfly figurine sits perched on my night table. I carry it with me as I dress for the day, attempting to cover the awkward lines and angles of my body: dark jeans with the cuffs rolled up, the horse necklace, tucked against my chest beneath a gigantic blue felted pullover that was my mother's once, a navy blue knit hat shoved low over my ears. I push my bangs up underneath it. But then the scar peeks out at me, white as chalk. I release the bangs from the fortress of my hat. My hair is dark and split-ended and long-suffering for a cut that I'm never quite prepared to give it. I'm just not good at parting with things, I guess.

I should be doing homework right now for Intro to Economics— the elective my father decided would be in my best interest to take. I should be researching and performing basic statistical analyses of inflation and unemployment, but I just haven't got any room for that: the only thing in my head right now is Sapphire; the moment she died. I don't think what happened was random—don't think it was just *bad goddamn luck*, as Mario would say.

I'm going back to Neverland, back to the puke-yellow house with the daisies. I don't exactly know what I plan to do once I arrive, but I've got to be there. I've got to reclaim her, whatever it is she was.

*   *   *   *

It takes me a while to retrace my steps and find the place. The painted daisies are even more glaring in full daylight. No one's here—no police officers, no one sniffing around attempting to right any wrongs.

I walk cautiously to the front door, crossed with police tape. I *tap tap tap, banana* and bite the tip of my tongue lightly nine times before I try the knob: locked. I don't know what else I expected. My heart's hammering splinters in my chest as I creep down the alley, toward the door in back. I pass the shattered window, also crossed with police tape, and notice that the bullet has been dislodged from the wall. A new, sick fear flashes through me, making me want to turn around. But I don't.

I reach the back door. It looks pretty flimsy, like it might be easy to slip through. There's a broken bit of wood by the knob; I start to work it with my fingers. It splinters quickly apart.

Suddenly, a pair of strong hands grip my shoulders from behind.

I let out a shout without meaning to and whip around, prepared to hit, prepared to run. I'm so scared that for a second what I'm seeing doesn't make sense—it's all fragment and fracture and *bear* and *teeth* and *boy*.

Then I realize the hands gripping my shoulders belong to a guy in a bear-eared hat. It's the boy from the flea market, the boy whose high-speed jaunt sent me crashing into Mario's table. His eyes narrow for a second and then widen. He must see a flicker of recognition pass through my eyes.

"What are you doing here?" he demands as I shake myself out of his grip.

"I'm—I'm not doing anything. What are *you* doing?" I spit back. "You're the one who—why would you—" My words tumble out, tangled fragments. "Why would you come up behind someone and—you could have been—" *You could have been the killer,* I almost say, but I can't get it out, can't tell this boy in a dumb bear-eared hat who I thought he was, what I thought he was about to do.

He stares at me hard, seeming to assess me. Then, suddenly, his whole posture shifts, and his face softens into a grin. "Whoooa, man. Don't shoot!" He puts his hands in the air like we're playing cop and robber and I'm pointing a toy gun at his heart. He has blue eyes and scraggly dreadlocked hair. Oddly nice teeth. "Just a simple question. Don't you remember me—Le Market du Flea—from yesterday?" He steps back with his left foot and bows, pretending to lift an invisible hat from his head in apology—but he leaves the actual hat with the bear ears on his head.

Freak, I think, but don't say it. "I remember you," I say, still angry. "You crashed into me. Why the hell were you running so fast?"

"Oh, you know. Just stretching the legs. Sorry about that. Where better for a quick jog than a crowded outdoor market?" Even though his words come easily, he's still shuffling his feet, hopping a bit from left to right. He's either got to pee pretty badly or he's nervous about something. "I saw you from the alleyway, thought I'd come over and say hi."

His long dreadlocks are dyed blond in some places, though the rest of his hair is dark brown, and I can see now that his eyes are somehow blue and green and gold at the same time, like the old marbles Dad gave me and Oren to play games with as kids. He's wearing scruffy black pants and big sturdy-looking brown boots without laces, tongues hanging loose.

I narrow my eyes at him and he rushes on, "I've just been over there"—he motions to the other side of the house—"doing a little treasure-hunting Dumpster-diving, and I thought to myself"—he puts a finger to his temple—"if that pretty girl goes to the flea market, and likes creepy old things, I just bet she'd appreciate a good scare and then, the rare and impossible chance to check out my newly salvaged wares. So, we've got the scaring part over with, and now, part deux."

Pretty girl. He just called me a pretty girl. The words give me an electric rush.

Or maybe I misheard him. Maybe I heard a word that just *sounded* like pretty.

He grabs my uninjured hand and leads me toward the Dumpsters, and I don't protest. This guy radiates something— something bright and big and open, something I'm not used to at all—and I'm drawn to him despite myself.

No. He did. He called me a *pretty girl*.

Pretty means the girls at school, with their blow-dried hair and matching silver heart necklaces.

Pretty means normal.

He stops next to the Dumpster, stooping to lift something. He turns back to me, holding a flat tire delicately between his thumbs and pointer fingers.

"You, um, found a flat tire," I say. I don't know how this boy expects me to react to a bit of rubber, which he has obviously pulled from the inside of a dirty, smelly Dumpster, in the very alleyway where I was almost *shot* three days ago. Not that he could know about the last part.

"Oh, I certainly did," he says, without irony. "Here, just come a little closer. It doesn't look like much now, *but*"—he removes one hand from the tire and, as a magician might do, waves it back and forth in the air—"wait till you see how it got flat in the first place."

I don't know why I decide to move even closer to this near-complete stranger, but I do. He lifts the tire closer to me and flips it around. Its entire backside is embedded with shards of mirrored glass, protruding from the ink-black tire like stars.

"Wow. That's—that's really beautiful." And I mean it, and move my fingers toward the glass. I've got to touch these stars pulled earthward, before they disappear.

"Hey—don't do that!" He yanks my fingers away. His hand is cool and big. I shove my hands into the pockets of my pullover, embarrassed.

"See?" He shows me the palm of his own left hand, covered in tiny red gashes. "I got all cut up earlier. Bleeding from the hand isn't as fun as you might think, believe it or not. But an artist's life is full of hardship! And I guess they're kind of like my battle wounds."

My wounded palm throbs inside my sweatshirt. My whole arm suddenly feels cut up—sharp and raw. He doesn't realize that I'm suffering from my own battle wounds—the kind of battle wounds you get when you stumble onto the frontline by accident. The thought of the bullet, the explosion—glass flying everywhere—once again makes me shiver. I blurt out, "Battle wounds, huh? So what are you battling?"

He hesitates for a second. Then his eyes light up. "My noble and single-handed fight for garbage rights!" He extends his uninjured hand to me. "I'm Flynt, by the way."

"Lo." I don't shake his hand. Shaking hands reminds me of something adults do, and therapists when they're meeting you for the first time and trying to prove *they respect you as a person.* I should know: I've been to a half dozen therapists in the past three years, including Dr. Janice "Call me Janice" Weiss; Dr. Aaron "This is a *safe space,* Penelope" Machner; and, most recently, Dr. Ellen Peech. Dr. Peech was straightforward, overworked, and obviously exhausted. By session number two, she'd already penned me a prescription for Zoloft and sent me on my way to Zombieland, where Mom lives. After two weeks of feeling dead numb, I decided the sewage system needed the pills more than I did, so I flushed them all down the toilet.

Mom and Dad don't notice, of course. They never notice. Anything.

Flynt doesn't say anything about the handshake snub—just puts the hand back into his coat pocket and bows again, still grinning.

"So, Flynt," I say, "you never answered me. What are you doing here? Besides fighting for trash-related justice?"

He looks up at the sky for a few long seconds before responding: "I'm an artist. Don't have the money to buy shit to make art, though." He shrugs. "So, I find materials wherever I can from this, our eternally wasteful nation-home of Neverland."

When Flynt says *Neverland*, he might as well be saying *heaven*. "Check it out. Great haul this morning." He turns around and plunks a canvas sack at my feet. He's always moving, never still.

"Open it up. Look around. Store's open till three." He rocks back and forth on his heels.

I pull out a ceramic lamp cracked down the center, a bag full of broken blue glass, a wooden board studded with a graveyard-like schema of rusty nails, a giant dented metal picture frame–like thing.

"So, what do you think?" He's grinning again, tugging at one of his blondish dreadlocks and then at the frayed bits and holes in his pants. I like the little imperfections in his clothes, the way they're kind of rumpled and don't really match and how his coat has colorful patches sewn onto its elbows. It all looks so right on him, on his lanky body. Really right. And soft. Not like the boys at school—overly pressed jeans and gelled hair and matching every-thing. All cold, clean, sharp lines.

"They're cool," I say, and mean it. I unconsciously go to finger the rusty nails and have to stop myself. Flynt is watching me closely and I blush, embarrassed. "What will you use them for?"

"Dunno yet. Something wildly, earth-shatteringly original. Or, you know, probably something ugly and terrible that will never let see the light of day."

We begin putting his things back in the sack, kneeling together on the dirty concrete. "You live around here, Lo?"

I stare at the ground, weirdly self-conscious that I don't. "No. Just outside of it."

"Where's just outside?" he asks.

"Lakewood. I can take a bus right here, though. It's easy." I can feel heat still burning through my cheeks.

"Never been there. I don't really leave Neverland much. At all, really," he says. "It's sort of my unbreakable rule." I look up at him and notice that he's blushing, too.

"You never leave at all?" I repeat. "Doesn't it get kind of . . . boring?" At the last second, I stop myself from saying *depressing*. I stare across the broken landscape of Neverland: all randomness and grit.

"Not really." He shrugs. "This is home, for right now at least. And Neverland is great."

I must be making a face because Flynt adds, "Trust me, it's true. There's lots of cool stuff around here. You just haven't had the right tour guide." The grin never leaves his face, but his eyes are sharp and alert, like an animal's. "So, Lakewood Lo, you never actually answered me either: what are *you* doing, ambling around these parts, fiddling with broken door handles? You"—he hesitates for a second—"ever been here before?"

I can't tell him the truth; I feel that, like a pulse through my body. I stand, wiping dirt from my knees; Flynt stands, too, watching the clouds of dirt rise between us. "Um, well, I have this old friend—or I *had* this old friend. She was murdered a few days ago. I saw her picture in the paper and a photo of where she lived." I point to the puke-yellow house directly beside us. "And I felt like I should come here and, you know, pay my respects or something."

Adrenaline is pushing words from my lips I hadn't, stupidly enough, been prepared to say. I rush on, clutching the horse pendent around my neck, spitting out invented details as they come to me, "We were really, really close as kids and then she moved away and my parents would never let me come out here to visit . . . and now she's, well, she's gone." Avoid eye contact. Deep breath.

Flynt gets quiet. He's tugging at an errant dreadlock again;

he's no longer grinning. "Hey. I'm really sorry about your friend. I heard about that. Well, I read about it, too." He looks back toward the Dumpsters. "It's rough. People are crazy, especially around here. Trust me. I know most of them."

"Yeah, thanks," I say. And then, all at once, in a burst: "The worst is that the police don't really give a shit. They've just written the whole thing off. They're not even investigating. Not really."

Flynt says nothing. I'm embarrassed by my outburst, and I bite my lip, turning away from him.

Silence: seconds like bricks, falling from the sky, forming a wall between us. I wrap my navy blue coat around me tighter.

"I should probably get home," I tell Flynt, who nods.

"Let me walk you to your bus," Flynt offers, linking his arm with mine, like we're old friends. I pull away. I'm not used to being touched, not by a boy, anyway. The few times it has happened have been by accident—like when J. R. Miller grabbed me around the waist at the sixth grade dance, confusing me for Grace Hull, or in eighth grade, when Micah Eisenberg put both hands on my lower back and pushed me out of the way so he could make the winning spike in our gym-class volleyball tournament. And that hardly counts.

Flynt doesn't try to touch me again but doesn't seem offended, either. We walk through Neverland's landscape of uncapped potholes and trash-strewn streets.

"You should come around sometime. I might just know a really cool guy with fabulous taste in head gear who can show you how great this shit-hole town can be," Flynt says when we're almost at the bus stop. He tugs on his bear-ear cap.

My heart leaps. Someone wants to hang out with me. A boy wants to hang out with me. I examine his face, his eyes, trying to decide if he's messing with me. But his expression remains the same: dimpled grin, wide, playful green-blue-gold eyes.

The moment I cast my eyes away from Flynt and to the sky, I see six blackbirds swoon past in a line—like they were put there, right at that moment, to reassure me. It's almost enough to distract me from my mission, from the images of Sapphire's murdered body still cycling through my head—an endless revolution, a bloody carousel.

I decide to play along. "That sounds like it could be all right," I say cautiously, and Flynt's smile gets even bigger. "So . . . how do I find this really cool guy? Does he have a cell phone? A bat symbol? A birdcall?"

"I wish!" he says. "He wasn't blessed with the whistling gene, unfortunately. See." He purses his lips and tries to whistle, releasing a stream of air, a flag of spit, nothing more; we both start laughing. "Doesn't have any of that other fancy robot stuff, either. I'm pretty sure I'm—I mean, he's—trying to stay off the grid as much as he can, you know? Just, meet me—I mean, him— in the same spot. I suppose you should give him your number, just in case he ever happens upon a phone booth. And don't be afraid to just ask around. Someone will know where to find him." He pauses and corrects himself, for real this time, gazing at me. "Where to find me."

The 96 is waiting at the stop when we arrive. I scribble my cell phone number quickly, nervously, in a soft-covered notebook Flynt has been keeping in his pocket. Then I *tap tap tap, banana* as softly as I can, face burning as I do, hoping he won't hear me, hoping he won't notice, board the bus, pay the fare. Through the reflective bus windows, I watch Flynt slip through a different alleyway to who-knows-where, tire slung around his neck, soft-side-down, like a fallen halo.

CHAPTER 5

Spring starts inching its way into Cleveland, devouring old snow, asserting itself in the parks and tree branches, and consuming the high school world with a kind of madness. Each and every wall of Carver is glutted with flyers when we return from the weekend: PROM! PROM! PROM! ONE MONTH UNTIL PROM! VOTE ON YOUR FAVORITE THEME! MAD JUNGLE DISCO? HIP-HOP-ALICE-IN-WONDERLAND-RABBIT-HOLE? OUTER SPACE?, then small print: TICKETS $25. FOR A LIMITED TIME ONLY, SUCKAAAAS. And: WHO RULES? YOU DECIDE. VOTE FOR YOUR PROM COURT TODAY! The entire science wing—papered with flyers featuring Annica Steele's face, a Photoshopped diamond crown atop her perfect hair, one word at the bottom of each flyer: BALLER.

Not only am I surrounded on all fronts by prom flyers, I'm also surrounded by Jeremy. He makes sure to grab a seat next to me in English class on Monday and, after lunch on Tuesday passes me a note, messily folded. I unfold it in the bathroom, in private. It says: *Study? Tonight?* I throw it out, then feel bad and have to dig for it in the trash, underneath balled-up paper towels and used-up lip-gloss containers.

By Wednesday, I can't wait any longer. I can't get my mind off of Sapphire or Flynt, the boy who called me pretty. I'm aching to scratch the growing itch of all of the details I've yet to discover about their secret sunken city. Instead of taking the bus to school, I hop the 96—*a good number, thirty-two threes*—and ride to the end of the line. I never used to dream of cutting school, as awful as it could be—I was too scared. But, suddenly, I understand: fearlessness comes when you realize there are more important things to solve than vocab questions and limits. I find my way back to the Dumpsters, hoping to find Flynt scavenging as promised.

Instead, I find three notes taped, one on top of the other, to the Dumpster closest to the street. Scrawled in mad, loopy script, barely legible, each one (with minor variations) says the same thing. The last one reads:

> *Dearest Lo,*
>
> *If I'm not here, it's because I've been called by darker forces to a place known, in the hush-hush, as Malatesta's. Walk due north two blocks and make a left down the alleyway marked with Xs in red paint. Be stealthy. Be brave.*
>
> *x Flynt*

My heart flutters; he's left me a note. Every day since we hung out. I follow his instructions—the whole time worrying that he won't be where he says he is, or that I'll get too lost to find him, or that this will turn out to be a joke or a prank.

Luckily, I spot the alleyway Flynt described in his note—subtle red markings, graffiti skulls, forming an ominous border around cement walls.

Farther down the alleyway is a clearing, and within it, a large lean-to, a huge M whose entrance is painted in drippy black. *Tap tap tap, banana*, again, *tap tap tap, banana*, and again, *tap tap tap, banana*, to be extra safe. I step cautiously inside. There are several tables and chairs, obviously Dumpster-scavenged, scattered unevenly throughout the space. People—pierced, tattooed, Mohawked—are seated or sprawled on the dirty floor, working on various art projects.

I find Flynt squatting in a corner, painting on a giant wooden board with his hands and elbows, his face furrowed in intense concentration. Every visible part of his body is covered in paint.

"Flynt?"

No one looks up.

"Flynt," I say, louder this time.

A girl sitting close to him leans over and blows on his ear. She has studded emeralds pierced into her cheeks.

"Hey, F," she says, "you've got a visitor."

He looks up and grins at me, bear ears standing at attention. I think there might be paint on his teeth. His eyes are fiercely green right now, cheeks flushed.

"Lo! You found me!" He gets up, wiping his hands on his patched jacket. "Give me a second to pack this stuff away. Then I'm gonna show you all around the mystical world of Neverland."

He stoops to lift the heavy board, simultaneously making introductions: "Lo, meet Seraphina—she makes killer wigs, and a million other things it would take too long to name"—the girl with pierced cheeks nods to me—"Marlow, resident puppet maker, poet, revolutionary"—a skinny black guy in rainbow suspenders with a half-shaved head looks up, confused—"and Gretchen, vegan chef, dancer, and illustrator extraordinaire"—a very tall girl in a tutu wide as a hoopskirt and heavy black lace-up boots curtsies to me. "These three pretty much run the place."

I wrap my coat around my (now) holey cashmere sweater—something Mom bought me in seventh grade from the Gap—and wave shyly at them. I've never been good at art, at turning the inside-out. Oren was the artist—the illustrator, the rhyme-maker, with a voice like maple syrup.

Flynt turns the wide board in his hands, yells over his shoulder as he travels: "I'll be right back."

He disappears behind a curtain. I count nine dislocated wooden planks in the ceiling of the old warehouse; the calm perfection of the number wraps itself around me like a second coat. It's going to be a good day—I can really let myself believe it now. Seraphina, Marlow, and Gretchen go back to their projects. Flynt reemerges seconds later, sans wood, but paint-smattered as ever. "Let's go."

He offers me his arm. And this time, I take it.

*   *   *   *

"So, I just . . . throw it?" I lift a chair between my legs, preparing to shoot it into the pyramid of trash cans Flynt has set up in an abandoned parking lot. Flynt is teaching me how to "trash can bowl"—a common game here in Neverland, apparently. I've never bowled with anything but duck pins in a big air-conditioned room at the birthday parties my mom forced me to attend as a kid.

"Yep. Just chuck it, hard as you can. But, you've gotta get a feel for the chair, aim it with just the right angle." He swoops his hands and arms through the air in demonstration. "It's beautiful, if you do it right." He smiles coyly. "No pressure, though."

Just as I'm about to send the chair flying, a car backfires some-where, and the noise makes me jump—still nervous, still twitchy from the memory of the gunshot.

My chair flies sideways in the air and splinters into several pieces as it hits the ground, three feet away from the perfectly pyramidal arrangement of trash cans. A half second later, Flynt, with a running jump, propels his body into the trash cans. They land with a tremendous clattering, and he leaps to his feet and jogs back toward me.

"Whoa! Lo! You got them all! Look at that!" He grabs me by my waist, spins me around, and cheers, trying to get me to do the same. My body feels like jelly, loose and uncontrolled, and I wriggle myself from Flynt's hold as quickly as I can. I stare down at the arms of my coat and realize they're covered in paint. Flynt's multicolored handprints—the paint he was using at Malatesta's must have been still-wet on his hands. I can trace the places where he's touched me—shoulders, waist, the backs of my hands. And I can't help but smile, hoping Flynt doesn't see how violet my ears must be turning.

"I broke the chair. I'm no good at this."

"Then how did all of those trash cans end up on the ground? Answer me that, Lo!" He quickly runs toward the Dumpsters and returns with a new chair. "And if you broke the chair, then why is it perfectly intact?" A smile spreads across his face. "Hey. What happened to your coat?"

I look up at him. His eyes are flecked with gold. I play mock-innocent. "What do you mean? It's always looked like this, Flynt."

"Right, right, of course. Sorry—the sun is so bright—makes me see things."

"Stop trying to distract me from my winning streak." I narrow my eyes, set my mouth into a line, and bend my knees and arms into a fighting stance. "Set those trash cans up. I'm gonna knock 'em down again."

Flynt sets them up for me. I raise the new chair over my head—a slim cherry oak missing a leg—close my eyes, and fling it ahead. A wild crashing—a tumbling explosion—makes my eyes pop open. I did it.

"Score!" Flynt cries dramatically, arms raised to the heavens.

There's a wind picking up, making my bangs blow off of my forehead, making the trash cans spin against the gravel, a dragging sort of beat. We skip to it in looping circles, hand in hand. And then I realize that our hands are touching and let his go and run to the other side of the parking lot to set up the cans for him. He knocks them down cleanly, easily, and we dance around some more—two people, victorious. Laughing.

Being with Flynt is strangely freeing. He's different from everyone else I've ever met. Which makes me feel less completely and totally abnormal, less alien. I just didn't know before that another person, let alone a boy, could make me feel this way.

I barely know anything about him, but he seems so familiar—as though I could flip through childhood photo albums and he'd be in every picture. Grinning. Swinging one-armed from trees in summer. Making three-armed snowmen in winter.

"All right," he says, pulling some red mittens from the pockets of his coat. Paper scraps and pen caps and a small plastic blue owl tumble out with them. "What say you we move on to the next part of our tour?"

I nod. Flynt grabs the chair we've been chucking and returns it to its resting place, near the Dumpster, for the next trash can bowlers to use.

I have a sudden aching wish, lodged in the pit of my stomach, for Oren to be here right now. He would have gone crazy for this, he would have come up with some way to give the game stakes, to make it more competitive, he always did; he would have won; we would have had to give him back-scratches whenever he wanted them for two weeks. I wonder if he ever went trash can bowling, when he left, before he left for good.

The piece of paper I always keep in my shoe slides backward from my arch, burning itself into my heel.

That's when I feel it: the *urge*, swelling in me like air being pumped into a balloon. I try to deflate it so Flynt won't see—push with my hands against my head to hold it in, but I can't. It's too powerful; it hurts; it pushes back until my hands fly from my forehead and I walk toward the fallen trash cans, touch each of them—six—in case Oren ever touched them too. Six trash cans.

Maybe I'll inherit his cells, take them into my cells, and maybe some part of him will grow back there. Six chances. Three breaths at each can. Six chances for him to come back. Eighteen breaths. Eighteen chances to breathe him in.

Flynt hollers to get my attention. I've been standing in one spot, lost inside my head, and he's yards and yards ahead of me now. I run ahead to him and he leads me on, farther into Neverland, the city of lost children.

*   *   *   *

"And this is where the junkies go to buy heroin, and the corner across the street is where the cokeheads go to buy cocaine, and this one over here is where they'll sell you meth, if you're really desperate," Flynt explains. "It's all very organized around here."

Everything he tells me about the workings of Neverland makes me feel very small and young. The worst thing that ever happens in high school world is when people get caught at the mall cutting class, or smoking cigarettes behind the science labs—nothing could possibly be worse than detention, than being grounded and not allowed to go to one of Sarah Moreland's infamous hook-up parties. No one thinks outside of the Carver bubble—how much worse things could get, or how much better.

Flynt steers me farther down the desolate-looking street. The few buildings still standing are window-cracked and look as though at some point they have all sustained major structural damage by fire.

Neverland is spread out like a dysfunctional maze where

nothing quite connects back to itself or makes sense. It seems like the whole place was laid out by a group of people who lost interest halfway through its construction: the church without a steeple; the rusted-out birdbath that acts as a kind of community P.O. Box where messages are dropped and exchanged; the empty lot full of sinks and toilets and cracked metal tubes and parts known as "the bathhouse." Flynt explains it is a common Neverland hook-up spot.

Half the people we meet are other runaways. They squat mid-sidewalk and part like the Red Sea to let us through, like Flynt is Moses. Some raise their fists to him as we pass, a motion of solidarity; some wolf-whistle at us, which makes him laugh, and then snort, which makes me laugh.

We turn a corner and head down an alleyway blocked by a heavy curtain. I put my right hand in my pocket, *tap tap tap, banana.* I *banana* the softest *banana* in the world; it's a new game, seeing just how soft I can *banana* while still *banana*-ing.

And then I gasp. Beyond the curtain is a Narnia; it's as though we've passed through to another, secret world. In it is a large, open space where someone has erected a series of random stone walls and stairs that lead nowhere. Everything is covered in brightly painted abstract murals and strung with twinkling lights and quilted bits of fabric. And there are people everywhere, in long skirts and patched black jackets with bolts in their ears and noses and lips and tongues, some with dreadlocks like Flynt's, others with shaved heads or hair streaked with color.

A circle of people are pounding trash can lids or pots and pans with their hands. Others play guitars and all sorts of tinkling, booming, hand-made instruments. Some of them are singing, or maybe moaning. I can't tell which. It's a thing both amazing and terrifying to witness, and I can't help but move to the rhythm. I forget the cold, the things I'd like to rearrange in my room, how Mom never stops sleeping and Dad never stops working.

I let myself go.

A tall, thin man in snowflake suspenders rises from the ground and approaches Flynt and me, holding out two sets of wind chimes. "Mind finding some sticks and joining us? We need some folks on chimes, yeah? We're going for something somber but celebratory at the same time, okay?" He gives a nod and rejoins the circle.

I'm about to shake my head, *no thank you*, but then Flynt says, "No problem!" and grabs my hand, pulling me back toward the curtain, the entrance of Narnia. We find two twigs: long, sturdy ones with their bark still on them, studded in frost. Flynt holds his up to me and narrows his eyes. "En garde," he cries out. "Produce your weapon!"

We spar for a minute before I knock the stick out of his hands and, faux defeated, he grabs it up, pretending to weep, and we run back toward the makeshift band and settle down to play.

I have never known anyone like Flynt.

The rhythm sweeps through me. I don't look up for three whole songs: three is a good number. Not as good as nine, but still very good. By that point, two people are arguing over who gets to play the largest trash can and someone has cracked open a bottle of Wild Dog and the guy playing the medium trash can is slumped over—he has just fallen asleep, or passed out, mid-drumming, mid-singing—and the rest of the band seems to be *dis*banding.

Flynt touches my shoulder with his twig. I touch my shoulder two more times to make it three. He laughs at me. I blush. "You're a natural on the wind chimes, kid," he says. And then, "You gonna be okay if I head over to that Dumpster"—Flynt points to a giant, dark blue basin—a makeshift Dumpster, I guess—"and scavenge today's wares? I'm looking for some new inspiration."

I nod. I see three leaves fall from a sycamore tree just beyond Flynt's head all at once, and I'm doubly reassured that this is the right thing.

Flynt flashes me a big, toothy grin before jogging away toward the Dumpster. I feel oddly comfortable here, among my own kind—the weird and the forgotten, the invisible and ignored. At school, I'm the girl who eats plain grape jelly sandwiches wrapped in tinfoil, alone on the front lawn, or in the library when it gets too cold outside. I'm the girl who can't enter or exit the bus, school, class, without tapping and *banana*-ing, the girl who doesn't raise her hand when she knows the answer because if she did, she'd have to put it back against her desk and raise it again and repeat. Three times, or six, or nine—depending on a whole host of other factors she could not control—how many words were in the question, how many other people had raised their hands, how many times the person in front of me had scratched the top of her head. I'm the girl who cannot shower after gym class because she'd have to do that, too, at least three times and, by the time she finished, the school day would have ended.

In Neverland, with Flynt, I'm a killer trash can bowler, a

musician. I'm—and I can hardly think the word before a warm, alien feeling flushes through my whole body—*pretty*.

Two boys several yards away begin to chant or sing again. They're not wearing shirts, despite the cold, and they're rubbing red tribal paint into their bare chests, and now they're laughing, looking ecstatic, like they've never been happier, and I want to be near them, so I rise. Maybe I'll even chant, too. Maybe I'll throw my arms up to the air and dance around and sing and howl.

But on my way toward them, a conversation catches my attention. A group of girls—about my age—are huddled together, looking nervous and tired.

A blonde girl wearing thick purple eyeliner and a long black coat is saying, "But I haven't talked to my parents in six months. They'll think I'm lying. It's what they've always thought." She looks between her friends, pauses, bites hard on her lip before going on. "I guess I could call my aunt. She might lend me the money. I'd share it. We could just go. Tonight, even. I mean; if she wires me the cash somehow."

"Yeah," says a girl with aqua feathers pinned into her black hair. "But where? Where else are we supposed to go?"

"I've got a friend in Philly," the blonde girl says slowly, like she's piecing together the plans as she announces them. "I'm pretty sure she still lives in the same place. We can crash in her basement. I just want out, you know?"

A third girl in big black combat boots blurts to the group: "I've got fifty bucks. That'll probably be enough for all of us, right? For the bus?" Her left heel hammers the ground nervously.

I hold my breath, also waiting—waiting for them to say why.

Why do they suddenly need to leave Neverland so badly? I think again of Sapphire, of the blood patterned up her walls. Maybe they knew her?

The first girl, the blonde, opens her mouth to speak again; then Black Boots sees me lurking nearby and elbows her sharply in the ribs. She whispers something to the others, and they move away from me.

I jog a little on my feet to keep warm, trying to act as though I haven't been standing there, eavesdropping. I continue walking down the alley, toward the dancing boys. But as I get closer, I realize that what they're rubbing into their chests isn't tribal paint.

It's blood.

They're cutting themselves, their chests and arms, with shards of glass from broken liquor bottles. The ground behind them is littered with empty bottles. One of them looks directly at me and smiles, wolf-grin, all teeth.

"Hey, you." He points at me with a bloody finger. "Haven't seen you in a real long time. You're, like, never around anymore. What's that all about, man?" His eyelids are fluttering. He reaches for me as though he wants to grab me; I gasp and turn, then turn back to him, and back away, again, again, again. Can't stop turning. My brain says, *No*. My brain says, *Not yet*. My brain says, *Six more to make it twenty-seven*. Three nines. Good. Clean. Good. Clean. *Done*.

I need to find Flynt.

Banana banana banana. I don't know if I'm thinking the word or saying it out loud. It bounces between the walls of my skull; I feel it pound, each syllable. Each piece. Each part. I hurry back down the alley. Suddenly, everything looks different, grotesque. Not a Narnia. A hell. The veil has been lifted and everything beneath it is covered. Stinking. Rotting. Everyone seems to be sick or about to be sick—shaking, moaning, twitching eyes rolling toward the sky. I don't know how I ever thought they were happy. Maybe it was just Flynt tricking me into seeing things that weren't really there.

Flynt Flynt Flynt. I say his name three times aloud. *Flynt Flynt Flynt* again. Once more. *Flynt Flynt Flynt.* I don't care if people can hear me. I stop and tap my right foot nine times. And then the left, another nine. And then I pull out six hairs. With each one I say his name. *Flynt Flynt Flynt Flynt Flynt Flynt.* Each a tiny death. Each a sacrifice that will bring him closer to me. *Come on come on come on.*

And then I see him—I knew it would work—appearing as if by magic, clutching a plastic bag spilling with trash. "Some *great* finds around these parts," Flynt says, as he approaches.

"I want to leave," I say. "I want to go. *Now.*"

His expression changes. He comes closer to me. "What happened?"

"I—I don't like it here. We have to go." I squeeze my fists, three times and mutter *banana* below my breath.

"Wait, what? Lo, tell me—"

"*Now,*" I say.

Find a wall. Tap three times. *Banana.*

CHAPTER 6

I think I'm shaking because Flynt puts his hands on my shoulders and starts hushing me like how my mother used to. He leads me back through the secret curtained entrance, where I *tap tap tap, banana* softer than I've ever *banana*-ed before, and onto the street.

Flynt says he's taking me to a better place, a place he knows I'll like. I try to tell him about what I saw—about the boys—as we pass through the curtained alleyway.

"Lo, hey, it's fine, you got spooked. You're just not used to the way people are around here."

"Yeah, maybe," I say, though I don't believe it. I'm not so naive as to think what I saw back there was okay—just the way people *are*.

"Look, you've got to understand. It's different here. We've got nothing to lose. We're not part of that other world, the dead world of TVs and gadgets, you know? We're more alive than that. We're the scavengers. The hawks, way up in the sky, giant wings, swooping down to earth when we feel like it. Know what I mean?"

Flynt takes a deep breath, watching me, his cheeks growing redder in the cold.

I stare at his bear ears, then his blue-green-gold eyes. I'm filled, suddenly, with a surge of anger. "And what about when people *actually* die? Is that part of your twisted version of fun? Does that make you feel more alive?"

Flynt's voice grows quieter. "I promise you're going to like this next spot, okay? No drum circles. We're almost there."

I continue to follow him, even though the anger is still there, low and smoldering. He's not listening; he doesn't care. All he's interested in is beautiful garbage.

We weave through alleys and tight corners and wide streets until we reach a tall building—tall for Neverland—and Flynt jimmies the lock to a door in back. I *tap* and I *banana* in three quick, secret cycles, the anger turning to a hot shame, praying he won't notice. If he does, he doesn't say anything.

Inside it's dark, though with the door still open I can see the winding staircase a couple of feet ahead of us.

"Someone rich used to live here, a really long time ago. It's been gutted by looters. Now all that's left of this place is the stairs." He leaps up onto the staircase. "Be careful climbing. There are some loose spots, and some of the stairs aren't too stable. Oh, and there's a monster here somewhere, too, a staircase monster. Be on the lookout for creepy tentacles."

"I think I can handle it, Flynt." I follow him up the staircase, picking my way over the broken or missing boards.

"It would just suck if you were eaten by the staircase monster. I'd probably be investigated in the homicide case sure to follow, and, to be honest, I don't think the Cleveland police would believe that a Staircase Monster ate you. If they *cared* enough to investigate around here, I mean," he adds, and even though his tone is still light, there's a hard edge running beneath it. I think of Sapphire. I wonder whether he is thinking of her, too, or of other cases, of other Neverland kids who have slipped through the cracks.

We make it to the top of the stairs safely, uneaten by monsters, and the tiny window at the top lets in enough light for Flynt to see the frozen door handle and jiggle it open.

We walk out onto a wide rooftop, and all of Neverland and the whole city of Cleveland and the distant quilt of the suburbs, too, are spread out before us—brilliantly pink and orange and yellow in the glow of the waning sun. From here Neverland and all of Ohio beyond it look more beautiful than I've ever imagined they could look.

Flynt was right. This is a good place. My head begins to clear now. Maybe I did just get freaked before. I can see seven church steeples and four domed buildings. Seven is a bad number, and I turn a complete circle until I spot one more steeple in the distance, stained ruddy red in the setting sun. Eight and four—both awful, suffocating numbers—but twelve, even if it's not always as perfect as nine, helps me breathe. Twelve is good for buildings. Twelve is solid, sure, safe.

Flynt moves to the edge of the building and spreads his arms out wide like he's a plant receiving nourishment. I move closer and watch him for a second.

"So, where do you live?" I realize he has never told me.

"I move around a lot." Flynt shrugs. "I find a different crash pad every two or three months. I've been on my own for five years, since I was thirteen, so it's something I've gotten pretty good at. Moving, I mean." His eyes glitter.

The roof is covered in something black and rubbery, and it's peeling away in patches. "How come you've been on your own since you were thirteen?"

"Oh, you know. I was ready to leave; there was nothing in Houston for me anymore. Thirteen is considered pretty much full-grown in my family." He squats low, starts aiming little rocks of gravel onto the rooftop across the street.

"Yeah, but what about your parents? They just let you go?"

"They were kind of checked out. It was no big deal." He looks away for a second, maybe remembering. Then he turns back, smiling big big big. "So, the view from this roof is pretty amazing, right?"

"Isn't it annoying? Constantly picking up and resettling?" I press, even though I know that, well, of course it is. I've done it my whole life.

"Actually," Flynt says, "it's not so bad. I've got a bag full of the essentials, and if I need to run, I run, and I find somewhere new, and that's where I stay until I feel like leaving again. A beautiful system, really."

"But what about, like, school and stuff?" I swallow, realizing I sound just like my mother. Or how my mother *used* to sound, before she retreated to her bedroom.

"Neverland is a *very* educational place," Flynt says, winking at me. I've never known someone who could hold a smile for so long. "I'm planning on getting out of here for good pretty soon, though. I'll probably head to San Francisco. Maybe Portland. I'll turn to ash and scatter in the western winds and become solid again somewhere by the ocean. Like a phoenix. Or, more like a seagull, with a phoenix-like sensibility."

Music drifts up to us from a bar on the strip below: slow, steady beat, languid violin, molasses guitar. Flynt gets up and flaps his arms like wings. He grabs my hand, pulling me with him and twirling me once.

"You're a pretty good dancer," he says. "Bet you didn't know that, did you? Just like you don't know that you're a good bowler, or a good wind-chimer, or that you're beautiful?"

Beautiful. That word makes all the other words dry up in my mind. "I—I'm not—"

He cuts me off. "So what's 'Lo' short for?" He spins me away and back again.

"Penelope."

"Penelllllllopeeee." He sings it. "I like that. It's kinda cool, old-fashioned or something."

"It was my mother's grandmother's name," I explain as he twirls me back in, then puts his hand on my lower back and begins a waltz. It makes me shiver, but I don't pull away. I blabber on, "My parents said that when I was born, my hair was thick and dark, like hers. They were going to name me something else but when they saw me, they were sure I was her, reincarnated." I pause; he dips me. Electric heat races up my back. "My parents are kinda weird," I continue, feeling Flynt's big hand around mine, guiding me in circles. I count each revolution in my head: *four, five, six.* "Or, I mean, they *were* weird. Now they're not anything." I bite my lip, wishing the words back. "So, what's the story with *your* name? I've never met anyone else named Flynt."

He drops my hand and does a goofy ballerina twirl, arms raised above his head. "Just a nickname. After Larry," he says as he twirls farther away.

"Larry?" I repeat.

"Larry Flynt."

Now that Flynt isn't leading, I don't feel comfortable dancing. I hug my arms across my chest, squeezing my fingertips hard into my shoulders; each finger, three times, *push push push.* Thirty; thirty pushes. The number relaxes me; my neck releases, I shake my head.

Flynt raises his eyebrows. "Mr. Flynt happened to be quite the porn-o-graphy mogul back in the day. He was a pretty famous smut publisher and owned a chain of strip clubs and all those sorts of things."

I squint at him. "So, what? You're secretly a porn mogul?"

"Not exactly." He laughs. "You actually never heard of Larry Flynt?"

I shake my head again and Flynt reaches out, chucks my chin like I'm six and not sixteen. "You really are from Lakewood, aren't you?"

"Just not too much of a porn buff," I say stiffly, jerking away.

"Hey, hey." Flynt's voice is soft. "I think it's cute. I think it's great, in fact."

Cute. Great. Like *beautiful*: words that have never applied to me, words I always thought were meant for different kinds of girls.

"People started calling me Flynt because when I first moved to Cleveland from Baltimore, I earned most of my money in strip clubs." Flynt hurries to explain when I raise my eyebrows. "I sketched strippers for their clients. You know, they don't allow cameras in the clubs. I was a one-man service industry for the service industry." I can tell he used to use this line a lot. He raises his eyebrows up and down, cartoon-like. Teasing me.

But his reference to strippers has distracted me.

"So, then maybe you remember Sapphire?" My voice sounds weak and high. "You know. The stripper—the friend of mine—who was murdered last week? Maybe you've sketched her?" My mouth and throat are dry, itchy, waiting for his response. *He's got to know her. How could he not?* The breeze picks up. The city below looks like it's on fire.

Flynt shrugs. "I don't know. I mean, there's like half a dozen clubs in Neverland alone, and strippers in and out of them constantly, too many to keep track of. I only know a few of them, really." He is watching me sideways.

And what comes to me, a certainty like a rock in my stomach, is: *he's hiding something.*

"She worked at Tens," I say, "Do you know Tens?"

A few seconds pass; he seems to be thinking. "Yeah, I know Tens," he says finally. "I haven't been in a while, though. Maybe Sapphire started there after I'd already stopped coming by to draw."

Another rock drops in my stomach. *He's lying.* I don't know how I know. I just do. My heart is a great thumping whale within my chest. I count rooftops in the distance. Eight red. Four deep blue. Five light blue. All bad. Bad bad bad. The nervous feeling is creeping in, wrapping itself around me, serpentine. *But*—I reason with myself—*if I group the blues together, four light and five dark makes nine.* Nine is very good.

"I'm thinking of stopping by there soon, actually," I say, wrapping my fingers around the butterfly in my pocket, relaxing my face, voice, attempting to sound casual. "I feel guilty about being out of touch for so long. I'm thinking it might help if I could talk to some people who knew her."

It's not difficult for me to make these sorts of lies sound genuine. The guilt is real enough. The guilt is always real. I dig my heel into my shoe, feel the mashed up piece of paper slide against my sock so I always know, so I never forget that anywhere I go, anything I do, there is at least one thing I'll never be able to undo.

Flynt looks at me hard, a look that makes me draw back. "I wouldn't get your hopes up about the girls at Tens." His cute dimples have disappeared, and his face is serious now. "The thing with strippers is this: unless you're a client or carrying a cocktail, they're not interested in talking. You'd be wasting your time." He stands up, all business suddenly. "We should get you to the bus. I've got some stuff to work on over at Malatesta's, and it's getting dark."

Just like that, he turns and walks back toward the stairwell. I follow him, feeling like the air has just been knocked out of me.

Tap tap tap, banana; I don't care if he notices or not. We exit the building in silence. Flynt doesn't make more jokes about staircase monsters or giant holes in the stairs. He doesn't look back to check on me. Outside, the darkness feels huge.

"So, do you need me to walk you to your bus?" Flynt asks flatly, like he hopes I'll say no.

There's a chance I'll get lost, but I don't want him around if he doesn't want to be.

"No," I answer. "I'll be fine. I'm fine."

"You're sure?"

"Yeah. Totally sure." I pull my cell phone from my pocket and pretend to check a text message that doesn't exist. I bet this annoys Flynt. I hope it does. "My friend . . . um, Jeremy . . . texted me to say that he's around here. So, I'll be fine. I'll meet up with him."

"Oh. Okay. Well, do you think you're gonna come by again anytime soon?"

"I don't know."

Flynt rubs his forehead, under his bear hat, and sighs.

"Lo, look, I'm sorry to break the news to you about Tens. It's just the truth."

"Yeah. Thanks." I don't look at him. I don't want to give in. Instead, I stare at the sleeves of my coat. They're dirty, covered in red paint, Flynt's hand-splatters. I was happy about it earlier, and now I'm not. Now I'm annoyed, off center. "I'm going to go, okay? Jeremy's waiting for me."

"Yeah, me, too. Got a lot to do." He chucks my shoulder with the back of his hand like nothing's happened. "Don't be a stranger, Lo. Come back soon. Really. You know I'll be here."

Flynt salutes me and walks in the opposite direction, toward

Malatesta's. I finger the dried paint on my coat as I walk to the bus, studying the street signs carefully. I'd be worried about Mom getting mad, except I know she'll never notice.

Thirteen and a half blocks to the bus stop. Left on Eastern Avenue. Right on 117th.

Maybe Flynt was right. Maybe he was genuinely trying to help. But when I mentioned Sapphire, it felt as though I flipped an invisible switch inside of him. Suddenly he became a different person—evasive and nervous. And mean, too.

He told me I was pretty.

He's a liar.

I run my fingers across the dried paint again on my coat. Six streaks. I see his hands in my mind. His long fingers.

I wish I could erase him. But he's stuck on me, now.

Six streaks. For good.

CHAPTER 7

The next day, school's as long as ever, but I'm distracted by too many things to notice its slow crawl. *Why would Flynt lie about knowing Sapphire?*

I space out for most of Brit Lit while Sidney Lourie and Brigid Crank, the girls in class with straight, silky blonde hair and beefy boyfriends, gush about *Pride and Prejudice* for nearly thirty minutes.

Why did he turn so suddenly, and then try and act as though nothing had happened?

I answer a vocab question out loud in SAT prep: the wound exhibited signs of (*copious*) drainage requiring medical intervention. I never do this. The answer comes to me and so I blurt it, automatically, "B: maximal."

During study hall, in the bathroom, I'm tapping out the six syllables of my name as I say it quietly aloud; three times to make it eighteen, which is an especially perfect number right after study hall. I start: *Pen-el-o-pe-Ma-rin Pen-el-o-pe-Ma-rin*

Pen-el-o-pe-Ma-rin; Pen-el-o-pe-Ma-rin Pen-el-o-pe-Ma-rin—
and then Keri Ram walks in and sidles up next to me at the mirrors, putting on oozy lip gloss that smells like watermelon. I have
four left to go, and I can't stop, even with her right beside me,
even though my whole body is burning, shameful. I mumble it,
tap so softly, hoping she won't notice. *Pen-el-o-pe-Ma-rin Pen-el-
o-pe-Ma-rin Pen-el-o-pe-Ma-rin Pen-el-o-pe-Ma-rin.*

"What did you say?" she asks me through the mirror.

There's a strange expression on her face. Mine is a deep, beet
red. I reach for the butterfly in the pocket of my jeans, squeeze
it three times so I can speak, so I can say anything at all, so I'm not
a total mute freak in front of Keri Ram.

"What?" I choke out. I want to run. I want to die.

She raises her eyebrows. "Did you just say something to me?"

"Oh." I tell her, hands fixed on my thighs to make them stop
shaking. "I was just . . . trying to remember, um, something from
English class. That T. S. Eliot poem that we read." I stare at my
awful clumpy bangs in the mirror. I pretend to fix my hair, though
it's kind of beyond fixing at the moment—just a tangled mass with
a rubber band wrapped around the end of it that I'm trying to pass
off as a braid.

"I'm *so* bad at memorizing poems." She caps her lip gloss,
pauses, assesses my reflection. "Where'd you get that necklace?
I really like it." She puckers her lips and admires them in the
mirror.

"Which one?" I ask, weirdly nervous, though I know Sapphire's
pendant is pressed beneath my shirt, out of sight.

"The moon."

I raise my fingers to the necklace, a crescent moon cut out of metal, a small, pale blue crystal dripping from its center; the silver horse burns, warm against my chest. "My father brought it back for me from Thailand a couple of years ago," I answer, shyly.

"Thailand." She sighs. "Cool. Have you ever been?" She reaches into her big leather purse and pulls out a thin black and silver tube of mascara.

I fuss some more with my braid, pulling out the rubber band and struggling to pull my fingers through the tangled nest of my hair. "My dad goes away a lot. But he never takes us. I mean, he used to take my mom sometimes. But, never Oren and me. And now"—I shut my mouth quickly. I never say Oren's name out loud. I glance at Keri in the mirror—she's rummaging through her bag again. Maybe she didn't hear me; she doesn't seem to be listening. "But I want to go. To Thailand. When I'm older I'll go." I force my mouth shut—when I talk, I have a tendency to babble—and go back to fussing with my bangs.

"Yeah, totally." Keri responds vaguely. I don't think she knows what else to say. "So, Lo," she begins, clearly trying to change the subject, twirling a loose strand of hair behind her ear. "Do you have a crush on anyone at school?" Her eyes pierce into mine through the mirror.

I'm so surprised by the random turn of the conversation I can only force out a "No."

"Really? Not anyone?" She's still staring at me through the mirror, like she's waiting for me to crack and expose the awful, secret truth.

I shake my head. "No. No. Definitely not."

"Not even . . . Jeremy Theroux?" She turns away from the mirrors to face me.

I make it look like I'm thinking hard—bite my lip, stare up and to the left, put my pointer finger over my lips—"Jeremy Theroux?" I repeat, like I've never heard the name before. "I don't think I even know who that is."

"That's weird. Because he stares at you in class. You really haven't noticed? And he's always trying to sit next to you. Like, obsessively. He's obviously got a crush on you. He's on the track team, too. He wins, like, every meet."

My face has gone tomato-red. "Oh," I say, acting like some light's gone off in my head, "*that* Jeremy." I sweep my bangs across my forehead three times in a row. To the right and to the left. Six times. "I wasn't sure who you were talking about first." I cough. "Sorry."

"So you don't like him?" Keri presses.

My face is violently red. "No." I shake my head for emphasis. "No." And again to make it three. "No." She's making me nervous—she probably thinks she's seeing right through me, that I'm blushing and saying no over and over again because I'm lying. She's probably going to leave the bathroom and tell all of her friends that I *do* like Jeremy but that I'm afraid to admit it, and then he'll find out, and ask me out for study dates a million more times, and it will never end.

She cocks her head, narrowing her eyes at me. "Yeah, okay. I got it the first time around." She looks almost disappointed in me. She swings her bag over her shoulder and heads for the exit, and with the door half open, says to me over her shoulder, "He's actually pretty cute, you know? If you really take the time to look at him?"

*   *   *   *

Jeremy approaches me by my locker as I'm placing my books in my bag, preparing to leave. His hair blazes in the late-afternoon light.

"Hey, Lo." He's wearing a soft-looking Cleveland Indians T-shirt and the same gray skinny jeans he wears every day. His bag is slung over his shoulder.

"Mm?" I turn away from him, pretend to be mining for something in the back of my locker. I keep thinking of what Keri said in the bathroom, and wondering if there's something wrong with me for not seeing how cute I'm supposed to think Jeremy really is, for not wanting him, like a normal person would.

Stupid. Of course there's something wrong with me. There are about a million of them.

"Did you get my notes? Either of them? I mean . . . I mean, I guess I know you got the second one because I was there. You know. In class and stuff."

"Notes . . . ?"

He coughs. "I know we've never really talked all that much before—outside of class—but you, like, you really seem like you've got this SAT stuff down, and I thought, sometime, if, you're ever not doing anythi—"

"I'm sorry, but I really can't talk right now," I interject. I can't look him in the eye to see the disappointment crowding in. "Mom needs me at home. Now. She—she's been kind of sick. We should talk soon, though, okay?" I force an apologetic smile. "I'm—I'm really sorry. See you tomorrow in class."

I slam my locker shut and walk quickly toward the big exit doors near Principal Powell's office.

"Okay. Um, see you tomorrow, then!" Jeremy calls out after me. I respond with a half wave over my left shoulder. Then, when he's not looking, I wave twice more.

Jeremy's nervousness makes me nervous. When his whole face goes red as he speaks to me, it gives me a sick feeling, because I understand it. I understand how every cell in his body must be burning and painful, just getting the words out.

Flynt isn't like that at all; he's not like me, or Jeremy. He knows how to talk to people. He has a million stories. Flynt makes my stomach hurt in a different way. Because he lied to me. Because he's free, unburdened by things. Because he's the most mysterious person I've ever known. I've never met anyone like him. And because he thinks I'm beautiful.

I count the tiles as I walk. Forty-nine between my locker and the back exit doors, five of them studded with gum.

*   *   *   *

For years I never had to walk home from school alone, no matter where we lived, because Oren was there. In the fall, in Minnesota, when the leaves were everywhere, he'd double back behind me and push me into the big leaf piles people made on their lawns. We'd get home and Mom would pick all the leaf-bits out of my hair and sweater while I sat on the carpet watching TV and Oren would bring me cookies to make up for pushing me.

He had a big wicker basket full of baseball hats that he'd collected since he was a little kid. He always liked baseball. He arranged them in a particular way, and he always knew if I'd gone in and touched them. And I'd go into his room sometimes when he wasn't there, when he was in the basement with friends or listening to music in the kitchen, and toss the whole basket of them all around his room, just to rile him up.

I always knew when he had come back to his room by the roars of anger, the pounding of his feet coming after me. Dad would sit us down, cross-legged on the carpet, insisting we apologize. Mom would come, too, stand beside him, nodding. She'd say, *You two are lucky you've got each other. Now, hug, make up.* By dinnertime he'd have forgotten all about it, and his hats would be back in the basket, just as he liked them to be.

Now I hold my breath when I walk past his room at home. Part of me is worried I'll breathe too hard and mess up his hats. No one's touched them; no one's touched anything.

We all thought he'd come back. He'd been picking up and leaving for days at a time for six months before he disappeared for good. He'd return home without a word, like this was a thing people did all the time, like Mom and Dad and I should have known our concern was not a factor in his comings and goings. And then weeks passed. And then months. We still thought he'd be back: maybe he'd left Cleveland, maybe he'd left the country, but he was somewhere, breathing. We were sure.

We were wrong.

*   *   *   *

I take Oak Street most of the way home from school, a straight shot along clean sidewalks and big, new cars. A cold mid-March breeze zips through the trees, and I reach into the pockets of my coat in search of the fuzzy blue mittens Mom knit for me three Christmases ago. My hand brushes against Sapphire's butterfly inside my pocket; I've started carrying it with me when I leave the house.

I notice the neighbors' old plastic Christmas reindeer has fallen over in their yard. And a few houses down, the Lowmans must have had their car washed today; it gleams. The winter sun is already beginning to set, casting long shadows off porches, all the houses on the block haloed in red-oranges and dark blues.

Nine ravens perch on the telephone wire stretched high across the boulevard behind my street, nine perfect black silhouettes. One reaches its wings to the sky, like it might fly off, but it doesn't. It stays and settles back down, and the nine of them—the perfect amount, a safe, full, comforting number—huddle closer, a family of solidly knit shadows. Watching them, a warmth fills me, like it used to on Saturday mornings when I was a kid and I'd wake before anyone else to watch cartoons, wrapped in my fuzzy pale blue blanket, waiting for everyone else to wake up, too, and for the kitchen to fill with the sounds of egg yolks being whisked in bowls, the hissing and popping of bacon, and the gurgling murmur of the coffeemaker: warm, buttery, earthy smells.

As I approach my house, I notice a package on the porch—a lumpy-looking dark thing—probably something for Dad, from work. Many of the companies he helps restructure send him products through the mail, compulsory sort of thank-yous; he used to give most of the crap they'd send to Oren and me. We'd build bridges of pen caps and robots of light-up key chains and beer cozies. Everything we built is saved in some box in the basement, a box we carry with us everywhere we move, its edges sealed in duct tape years ago.

I climb the steps of my porch, preparing to scoop up the package, when I stumble backward.

Not a package.

A cat. Scrawny. Mangy. Dead.

I curl into myself in horror; I might vomit. I force my eyes back onto the animal and see the white spots around its neck and torso matted in dried brown blood, its throat spilling something sick and foul-smelling. There's a note pinned to its neck.

Hands trembling, I rip the note off. I breathe slowly as the words swim into focus.

Now you know what curiosity did.
Be careful, or you'll end up like the cat.

CHAPTER 8

I barely make it to the edge of the porch before I puke over the whitewashed wooden rail. I thud to the ground, trembling, my throat burning, then *tap tap tap, banana* and push through my front door, pull my cell phone from the pocket of my coat. Nine-one-one. I say it aloud, twice more, as I dial. Through the ringing, through the heavy seconds of waiting: nine-one-one; nine-one-one.

Click. A man's voice; low, throaty: "Nine-one-one. What is your emergency?"

The words sputter from my throat, choked shards. "I—someone. Someone—" I hiccup, try to make the words clean, even—"killed a cat. There's a dead. A dead cat on my porch."

A sigh on the other end. Buzzing. "A dead cat, Miss? And where is it that you're located?"

"Lakewood. My porch—it's on my porch, here. Lakewood."

There's a pause. "Let me get this straight. A cat *died* on your

porch? *Somewhere* in Lakewood? I think this might be an issue for
the humane soc—"

"No!" I shout, bubbling with a tugging, tiding anger; "A cat was
killed on my porch. It didn't die. It was *killed.* There was a note—"

The operator cuts me off. "All right, calm down, Miss. This
sounds like some kind of prank to me. Are you having a conflict
with anyone? An ex-boyfriend, maybe, or a current—"

I hang up.

I press END again. And once more. To make three. I glimpse
the cat from the window and double over—almost puking, but
not—before going to the kitchen and pulling out a plastic trash
bag from under the sink. My mind is on an endless loop. *The cat's
out of the bag,* I think. *Look what curiosity did.* Everything beneath
the sink is in complete disarray, terrible. I *tap tap tap, banana* and
return to the porch with the bag and wrap it around the dead cat,
grimacing as I slide its body in, gingerly, and then push the lumpy
mass into a darkened corner of the yard, near a tree. I will bury it
later in the backyard. My hands are shaking fiercely, stomach still
turning. I *tap tap tap, banana*, go back inside, and rearrange the
cleaning products underneath the sink by color and height, sepa-
rating them into three groups of three and placing the additional
two bottles—squat, heavy, opaque white—in a separate cabinet
because they don't fit in, and I can't stand to see them beside the
slim-necked, transparent things that do.

I'm still shaky, foggy, so I crawl upstairs to my room and
move all twelve antique brass wall-clocks to the opposite wall,
breathing in and out in six-second increments. I lift the first
of the Roman-numeral clocks (nine in total, three regular

numbered)—this one salvaged from a musty little junk shop in Baltimore—and hold it to my chest to feel our hearts beating in tandem, twin metronomes.

Six seconds in, six seconds out—no choice anymore. *Don't mess this up.* If I mess up, even by a second, I have to start the breath cycle all over again. That's the rule. The unbreakable rule.

Now the first Roman-numeral clock needs to be where the long red Minnesota sundial clock hangs and every part of me knows it, to the smallest atom, and I have to fix it—*now.* How did I not see it before, that I'd arranged them totally wrong? I fix it. Then I lift my Cleveland Flea mantle clock with the three birds dangling from its underside from the wall to give it a dusting-off. Three swift swipes between its mottled top ridges; back to the wall.

Six seconds in, six seconds out: I don't mess up the breathing. I get it right. It feels good in my stomach to get something right. It feels good in my hands.

I step back and assess my work on the wall. Twelve clocks. The number spins through my head. Twelve clocks. The number starts to calm me until the dead cat vibrates once again into focus. The note seems to write itself into the air before my eyes—*Now you know what curiosity did. . . .* I see matted fur and blood in sick flashes, the wooden planks of the porch sodden with stain, with death.

I heard the gunshot. I bolted. Could the killer have seen me? Could he have identified me? He *must* have seen me, followed me without my knowing, seeing, hearing. Now he's warning me. No—threatening me. I move to the window and scan the street below—whoever did this might still be around, might be watching the house, might be watching me right now.

Clouds are gathering in the sky. Maybe a storm will come and wash the cat blood away—wash everything away.

Boom. Thunder, breaking through the rain-streaked sky. I shiver, scanning the parked cars and high trees and streetlights beginning to click on for the evening. Sapphire's murderer could be anywhere, everywhere.

I reach for Sapphire's butterfly inside the pocket of my coat and clutch it tightly in my fist. Something hot rises in my throat as the reality of the situation clarifies itself in peaks and jolts: I've got to find him before he finds me.

Because if I don't, I'm going to be next.

*   *   *   *

I stay upstairs, arranging, rearranging, as the sun disappears behind the trees and my room grows dark. I'm moving the Italian glass medallions to the second shelf above my desk, one by one, when I hear the garage door groan open and close, the back door click and twist and shut downstairs. Dad's briefcase clunks onto the floor. By the time every medallion has been rearranged, three-inch spaces measured precisely between them, there are new sounds, new smells: banging and clanking from the kitchen; flour and butter and warm things stewing. I'm sure I'm either dreaming, or I'm smelling something from the neighbor's house that's just so powerfully good-smelling that it *seems* like it's coming from our kitchen. My parents don't cook—haven't cooked since Oren died. It's take-out or cold sandwiches every single night. Mom doesn't really eat, anyway, and Dad's usually not home before ten. I must be hallucinating.

I let the good smells of an imaginary dinner weave around me, calm me, when something Flynt had said, in his low, soft voice, pops into my head: *Unless you're a client or carrying a cocktail, they're not interested.* I'm pretty sure he just wanted to shut me up after I'd asked him about Tens, but—I realize, sitting up in bed and throwing my blackbird-patterned comforter off my chest as something akin to lightning jolts through me—maybe it's not impossible. Just because Flynt says that's the *only* way, doesn't mean there's *no* way to get them to talk to me.

I've just got to be carrying a cocktail.

I sprint downstairs to get the makeup Mom keeps in the bathroom near the kitchen. When she used to go out, in every house we've ever lived, she'd always get ready in the downstairs bathroom because she said it had the perfect "evening" lighting— slightly dimmer than the other rooms, more flattering, more "movie star." I remember standing behind her as a kid, watching her; she'd dust her cheeks with rose-colored blush flecked with tiny sparkles, so her skin looked like it was made of diamonds. After she left—usually with my father, arm in arm, headed to a dinner—and Oren, as babysitter, was fixated on baseball on TV or playing guitar, badly, in the basement—I'd sneak some of the diamond-blush and put it all over my face and arms, prancing around the house, sparkling, pretending I was a fairy.

Before I reach the bathroom, I see the kitchen light on and my dad standing there bent over the stove, his broad back in a white undershirt and his silky black work pants. It wasn't imaginary dinner after all.

"Lind? That you?" he calls—clearly hoping it's my mother— hoping the dinner he's cooking will rouse her, at least for a few minutes, from her deep black hole.

"No, Dad. It's me."

A pause. "Lo?"

Who else would it be? I think, but don't say. "Yes. Lo."

"Dinner's ready in a minute."

It's heartbreaking, seeing my dad stirring things in his undershirt, seeing cutting knives and vegetables laid out on the kitchen counter (all in the wrong order, the colors all mixed), watching him wipe his pale hands on the dandelion-print towel hanging from the oven that Mom used to put out around Easter. He used to make us elaborate gourmet meals, every Friday night. We'd all wear dress-up clothes to the kitchen table like we were at a fancy restaurant, and Mom and Dad would let Oren and me take sips of wine, like families do in Europe. Seeing him, now, makes me half believe that things might be normal again. Even for a night. Maybe Mom will emerge. Maybe we'll light a fire together after dinner and I'll tell them everything. And then, they'll make it all better, like parents are supposed to do.

"I—I'm not really hungry," I tell him, which is true.

He turns around, looking crestfallen. "I made linguini with pesto. You like pesto, right?"

I hate pesto, actually. It's not the taste I mind, it's the texture, and the way it sticks to my tongue like green sand. But I force myself to smile. "Pesto sounds really good."

"Have a seat then, hon." He gestures to the table. He has set up three placemats, as though he is still hoping that Mom will come downstairs. Oren's chair is missing. My dad must have taken it away from the table at some point, moved it to the basement, so it would not stare at us every time we passed it, confronting us with its emptiness.

I sit down as Dad serves pesto-drenched noodles and peas onto my plate, and then onto his own. Green. All green against white. He scoops a dollop of food onto a third plate and places it at the other end of the table, plunking forks down as well, each one clattering too loudly.

"So, how's school going?" he asks, taking his seat.

"Fine," I say. We sit in silence for a moment as he starts eating. I stare. It's almost like I've forgotten how to do this.

Finally, he breaks the silence. "I'm sorry I haven't been around much, Lo. I've got to figure out how to handle this damn company I'm working with right now. Trying to pull the wool over the city's eyes . . . industrial chemicals shipping. It's disgusting, really. This guy thinks he's a hot-shot . . . thirty years old and already a big-time CEO . . . trying to get away with this sneaky real estate bullshit."

When he speaks again, his voice is quiet. "Anyway, I want you to know, I'm trying, Lo. You know that, right? Your mother and I—we're doing the best we can. I left work early tonight to spend time with you."

"I know. Seven thirty. So early." The words feel huge in my throat. The peas look grossly disordered on the plate, the pasta a tangled mess.

"And I'm going to try to be around here a lot more." He picks up his fork again. "By the way, I saw a garbage bag in the yard on my way in tonight. Were you cleaning your room like we talked about?"

The dead cat. He must have seen it, before I buried it.

"You didn't go in there, did you? To my room?" I ask quietly, patiently dividing the peas across my plate. Three even groupings. Seven peas per group. Not as good as nine but not terrible. Not the worst. "Because that's really *my* space, Dad, and I don't like anyone to—"

"Relax," he tells me. "I haven't gone into your room. But I *know* I asked you to clear away some of your junk over six months ago, and I just want to make sure you're on top of it, honey." He glances over at my plate and sighs. "Stop moving your food around and just eat it, okay, Lo? You used to love peas."

But I'm working and his voice is a low mumble I can barely make out. There's still this hideous *pile* in the center of the plate. I cannot rest until each pea is given a proper home on one edge of my plate. Three options. Six peas left to administer. Five peas left. Four. Three.

Dad watches me out of the corner of his eye as we sit there for a while in silence; the only sound is the clinking of his fork against his plate and the spreading, rearranging, mashing sound of mine.

I count each group of peas, confirming their symmetry. *One, two, three, four*—

But Dad interrupts. "Lo. I *told* you to stop *doing* that." So, I have to start again, hands beginning to shake. *One, two, three, four, five, six. One, two, three*—"Lo. Look at me. Please. Have you been taking your medication? Lo? Answer me."—again: start over, face burning, body bubbling over, a mix of rage and shame. He doesn't understand—I don't want to be like Mom—cripplingly numb, blank headed. I'd rather this. Groups. Order. Systems. Patterns. Safe safe safe. He shoots his hand forward, trying to grab my fork. I yelp, pulling it away from him, beginning again as I have to begin.

Group one: *One, two, three, four, five, six.*

He's glaring at me; I keep going.

"Eat your *goddamn* dinner, Penelope."

No—no choice. Can't stop. Group two: *one, two, three, four, five, six.* Group three: *one, two, three, four, five, six.*

I breathe, deep. Finished. Done. Each group even, a perfect amassment of color and form and figure.

I press my palms hard onto the edge of the table as I scoot out my chair and stand up. My dad is staring at me with that look he gets, the horrified look, like I'm a mutant animal in a cage. "Sit back down, Penelope. We are going to have dinner like a normal—"

"I'm not hungry." I repeat, stepping quickly from the table, hands clenched into tight fists. "I hate pesto. I've always hated pesto." I go into the hallway and torpedo into the bathroom. I close the door and lock it, half expecting for my dad to come banging on the door, demanding that I sit down again. But he doesn't. A minute later I hear footsteps pass by the bathroom. Then his study door opens and closes.

I exhale three times and count three spaces between breaths. Time to go.

I find my mom's makeup bag wedged between facial

moisturizers and two three-bottled rows of nail polish in a basket to the left of the sink, a thick layer of dust covering everything. I jog the dust off the bag and then just hold it for a minute, stare at it. From the corner of my eye, the Ghost of Mother Past sits in her queenly bedroom chair in front of the mirror, glittering there in the evening light.

I exit the bathroom and creep quietly upstairs to my room, moving a cluster of antique silverware; disembodied china doll heads, hands, feet; a tall stack of crumbling photographs of other people's families and dogs and vacations, carefully, against the foot of my desk. When I finish and there's room, I sit at my antique, cherry wood wardrobe and stare into the big, oblong mirror.

Whoosh—I slide the blush brush back and forth across my cheeks, watching them grow rosier and rosier, the thick fist of bristles stinging a little. They've grown stiff from lack of use. I am filled, now, with a jittery excitement. I can hardly keep still enough to rub foundation into my face evenly, or to draw the eye-liner pencil—a dusky, deep blue-black—around the border of my eyes. My hands are shaking like plucked rubber bands.

My face in the mirror, heavy with makeup, doesn't even look like my face anymore. I look *older*, like I'm seeing myself in the future, and if I passed this future-version of myself on the street, I'd think she was in college, at least.

An odd rush of satisfaction hits my body like a sugar high—I didn't realize it was so easy to become someone else. To shelve myself away, in a kind of dark distant storage, and then emerge—new—a cakey, sparkling, womanly apparition.

I look at this new girl's unblemished, even-toned skin—she has no scars. And then, in a blink, the apparition fades away. It's just me again. Scarred and plain. It occurs to me that I'm lying to my parents and sneaking out to a club when I'm supposed to be studying, almost like a Normal Teenager.

The irony of it makes me laugh out loud, and I clap my hand over my mouth to muffle the sound. Don't want Dad to think I'm any crazier than he already does.

I step away from the vanity for a final survey of my room as new jitters creep through my body, my fingers ticking madly into my fists—and it's a good thing I do, because I notice immediately that the stone wolves need to be moved five inches to the right, all nine of them; I need to reach them in three big steps, or in twenty-seven very small steps to prevent getting caught tonight. I get there in three big ones, rearrange them quickly, then take twenty-seven tiny steps back to my purse and do a final survey over my little kingdom. In order. Ready to leave the safety of my warm cocoon and spin outwards, new. Sort of.

Quickly: I remove the crumpled piece of paper at the bottom of my Converse and place it in the heel of a pair of mom's old heels. I'll wear them tonight, to blend in. Finally, I press my hand against the horse pendant, resting on my chest, and feel for the crumpled piece of paper in the bottom of my shoe, for Sapphire's butterfly in the pocket of my coat. I grab a purse from the arm of my desk chair, shove my wallet inside of it. *All systems go.* I reach my bedroom door in nine medium-size steps and creep downstairs, my heart thudding noisily. There is a thin sliver of light creeping into the hallway from my dad's study; otherwise, everything is dark. I grab some stale Cheetos from an open bag in the pantry, suddenly starving.

I *tap tap tap, banana*, open the front door, pausing for a second as I stand, sandwiched between warmth and frost: in the darkness, the killer could be waiting.

I hesitate for another second before sliding outside into the frosty air, clicking the door shut quietly behind me.

CHAPTER 9

"A cocktail waitress? You've got to dance, too. You know that, right? Not your average everyday drinks-and-dinner kind of thing here," says the manager of Tens: a short paunchy man with a thick golden mustache and forest green sport coat. He has taken my coat and draped it lazily on a hook by the door, and now he's sizing me up. He quickly glances between my face and chest, seeming to peer, X-ray vision–style, through my black skirt (the shortest I had), purple spaghetti-strapped tank-top (the smallest I had), thin, knit shrug covering my shoulders, and Mom's old patent leather heels from the eighties that I used to play dress-up in (the only pair in my closet that were remotely right). I'm trying to pretend this isn't happening without letting on that I think he's kind of creepy.

I push my bangs to the side, back and forth, three times, and then plant my hands against the sides of my thighs and stare straight ahead. I need to seem fearless. I need to do more than *seem*, I need to *be*.

I stare into the crowd—the profile of a man sitting close to the stage looks very familiar—greasy hair tucked under a ratty old cap, leathery skin. *Mario.* But, seconds later, he takes the hat off to wipe his forehead, and I see his hair is muddy brown, not Mario's dyed shock of red. He's just another greasy middle-aged man, a pack of Winstons peaking out of his shirt pocket. My heart skips wildly in my chest.

I try to hide my hands behind my back, tapping. Nine, nine, six. Nine, nine, six. Nine, nine, six. "I love dancing," I say, smiling, flashing him rows of white teeth between painted lips.

So far, everything's going smoothly. I made a plan on my way here:

1) Find club

2) Find manager

3) Find out more about Sapphire, in whatever way I can

4) Try not to get killed

One and two I've got down. I'm working on three and four.

"Work experience?" he asks.

"Oh, yeah. Yes. Absolutely." I put my hands on my hips and push my chest out—normally, I try to hide my C-cup boobs, but now, they might be just what I need—just a little, three little juts, as I gaze around the club, formulating answers: I've never been to a strip club before, and Tens is not what I imagined. I thought it would be glossy, larger-than-life and distant, like a movie.

Instead it's just a dim room, and there's a lingering cigarette smell in the air and a half sweet, half sour liquor-y smell layered somewhere beneath it and big men dressed all in black clomping onto the main floor from what must be a basement or secret level below, watching, waiting.

The customers—the men lined up at the bars and at the tables—look surprisingly normal. I guess I expected some leering, bug-eyed creepers. But they look like guys my dad might play golf with, newly beer-bellied and taking a load off in their post-work polos. One table is full of boys just barely older than I am. They're laughing too loud, at jokes I'm sure aren't funny.

A girl with feathery dyed-red hair slides down the pole cross-legged, her back arching toward the audience. *Look. No hands.*

Her skin puckers slightly against the slick-looking metal, thigh-sliding, ankle-gripping, all of her skin flashing in the light. She seems to be floating through air, her body pliable and shiny as bubble gum.

She makes it look like the whole thing's a breeze: capturing metal between thighs, making it melt between warm skin and muscle. I can't imagine being her, being up there, eyes snaking over every inch of my skin.

I focus my eyes back on Mustache. "I just moved here from . . . Chicago. But I was working there, for a while, in a club. Waitressing."

His eyes rove up and down my body, lingering momentarily on my slightly lopsided boobs (can he tell?); a sick feeling floods my belly. I force myself to keep smiling.

"You seem like a good girl. Good body, good attitude, good face, nice long, thick hair—you got an Irish look to you. You Irish?"

I shrug, again, again, trying not to shrink into myself. "I don't think so." Hearing his "assessments," I feel both weirdly

THE   BUTTERFLY   CLUES   95

satisfied that *I'm good enough* and disgusted with myself for caring and then, again, more of the half-sick-feeling excitement.

"That's what we're looking for around here," he continues, rocking back and forth slightly in his leather shoes, lips pursed and hands perched on his hips in a way that makes him look oddly feminine. "Just lost a girl, so we're definitely looking for, uh, some, uh, new blood." His eyebrows crease together. "You're eighteen, right?"

The way he so casually throws out the phrases *lost a girl* and *new blood* makes me stiffen, though I answer yes with three curt nods.

"Let me get you an application," he says. "Stay right here." He pushes through swinging doors just next to the deejay booth; I make out a dimly lit hallway, and what must be the entrance to the office, before the doors swing shut again.

A new girl takes the stage. She is wearing sparkly pink underwear, and sprawls majestically onto her taut stomach, then cat-crawls, lollipop in mouth, toward a wide-eyed customer in the first row. She's Tens' answer to Carver High's Jessica Fisk-Morgan: The Cheerleader. All sugar and fluff. Ever vapid, ever bouncy, she earned yearbook superlatives "First to get Married" and "First to get Pregnant" four years in a row. It makes me feel better to think of the girl onstage this way, less freaked out and out of place.

Mustache returns with several slips of paper, clipped together, and slaps it on the bar. "Go ahead and fill out the forms and I'll give 'em a look-over, ask you some questions, see if you're a good fit." His head bobs as he talks. It never stops bobbing.

On the application, I make up a whole list of clubs and

restaurants, change the year of my birth to make myself eighteen, then write out my fake name: *Juliet*. There isn't even a space for a last name. They don't want to know, I guess.

The Jessica-like girl onstage has transferred her lollipop into the wide-eyed customer's mouth. A whooping holler breaks across the small crowd of men. Mustache comes back toward me, pulling my application from the bar and scanning the pages quickly, mumbling *hmm*s and *uh-huh*s, as he reads.

"So . . ." I swallow hard, tap again against my back. Nine, nine, six, counting the numbers silently, quickly in my head. Time for part three of my plan. "Would I be able to take a look around the club, you know, to get a better sense of the place?"

Just as he looks up from the paper and opens his mouth to answer me, one of the waitresses cuts between us.

"Howard, look, I was supposed to be out of here *forever ago*, okay? And I finally convinced this dipshit at table twelve that he needed to pay his twelve-hour eight-hundred-dollar bill so that I could *go home*, and now the piece-of-shit credit card machine decides it doesn't really feel like *working* right now. So, can we figure this shit out? My night off started, like, six hours ago." She taps her foot, twitching as she speaks, glaring at him and ignoring me. I start twitching, too, just watching her.

The manager puts his hands on her bare shoulders, glancing quickly at the sparkling triangle of thong between her thighs. "Take it easy, Amber. I'll fix it, all right?" He turns back to me. "You can take a walk around the club, talk to some of the girls, you know, whatever you want." He says it like it was his idea in the first place, like he's already my boss.

I weave through a cramped maze of red and black tabletops with *Tens* written in cursive across the face of each. The air has a thick look to it. The floor is covered in wall-to-wall plush black carpeting. About a third of the tables are occupied—small clots of customers between big pockets of emptiness. Most of the tables are just a mess of paper napkins and plastic multicolored toothpicks and green olives and different size glasses and hairy forearms and wedding-banded fingers.

The underage-seeming boys are closer to the stage, sporting matching SIGMA TAU GAMMA T-shirts in matching navy blue—I bet these are the boys that Kevin DiGiulio and Brad Kemp and Tony Matthews will become in a maximum of three minutes post high-school graduation.

A waitress pushes past me with a tray of drinks, flashing me a look of frustration. She's the Simone Rothbait of Tens, I decide: she looks way too old to work here. Some people think that Simone is secretly on parole and can't graduate until it's over—and that she's been on parole for fifteen years. That's why she's always so pissy, and in all the slacker classes—at this point, she's given up the jig. Simone Rothbait will be in high school *forever*.

I move quickly out of the waitress's way, as I do with actual Simone when I cross her path at Carver, and grasp harder on to the butterfly in my pocket. *Five rows of six tables. Thirty tables. Three x ten.* I focus on the three, push the ten somewhere else for now. I'll deal with ten later. The red-haired dancer appears from behind the stage, and I follow her, into the hallway that stretches along the back of the club.

Remember. You're not Lo. You're Juliet. You're new.

"Excuse me." I tap the red-haired girl on the shoulder and resist the urge to tap her other shoulder as well.

She whips around, the look on her face fading quickly from anger to confusion. Keri—I realize—she's the Keri Ram. Teen Queen. Pretty Princess, but with enough very minor imperfections, close-up, to render her unhateable to even the very jealous types. "Can I help you with something?"

"Uh, hi. Yes. I'm, um, applying for a job, and the manager told me to look around the club, talk to the girls. So, can I? Talk to you about the club, I mean?" I don't know where to look as I speak to her. My eyes keep gravitating down toward the sparkly purple thong hugging the sides of her waist, capped in hot pink fringe and swaying gently as she moves.

I tug at my Gap tank top and just-barely-above-the-knee-length jean skirt (from eighth grade), Mom's tacky old heels from the eighties, suddenly aware that I must look, to her, like a child, a narc, a visitor from a foreign land.

But her face relaxes. She runs a hand through her hair. "Oh. Yeah, sure. I mean, it's the same here as anywhere, but . . ." She shrugs, then bends over to remove her black rhinestone-studded high heels, one by one, wincing slightly and motioning to a hallway in front of us. "I'm heading to the break room right now if you wanna come. Quieter there. Easier to talk."

A security guard grants us entrance into a cordoned-off hallway. I *tap tap tap, banana* so so softly.

"Duck," the redheaded girl warns me. "Ceiling's too low."

*   *   *   *

There are five girls in the break room, six including me, and we've just finished making introductions. The girl who reminds me of Keri Ram is named Marnie, and the others introduce themselves as Suzie, Randi, Lucy, and Lacey. I can't help but assume they've all got made-up names. They reapply makeup, toy with different styles of too-small lacy G-strings, spray perfumes onto their wrists and ankles and necks. Two of them finish smoking their cigarettes at nearly the same time, both pulling new ones out of separate packs almost immediately after stubbing out the old, becoming visibly less twitchy as soon as they relight. For some reason, seeing this relaxes me a little—they're nervous, too. Masking it as best they can. Just getting by.

Lacey has a mole on her cheek. She has just finished giving me a rundown of club rules. Nails must be painted at all times. No full nudity on the pole. Two sick days a month, suspension for no-call no-show. No drugs.

"But don't worry"—Suzie exhales a cloud of smoke—"they're *so* not that strict about that."

"So, you feel pretty safe here?" I try and steer the conversation toward Sapphire. "I mean, nobody creeps you out?"

"Once in a while there are situations—you know how it goes." Marnie shrugs. "Sometimes someone makes it past security, comes charging into the dressing room all lit up. But nothing crazy. Same shit as everywhere, you know?"

"And the customers aren't allowed to touch us," says Lacey. "No hands. Not that that stops most of them from trying. If they try to get up onstage or anything we're allowed to throw a shoe at their heads. It's in our contract."

"But that doesn't usually happen?" I ask, working at the hem of my skirt. There's a slightly twisted expression on Randi's face; she's staring at me through the mirror.

Lacey continues, furrowing her brow: "Most of them definitely *try* to see how far they can get—usually some drunk old guy with a lot of money who thinks he can do whatever he wants. But the bouncers are usually on top of it."

"And," says Marnie, "we got some great regulars, too." She pulls a wad of sweaty cash from between her symmetrical cantaloupe boobs and zips it into the interior of the black leather purse slung across her chair. "Moneybags in business suits, dumb frat boys with a trust fund. Bachelor parties."

"I *hate* bachelor parties." Lacey pouts.

Marnie ignores her. "You've got such a baby face, you'll do great. Wednesday's costume night—put on a school girl outfit, or some cat ears . . . the guys'll love it."

The dead cat flashes into my head. It keeps doing this: assaulting my field of vision, not letting me forget. The big question—the reason I came here in the first place—stretches itself long between my teeth and practically leaps from my mouth. *Time to go for it, Lo. Just. Ask.*

"Didn't you work with a girl who was just killed? Sapphire?"

The girls all stop dressing and lip-sticking and hair-curling and are still for a moment. I hold my breath through the agonizing pause. *One, two, three . . .*

The dam breaks.

"Sapphire," Suzie cuts through the new silence in a quavery voice. She looks at the other girls, as though asking permission to speak. But the mood in the room has shifted: they're all looking somewhere else—at their feet, at the walls, at their long polished nails. She begins anyway, hesitantly at first: "Yeah, we knew her. She was one of the good ones—you know, showed up on time, would lend you a twenty if you were having a slow start and needed a drink. She was funny as shit, too. Not a pissed-off drunk, like the rest of us." She tries to laugh, but it comes out more as a cough.

"She used to cover for me whenever Colin got sick—he's my son—even if he just had a cold or something," Randi adds, lacing a pair of stilettos higher up her thighs than I knew boots could reach. "She cared. She really did. Yeah. She was good people." She finishes lacing with remarkable speed and goes over to the lockers, pointing to one with long French-manicured fingernails. "This used to be her locker. It'll be yours, now, if you take the job. She left some crap in it. You can just take it, I guess."

"Really?" I ask her, uncertain if I've misheard, worried that I'm somehow being tested.

She shrugs. "She's not coming back for it, right?" Her tone softens. "Besides, she would have probably given it to you, anyway. She was like that. Generous. Always shared her makeup, clothes, whatever."

"Except for her ugly-ass lipstick," Marnie says, but she says it with affection. The other girls groan, and laugh: they are caught in the cycle of remembering, now, distant-eyed and hazy. "You couldn't *pay* homegirl to give that purple shit up."

I put my hand into my pockets to grip the butterfly as I walk toward Sapphire's old locker and put my fingers around the handle—the whole thing feels a lot like a dream, like I'm observing my body from somewhere far away. I shut my eyes for a second and imagine that I'm her, that she's me, that we've melded into one, solid, living person, going about our daily business, getting ready for work. And my hand, gripping the handle of her locker and swinging it open, is also her hand, granting me entrance.

Inside the locker is a bag of makeup and, taped to the inside of the door, a small black-and-white sketch of a bird winging through the sky. Beneath it is a tiny note, neatly printed and shaded in block letters.

I love you, Sapphire.

The note is signed *Bird*.

My fingers feel like they might shake right off as I reach in to grab the makeup bag and shove it into my marigold linen purse. The makeup bag is dark blue with a purple zipper—I feel like it was made for her, or of her. Like she wove herself into cloth and thread in the night and, when she died, simply unraveled, slowly, in little parts and pieces, to prevent herself from ever fully disappearing.

I leave the bird drawing where it is, but detach the note and fold it carefully into my pocket.

"Girl would reapply that stuff every ten minutes." Marnie laughs as I squeeze the bag into my purse. "She never took it off before she left, either." She looks around at the other girls. "Did you guys *ever* see Sapphire without her face on?"

"Nope," says Lucy. "We used to joke she secretly had a hideous monster face under there. She always played along, too." She sighs, a heaviness in her voice. "She could be pretty funny."

"It shouldn't have been her," Randi puts in with sudden

intensity, white teeth bared, extra-bright against her dark skin. She glares at me through the mirror, as though I'm somehow to blame. "It doesn't make sense. She had class, you know?" She shakes her head. "She never did extra to a guy for a hundred bucks, never went out with the guys from the club, not even the regulars. Not even the *bouncers*."

"I can't believe she's only been gone a week," Marnie puts in. "It feels like she's been gone forever."

My head is pounding slightly—all the crowd sounds from outside and the hot, bright lights and the mingling smells of sickly sweet perfume and hairspray. "Did she—did she maybe have a boyfriend?"

A few of the girls shrug, look between each other.

"She didn't ever say. She kept private about a lot of shit, ya know?" Randi says.

So, she was kind and generous and responsible and private. I think of the note from Bird. Maybe a boyfriend? Or a best friend? Someone who loved her, in any case.

Then why was there no one to claim her body?

I check the time on my cell phone: it's almost twelve thirty. I have to wake up for *high school*—the whole school thing seems even more absurd than usual right now—in six hours and eighteen minutes.

"Hey, thanks for your help," I say. "I appreciate it, you know?"

Marnie says, "So, when you think you're gonna start?"

"Oh. Yeah. I have to talk to"—I almost say *Mustache*—"the manager about that. But you guys have been great. Really."

"Yeah, no problem." Marnie bends forward, lifts a pack of

matches from the long dressing room countertop and lights a cigarette. "See you around."

I *tap tap tap, banana* as quietly as possible and duck into the low hallway and make my way back into the club and toward the exit, feeling empowered by the information I've gathered, feeling really good. *I did it. I didn't freak out—not really. I acted like a normal person.*

On my way out, though, a gleam of silver catches my eye. I spot an area I haven't seen yet: the VIP room. It's a red-carpeted section at the back of the club, full of marble tables, each one topped with delicate, intricately engraved silver ashtrays, and blocked off by velvet ropes.

And I can't leave just yet.

Because I've got to have one of those ashtrays, *got to got to got to.* It's the *urge*—there's nothing I can do—my head is full only with this, this intense *need*. Something beyond need, even. The sparkle and flash of it courses through my whole body, every nerve, every cell. It pulls me forward, inch by inch. I cannot choose. I cannot stop it.

I wait until the big, burly bouncer turns to scold a customer in the regular area for trying to paw one of the waitresses before I sneak past the velvet ropes and grab the closest ashtray within reach. A rush fills my whole body as I do, clears up my head, makes me feel instantly like everything in the whole world is okay, like the universe and solar system and every big, holy planet and blade of grass and flake of fresh-fallen snow are rotating and growing and falling just for me right now. When I find where it belongs, where it fits, everything will be whole: I will plug up the emptiness, the swirling, sucking drain of the universe spinning into chaos.

I'm about to slip the ashtray into my handbag when a small curly-haired girl and her customer—escorted by another huge bouncer—come up the stairs and around the corner, heading directly toward me. I pocket it, quickly, praying they haven't seen me as I duck behind one of the heavy velvet curtains hanging to my right.

I trip through a different curtain that sends me falling backward into an enclosed big leather booth and onto something warm and shifting.

A low voice very close to my ear says, "And where did you come from?"

Not something. *Someone.* I turn my head to face a man: surprised, smiling. Gorgeous.

I'm so shocked that it takes a second to register: I'm sitting on his lap.

CHAPTER 10

The man and I stare at each other and my body feels like it has completely stopped working. All I can think is *handsome. So handsome.* And for a second I forget exactly where I am and what I'm doing here in the first place.

After what might be seconds but what feels like hours, he speaks again:

"I'm going to take a wild guess that you didn't intend to end up on the lap of a random stranger?" He laughs, his eyes crinkling as he smiles. He looks like Mr. Hamilton, my very cute tenth-grade English teacher who, after Oren died, had given me a long, genuine hug and said, *Lo, you take as much time as you need with everything, okay? I can't even imagine what you're going through right now.* Mr. Hamilton—the only one who came to the funeral, the only one who had the balls to admit the awful truth: that he *didn't* and *couldn't possibly* know. That the grief might last forever.

I try to say something, but the only sound that emerges is a low *hhnnn*.

"Sorry—how rude of me." The man laughs. "I'm Gordon Jones. I'd offer you a handshake, but . . . I suspect we may have already progressed beyond that." He does a little sweeping motion with his hands to indicate the (very short) distance between us, brushing my neck, briefly, maybe accidentally, with his fingers. My breath catches in my throat, but I don't shrink away.

"I'm Penel—" I say before catching myself. "Juuuliet." I drag out the *u* as I say it, hoping there's a chance he'll ignore my blunder.

But he doesn't. "Well, *Penel-Juuuliet*, forgive me for saying, but if anyone was going to fall out of nowhere and into my lap—literally and metaphorically speaking—I'm glad she happened to be so beautiful." He looks into my eyes as I sit there, still frozen into complete and total immobility.

That word again—*beautiful*—makes my cheeks burn straight through to my teeth, my gums. And Gordon Jones, with his jet black hair and big green eyes and clean, square jaw and silky black-and-gray business suit, thinks this word applies to me.

"I—I'm new here," I finally manage to squeak out.

He puts his hand on my back, in a fatherly kind of way, and says, "Hey, it's okay if you're nervous. These places kind of make me nervous, you know? But I promise I don't bite—okay? Juliet?" He catches my eye as he speaks to me, looks into me like he wants to reach way down into my belly and wrestle with the darker parts of my soul, or something. "We can just sit here and talk to each other. That's more than fine with me. I'd like to do that, actually—it's a kind of hobby of mine. So, you don't need to worry about anything, *really*." His eyes move down to my neck, my chest; he cocks his head, staring. *So cute. He's so cute.* "Where did you get that?" His fingers brush the horse pendant, Sapphire's horse pendant, loosed from within my shirt.

"My friend." The words bubble out. "She, um, she died. She left it for me."

"You guys were close?"

I nod. Because I feel closer to her than I've felt to most living people.

"It's very nice. Elegant." His voice calms me, his eyes calm me, and I can't help but wonder why *this* guy is sitting in a VIP booth at a strip club in Neverland. He's gorgeous and rich looking—probably no more than thirty—and seems genuinely nice. And he's not the strip club–type, at least not the type I've pictured: the hooting, hollering, beer-bellied drunks who fill the seats out front, slobbering onto the stage at the sight of a bare breast.

I notice the freckles above his left eyebrow and count them: six. Good. Perfect. The right amount. I decide to let myself relax. I move off of his lap and onto the plush leather couch beside him, blurting out: "So, what *are* you doing here? If these places make you nervous, I mean."

He smiles at me, patient, as though he expected me to ask. "Hazards of the job," he says. "I'm thinking of buying the place." His smile curves up the right side of his face like a lopsided crescent moon.

I can't tell if he's joking or not about the whole "buying the place" thing, but either way, his answer, and the *way* he delivers it, reassures me even further.

"And what about you?" He reaches out and places one of his hands on top of mine. It is warm. Dry. Comfortable. "When did you start?"

The feeling of his hand on mine somehow radiates through my whole body, making every cell feel warm. "It's kind of a long story," I say, but before I can say anything more, a giant, awful-looking bouncer with a nose like a squashed tomato and squinty little eyes pokes his head into the curtain.

Without thinking, I spring immediately to my feet and begin a clumsy dance in front of Gordon, hoping neither man can tell that I have no idea what I'm doing.

The bouncer sneers at me. "Mr. Jones, you need another girl?"

I keep dancing, just keep dancing. I see Sapphire's face in the folds of the curtain, watching me, willing me on, her apparition folding into and out of itself like slow-moving wings. We're in this now together, Sapphire and I; we've become responsible for each other. Our lives and our deaths. No turning back.

"No, Vin. I've got a girl, thank you."

"You sure you're all set, boss?" he asks.

"Absolutely sure, Vinnie. Thanks for checking in." And with that, Vin, the tomato-nosed bouncer retreats behind the curtain and into the smoke and noise and thick purple air.

I continue to sway awkwardly for a minute before Gordon reaches his fingers gently to my wrist, stilling me. "You don't have to keep going." His eyes are kind and serious. I fold my arms across my chest, embarrassed yet oddly comforted—like a little girl who has spilled her cup of punch all over the new white carpet but who is promised a pony, anyway. He keeps his fingers on my wrist and pulses softly. "Sit down. Let's just talk."

He looks down at his wrist, as though to check his watch. But there's nothing there. Just a white watch-shaped silhouette where a real watch should have been. He looks temporarily panicked, puts his hands to the pockets of his suit pants and feels around.

"What happened?" I ask him. "Did you—did you lose your watch?"

He fumbles for a second, covering up his empty wrist with the other hand; he smiles at me. A clean, tan smile. "I guess I did." He laughs. "Always a bit of a shock. Losing something."

I reach into my bag and check the time on my cell phone: "It's almost one A.M.," I tell him, as an unnamed panic starts to flood me. I have to go, have to get out of here. My salvaged ashtray needs to be placed and ordered, and I need to sleep. Juliet is going to turn into a pumpkin, and the old, ash-covered Lo will be back, with her stupid bangs and bumpy nose.

"I—I have to go, now," I stammer. "I didn't realize what time it was. . . . I have to be onstage. I'm supposed to be, dancing, and . . . not here. I'm really sorry."

I grab my purse from the floor. Gordon creases his brow, looking perplexed. I turn away from him, and as he begins to protest I *tap tap tap, banana*, push my way through the curtains, and start heading for the exit, head down.

I make it just outside the velvet VIP ropes when a voice, close by, stops me: "If I were you, I would *not* be walking out on Gordon Jones."

I whip around and Randi, dressed now in a leather corset, is standing right behind me, holding the edge of an empty drink tray in her left hand.

"He doesn't even usually go for the new girls, hun, so, you should feel downright *blessed*, especially in *that* thing." She motions with her French-manicured fingernails toward my skirt and looking me over like I've just committed some unbelievable crime.

"I—I didn't know," I say, sheepishly, tugging on the silver horse. "I don't know anything about him. I just started tonight."

She sighs and puts a hand to her hip. "Look, sweetie. Mr. Jones basically *owns* Cleveland. Real estate, or development, or some shit. Totally loaded. Good tipper, too. And he's also very, very super particular about his girls, *and* he's not a creep. Never pulls anything shady in the booth, you know?" She points a finger at me like Mr. Crawson, the sex-ed teacher, does when lecturing the class about all the STDs we stand to get if we so much as kiss another person without a condom on. "Tip for the future: if you ever get another chance with Gordon Jones, don't blow it. For real." She shakes her head and walks back toward the tables of men.

I stare momentarily at the curtained booth where Gordon Jones sits: loaded, sweet, handsome, maybe wondering where I went. I can still feel the warm leather on the backs of my knees, his whiskey-pepperminty breath between us in the air, hear the strangest word in the English language forming on his lips and sliding, warm and velvety, into my chest: *beautiful*.

I could go back to him. We could talk—just talk. I think of those six freckles above his left brow: a perfect number. A safe number.

Maybe he'd even want to help me if I told him what was going on, what happened to Sapphire, he'd care. He'd definitely care. And then he'd whisper: *You're safe here. I'm going to make sure of it.* And then he'd kiss me, kiss me as he whispered: *Safe* (left eye). *Safe* (right cheek). *Safe* (middle of clavicle). *Safe . . .*

Thunk, thunk, thunk. A bouncer pounds up the stairs, startling me from my daydream.

Time to go.

As I'm darting to the exit doors, I see something out of the corner of my eye that stops me in my tracks, roots me to the spot.

He's talking to Marnie, kicking his legs around on a tall stool by the stage, grin big and dimpled as ever. My heart jumps straight up my throat, shorting my breath to a gasp as I croak out:

"Flynt!?"

CHAPTER 11

Flynt swivels around to face me. His face goes instantly pale, his eyes widening. He jumps to his feet and threads his way toward me.

"What are you doing here?" I practically spit.

"I might ask you the same question," he says. "You headed out?"

I nod, not knowing how to feel or what to say.

"Oh, what lovely happenstance," he continues. "I'll follow you."

I *tap tap tap, banana* quietly, pulling my coat from the hook by the front door and wrapping it around me. Something doesn't add up. He told me he didn't hang out at Tens anymore.

We pass onto the street, and I begin walking in the direction of the bus, trying to gather my thoughts as I count and avoid the cracks in the sidewalk. *Twelve, thirt—*

"So . . . you came by here after all. And what'd you find out about your *old friend*? Anything juicy?" He plays with one of his dreadlocks.

I widen the gap between us, start the count over again. *Old friend*—behind his words, he's saying, *Liar*. He knows. My hands start burning.

"Okay, fine, Flynt." I stop under a bright streetlight and look into his face. "Sapphire wasn't an old friend of mine. I didn't know her at all."

Flynt snorts a little but he's still smiling. "Well, *that* much was obvious."

"But I—" I almost tell him about the dead cat and Sapphire's voice, constantly in my ear. "I can't stop thinking about her. I don't care if you understand, and I don't care if you want to help. But I need to know what happened."

His face softens, those blue-green-gold eyes shining in the light of the streetlamp. "You didn't have to lie, Lo."

"What about you? Didn't you tell me you hadn't been to Tens in years?"

"Oh, you know." He waves a hand. "Years, days. In Neverland, it hardly makes a difference." He pulls the moth-chewed scarf from his neck and comes toward me, wrapping it around my shoulders. "Bet you wish you had pants on right now."

I tear the scarf off and throw it back to him. "Stop trying to distract me, Flynt." I shiver. "Why *were* you at Tens?"

"If you must know," he says, sighing, "our little chat the other day reminded me that I hadn't been around in a while, you know, to draw, to take money from those sleazy rich guys." He puts a triumphant finger into the air. "And I made forty bucks tonight!" He starts walking again.

I hurry to catch up, still careful to avoid the cracks but no longer bothering to count them. "Is that supposed to be a lot?" I fire back, refusing to be baited by his charm.

"Look, Lo. I know what this is all about. You're pissed I didn't offer to show you my sketches. Right?" He puts a hand on my shoulder to stop me, and I finally look at him, grinning his sweet, goofy grin, even though it's the last thing I want to do. He wraps the scarf around my neck again and pats it, three times, which makes me think I should keep it on this time. "Look, I would have. I swear. But they sold like hotcakes. In a flash, I'm telling you." He taps the pocket of his patched, dusty black pants with his palm, holding it there protectively.

It's hard not to start smiling, too, standing beside him, even though I still don't know whether or not to trust him. I can't forget how weird he looked when he saw me. Almost like he was . . . frightened.

"Hey—can't hide a smile from me, Queen P. I'll find it. Always." He points at my lips, touching the top one softly with his warm pointer finger. I shiver, batting away his hand with my own.

"I'm glad I helped make you so rich," I say to him, trying to relax, trying to keep my voice neutral. "I should probably take commission."

"You're a slippery one, you know that, Lo? Always after my riches. I'm not saying you're a gold digger, but . . ." He ticks his tongue against the roof of his mouth. "How about this: I'll pay your percentage in the form of late-night pizza. Deal?"

A quiver runs through my chest. It's so late. I should be home.

"I know a great place," he goes on, "not so far from your bus stop, in fact. So, what do you say? Want to sign on it? Or shall a gentleman's agreement be sufficient?"

"You *do* owe me," I reply, even though I shouldn't go. He grins, grabs my hand, lets out a whoop into the thin night air.

And just like that, a good feeling flushes through me. Maybe I'll run into Keri Ram in the bathroom tomorrow. She'll be fixing her hair; I'll be dabbing concealer under my eyes. *I stayed out way too late last night,* I'll say, shrugging. *I was with my friend, Flynt. Got some pizza at a twenty-four-hour spot in Neverland. Oh, you don't know Neverland? It can be pretty cool, actually. If you know people, I mean.*

I follow him through the cold night down several mostly deserted blocks to what looks like a rusty old shed. He knocks: four times quickly and then another three. I clap my hands softly under my coat seven times to match before I *tap tap tap, banana.* "What did you just say?" Flynt asks as we wait, blowing hot air between his fists.

"I—nothing." My cheeks burn. Thankfully, Flynt lets it slide.

A guy with hair like a dirty-blond mushroom cloud finally opens it. He gives Flynt a short nod of recognition and a clap on the back before pointing us to a table in the corner of the room.

Inside it's like a cozy little cottage, equipped with a wood-burning pizza oven in one corner and six small tables pressed into the tiny space, the smell of wood smoke and dough and a thousand delicious things wafting through the air. Multicolored Christmas lights hang in clumps from the ceiling and the floor is an old diner–looking pattern of small tiles in black and white.

Flynt puts a hand on the small of my back for a second, inching me forward. My breath catches in my throat feeling his hand there, pressing, his fingers long and firm and warm.

"Pretty cool, right?" he says to me as we sit, hands resting on the warped wooden tabletops. "Not many people know about it, but I come here whenever I've got the cash. And then I blow it all on pizza and giant ice-cream sundaes."

"Good, Moneybags," I say to him. "Because I'm feeling *very* hungry all of a sudden."

While we wait for our food to come—*quattro formaggi*, mushrooms, olives, basil—Flynt inches his hand on the table closer to mine. "You know, Lo, you should tell me the next time you plan to wander around Neverland by yourself. It's not safe around here."

I take my hand off the table and put it inside my coat pocket, feeling for the butterfly, rubbing it between my fingers as the horse pendent burns against my chest. My suspicions bubble up again. I can't tell if he is speaking out of concern, or as a warning.

I think again of the blood-spotted note: *Now you know what curiosity did. Be careful, or you'll end up like the cat.*

"I'm fine, Flynt," I say stiffly. "I can take care of myself."

"I'm just saying. There are some pretty shady people around here. It's fine for me; people know me. I get a pass."

Something occurs to me: people know Flynt, and Flynt seems to know everyone, at least around here. "Do you know anyone named Bird?" I blurt out, a shot in the dark.

"Hmmm." Flynt puts a finger on his chin, the picture of thoughtfulness. "Can't say that I do. I know a Raven—he's cool, amazing graffiti artist, you should check out his stuff with me sometime—and a crazy woman who calls herself The Lizard. Of course, lizards are reptiles, although it's quite possible they share a common ancestor with our feathered friends, just like the dinosaurs." He has spoken the words in one long, pitter-patter sentence. Now he pauses and sucks in a breath. "Why do you ask?"

"No reason," I say, and then, when he raises his eyebrows: "Just something to do with Sapphire. Someone who knew her."

For a second, a look of pain crosses his face. "Look, Lo, just promise me you'll be careful." He spreads his hands and leans forward. "I'm only saying this because I worry about you, okay?" The last part comes out in a rush.

My throat squeezes shut. I don't know what to say.

Thankfully, just then, the snowy-eyed waiter comes toward us with the pizza. "So, what else did you find out about Sapphire?" Flynt says in a normal voice as the pizza is plunked, swirls of steam rising into the air, on the table between us. He grabs a slice and blows on it, sliding it in big bites into his mouth, his eyes on me.

"Well . . ." I hesitate. "The girls gave me her makeup bag. But they didn't say much."

"I told you," he said.

"They weren't rude, or anything. Just busy. And I guess they didn't really know all that much about her life outside the club."

Flynt is already reaching for a second slice. Our hands collide over the plate, and he laughs, backing off so I can take a slice.

"So, that's it, huh?" he presses. "That's all you got?"

"Well, I mean, I talked to the manager . . . but I was just asking him for an application. You know." I center the slice of my pizza

THE BUTTERFLY CLUES 119

on my plate, waiting for it to cool. I don't want to tell him about my time with Gordon. I don't exactly know why.

Maybe I don't want him to know I *enjoyed* it.

"I was thinking," I continue, returning my gaze to Flynt, focusing on the silky strand of cheese now fastened to his bottom lip, "since you know the lay of the land and all that . . . I mean, maybe you could help. You could ask around for me. You know everybody, and I don't." I lift my slightly-less-scalding slice of pizza to my mouth, taking three small bites.

He drums his fingers on the table for a few seconds, wiping up some sauce with his napkin and balling it into his fist, grabbing a third slice and sliding half of it into his mouth. I haven't seen anyone eat so ravenously in a long time. "It's really not my business," he says finally. "It's not your business, either. I hate to break it to you, but people die all the time around here."

I close my eyes, open them again. I grip the sides of the table, willing the anger down. "I know it won't bring her back," I say. "I didn't even know her. Okay? I didn't know her at all. But . . . but this is the right thing. And I *need* it. For her, yeah. But mostly for me."

I watch him, holding my breath, counting to six. "And," I continue softly, "I guess I kinda need someone around who . . . cares. When it comes down to it."

"I'll think about it," he says finally, raising his eyes to me slowly before moving them to the center of the table, to the last two slices of pizza, beaded with grease on the silver pie pan. "You gonna eat that?"

*　*　*　*

An hour later, 3:00 A.M., I'm home and unable to sleep.

I study my face in my bedroom mirror and hear Gordon say that word again: *beautiful.* My finger traces the scar above my left eyebrow, like a big dent in my face. I got it the time I fell into the creek at the bottom of the hill near our house in Minnesota (Oren christened it "Butt Creek" the first time we found it). We were looking for pennies. We made finding them a contest, of course. Oren made everything a contest. He spotted one of our flattened pennies on the edge of the bank, gave me the *let's race* eye, and shouted, *"Go!"* Running too fast, desperate to win for once, I caught my left foot under a branch and tumbled headfirst into Butt Creek.

All I remembered after that was the rush of ice-cold water, which knocked the air out of me like a punch, and being sure I was going to die—and then Oren's arms, pulling me back to the bank. He realized I was bleeding before I did—I didn't even feel it, until I put my hand to my head and it came away covered in blood.

After that, every time I'd get angry with him he'd just raise his eyebrows at me and say: *Remember that time I saved your life?*

I stare at myself so long my eyes start to cross and a third giant green-gray Cyclops eye floats up in the middle of my forehead. I refocus my eyes until they're two again, and the Cyclops eye disappears.

I pull Sapphire's makeup bag from my linen bag and set it on my nightstand. I paw through its contents, drawn immediately to the eye shadow—a dark, night-sky blue called "Midnight"—and rub it across my lids. As soon as I open my eyes, a weird sensation overcomes me. For a second, looking into the mirror, I swear it isn't me sitting here, staring at myself in the mirror, but her. Sapphire.

I reach my fingers back into the bag, feeling around for the most important part of Sapphire's look—her signature bruise-colored lipstick—but it's not here. I dump everything out onto the table, much of it just multiple copies of the same thing; it's not in the bag.

I glance back at myself in the mirror one last time, at my eyes, looking so much like Sapphire's now, before returning to the bathroom to rewash and rewash and rewash my face. Back in my bedroom, I scoop all of Sapphire's makeup back into the little bag before arranging it as the center point in a circle of six looming silver candlestick holders. It looks like the dark, bulgy center of a flower there, and the candlesticks stand guard around it, protective. It's then that I remember the ashtray, resting patiently in my bag. I remove it with both hands and place it in a staggered row beside a slightly rusted cigarette case with the initials *GTB* engraved onto its face and three long, flutelike cigarette holders.

I think of Sapphire, a dark, patient silhouette floating gracefully between tables stacked with gleaming hand-engraved ashtrays, the floor, the ceiling, the walls—everything—covered in them. I wonder if she smoked.

I'll find out, I silently vow. I'll find out everything. Somehow.

CHAPTER 12

"Penelope. Hellooo? Are you with us?"

I snap suddenly to attention. Mr. Keller is frowning at me.

"I'm sorry," I say. "I didn't hear the question."

"There *was* no question, Ms. Marin. We were going around the room and giving our answers to the homework you were assigned yesterday dealing with differentiation using the Chain Rule."

I feel like my eyes might roll back in my skull. It's not even that I'm completely exhausted from getting less than four hours of sleep last night—which I am—it's that I can't get my mind off of Sapphire, her missing lipstick, and her killer. I can't stop thinking about Flynt, too, last night; if he's really going to *think about it*, or if that was simply the best way he could think to brush me off. I just want to know. Have to know that he'll help me. Have to know that he'll *commit*.

"Problem nineteen, page one-eleven, Ms. Marin. What was your answer?"

Keller's one of the teachers who notices my patterns, probably because he's a math freak and hyper-attuned to numbers. He tried to talk to me after class once; he told me he *understood*, but that all the tapping during tests was distracting to other students. He tried to get me to talk to the guidance counselor about it, as if that would help anything. And when he confronted me, my face got so hot, and my mouth so dry, that I couldn't respond. Not even to lie and say that I didn't know what he was talking about, to make the insane promise that I'd never tap again. He didn't *understand*. There's no way he could possibly understand.

Since that conversation, it is like he takes my tapping as a personal insult, like I'm deliberately doing it just to distract him during lessons.

I flip the book open and stare at the problem, computing quickly.

"This couldn't have been our homework, because it's next week's lesson," I reply, "but, if the outside function is the sine, and the inside function is three-x-squared-plus-x, then the derivative would have to be six-x-plus-one times the cosine of three-x-squared-plus-x."

He clears his throat, raises his eyebrows. "Good, Penelope." He clicks his tongue once, uncertain how to reprimand me, turning to the board to explain a new series of problems to the class instead. I try to focus and can't. No way. My head is in the club; in Sapphire's makeup bag; in the tall mirrors of the dressing room; in Marnie's long, dyed red hair; in the dead cat, growing bloodier and more disjointed each time it claws its way into my head. Everywhere but here.

I have to find out more. But where? And how to find it?

After last period; I turn the combination and shove things into my book bag as someone, walking past, shouts: "Screw derivatives!"—a husky, hard-edged, cool-girl voice. I turn my head: Annica Steele smiles briefly at me, and then runs ahead to catch up with the rest of the Perfect Girl Brigade at the end of the hall.

My breath catches in my chest. "Yeah!" I chirp after her, sounding way too excited. She doesn't turn back around. Maybe she didn't hear me. Or maybe I just imagined the whole thing.

I slam my locker and say my name again and again under my breath as I walk out of school: *Pen-el-o-pe-Mar-in Pen-el-o-pe-Mar-in Pen-el-o-pe-Mar-in.* Six syllables. Three times. Eighteen.

The cold air makes my eyes sting on my way home. I think of all the other things the newspaper neglected to mention about Sapphire. Maybe she *did* have a family—a sister or brother or a lot of sisters and brothers, parents who loved her, who lost her. She didn't do drugs, she didn't drink, she didn't break the rules. She was kind, helpful, *good*, according to everyone I spoke to at Tens. Her murder doesn't make any *sense*—that's what the girls kept saying last night. *It shouldn't have been her.*

Scuff, scuff, scuff—my whole body goes stiff and jerky at the sound of another person's feet, dragging through the snow. And then I start to feel it—the heat of another person's breath fast approaching, the *scuff, scuff, scuff* coming closer. *Oh God,* I think, *oh God, not now.* I turn on my heels, fists balled and close to my chest.

But, guess who: Jeremy. Of course. Jeremy.

"Holy shit," I say under my breath, letting it pass from my lips in a cloud of cold air.

"Lo! Wait *up*!" He's panting as he finally reaches me, a piece of paper in his hands.

His face is all splotchy and red from the cold, especially his button nose, and it clashes with his hair. His jacket isn't even zipped, and I see that his Neil Young T-shirt has developed a little rip near one of his armpits, a little tuft of hair poking out.

"You left this on your desk in English." He hands me the piece of paper—a handout about all the different words Shakespeare added to the English language that I'm pretty sure I already have or could get online if I really had to. "And I've been chasing you all day, but were you, like, avoiding me or something?" He laughs a little, like this couldn't *actually* be true. "I saw you walking out the door. We need this for the homework tonight." He rubs his hands against his thighs and smiles. He's got a little cleft in his chin.

Keri's right: he is cute, in his own track-star way—his muscle-y little body, the shadow of scruff across his cheeks and chin, the wild blue of his eyes that turn all little-kid sparkly when he gets a right answer in class, the freckles dotted across his nose, the way his mouth curves too far to the right when he smiles—even if he has a dumb laugh. And I'm probably only feeling irrationally pissed off right now because I'm so on edge. The fact is: I've been completely terrified since the dead-cat incident.

Jeremy's still talking, following me down the street. I can only half pay attention to what he's saying. "And, like, as a side note: it would be so *rad* if we could study SAT stuff together sometime. My mom's all like: 'Jeremy are you studying? Jeremy are you study-ing? Blah blah blah,' and, like, she's got some serious bored-housewife problems and has nothing better to do than harass me, I guess." He laughs again, high-pitched, girly. "Parents, man. Right?"

I nod. Six times. Nod nod nod nod nod nod.

"So I told her that there's this girl in class"—he jabs his finger at my chest—"that would be *you*—who is supersmart and who I'm going to beg on my knees to be my study buddy if necessary. And that kind of shut her up. So"—he flashes me a coy smile—"now you kinda *have* to be my study buddy, or the Moms will freak."

"Jeremy—I—" I need him off my back, need to be alone. But I can see that he won't let up until I give in. I stop at the corner of the street and fire my answer at his chin: "Great! Let's study together. In the library after school tomorrow, okay?"

He grins, his face lighting up. "Awesome, Lo! I knew you'd come through. You're saving me some serious parental grief."

"Yeah, okay," I say. "No problem."

"See you tomorrow, then!" He backs away from me, practically skipping. "I'll bring snacks!"

I wave him a fast good-bye and turn the corner, walking toward the 96 Line—the bus that will take me to the border of two worlds—where Neverland and the rest of Cleveland meet.

The fact is: I need Flynt. I wish I didn't, but I don't know who else to ask. No one else knows Neverland like he does, and he's going to help me, whether he likes it or not.

The bus lets off several blocks from the now-defunct birdbath that Flynt once told me serves as kind of community P.O. Box.

I keep my fist clenched tightly around the butterfly in my pocket, pumping it in my hand. It's like a heart sending blood to the rest of my body; I have to keep it from shutting down.

As I walk toward the birdbath, I try to think of what I will say in my note: *Flynt, please meet me tonight. Here. I will wait for you.* No. Too pleading. *Flynt, meet me tonight. Here. Need your help.*

I keep my eyes down, counting the cracks in the pavement out loud. I get to twenty-seven—*three nines; really good*—before I look up and see what I didn't expect to see but secretly, desperately hoped I would: a pair of fuzzy bear ears, bent over the edge of the birdbath, scrawling something onto a piece of paper.

"Flynt!" I say, practically bursting, wanting to run to him and squeeze him and bury my head in the dark shadow where our chests meet. Instead, I tug at the edge of my sweater, pulling it, pulling it, pulling it to the top of my thighs, wanting to stop but not being able to make my fingers cease and desist.

He snaps his head up and sees me, his dimples growing deeper. "Lo!" He jogs up to me, folding up the piece of paper. He hands it to me with a little bow. "I was just about to leave this for you."

I unfold *his* note and read it to myself while he's standing there, watching:

Dearest Penelope,

I am a giant jerk. I don't mean to imply that I am an abnormally sized human who happens to also be a jerk, but, instead, that I am a normal-sized human who happens to sometimes be an extra-large jerk. When you buy me an ugly holiday sweater next Christmas, it needn't be an extra-large men's sweater, but it should probably feature some much-despised public, or private, figure that will serve to indicate to the world the immense degree of my jerkiness. What I'm really saying is . . . I've thought more about it, and I'd like to be of help to you in your quest so that come Christmas you can just find me a basic ugly holiday sweater that has no other object but to be a basic ugly holiday sweater, and I can wear it the next time we beat god and the devil alike at trash can bowling.

Yours,

Flynt

The *Yours* part makes me warm. I fold up the note and put it in my pocket, looking at the triangles made in the branches of the trees. I wonder what made him change his mind but can't even let myself care right now. I need him. He's going to help.

"I'm sorry, Lo, for before," he says, focusing his big eyes on me. "I've cleared out my calendar. All of the Dumpsters in the world couldn't tear me away from your side. I'm all yours, okay? So what now, Private Penelope?"

I squeeze the butterfly hard, feeling Sapphire pulse through my palm. "Now," I answer, nerves winging furiously through my chest, "we need to figure out what happened the night she was killed. We need more clues."

"And how do you propose we do that?"

I swallow, will myself to speak the idea I've been mulling over all day. "We go to Sapphire's house," I answer, starting to walk, "and we break in."

*   *   *   *

Flynt slides a bobby pin from his pocket into the rusted lock of the odd yellow house and jimmies it open easily, like breaking into houses is something he does every day. He swings the door open, waiting for me to step inside first.

"You're *really* good at that," I say.

"I have to break into storage sheds and locked buildings all the time when I need a quick place to crash," he replies, without hesitation. "Believe you me, Lope—hey, has anyone ever called you 'Lope' before?"

A tightening feeling in my stomach: Oren used to call me Lope once in a while, because he knew it annoyed me. "No," I answer shortly. "Never."

"Anyway, *Lo*, I wasn't this good when I started. I had to sleep in the alley all too frequently on account of my poor de-locksmanship."

"That must have sucked in the winter," I say, trying to push away my suspicions. *He's here. He's helping me.*

"Ho-Lee shit—*yes*. It sucked. It more than sucked. I don't even think there's an adequate word to convey the intensity of the suckiness I endured." He winks, but there's a weird curve to his lips—like it's taking every single cell in his body to force them into a smile. "M'lady," Flynt says, motioning me inside the open door.

But I can't move—the weight of a thousand hands suddenly pressing pressing pressing into my chest, sucking all the air out with a single downward shove. The whole thing feels like a dream—this threshold before me—the insides of Sapphire's daisy-yellow house trembling and vibrating with a deathly cold.

"Lo," says Flynt quietly, "we shouldn't just stand here."

Six deep breaths. Nine taps. Three *bananas*. Again. Again. Again. I don't know what Flynt's face looks like right now, and I don't want to know. And, right now, I can't care; it's the *only* way.

Finally, I finish the cycle, and I can enter: yellow arch of the doorway shuttering as I pass, Sapphire's voice whispering through all the walls. Flynt follows, closing the door behind us, locking it. "Lo," he says again softly, "why do you do that stuff?"

Stepping inside, the darkness wraps around me with a watery thickness. He saw; he knows. My throat burns as I answer, the only words that come: "Have to." I shake my head and say it again: "Have to." And once more, to make it three: "Have to."

I think I see him nod, but I don't know. Too dark to know. A chemical smell comes up from the floor like sanitizer and metal and must. I shiver. The landlord must have shut off the heat pretty soon after they found the body. Flynt flips a light switch in the hallway and nothing happens. The dark beats its way around us, threatening. *Just try me*, it sneers. Flashes of waning light cut through the dark from a billowing curtain, sharp and sudden. My eyes work to adjust.

"I'm going to look in the kitchen for a flashlight or some candles," Flynt says, his voice shivery; I feel the heat from his body retreating as he walks forward, and, seconds later, I hear clanging, reaching, searching sounds resounding from a different room. Moments later, he reemerges with flashlights beaming. Two. One in each hand. He comes to stand next to me, handing me one. My hands feel suddenly massive and too heavy to lift.

We both just stand there for a minute with our flashlights,

sucking cold into our lungs. Sucking in the smells of covered-up dead person. And blood.

The cat again: yowling through my head, mouth open, frozen in terror. My stomach cinches up, curls into itself like a freaked-out animal. The curtain billows like someone's punched it: a square of weak light fills the room and disappears again with the wind.

Flynt clicks his flashlight on and off. I see Sapphire's bruise-colored lips, patterned up and down the walls, flicker in the stream of the flashlight. I blink and they're gone, and she's gone, too. I put my hand into the air, wave it around. *Can you feel me?* I think to her, waiting for a sign. *Are you here, somewhere?*

Flynt waves his arm through the air, too, aping me. "Christ, it's cold," he says. "I'm going to explore, okay?" He walks forward, shining his flashlight into corners, walls, floorboards as he goes.

"Me, too," I say to his back. I turn my flashlight on and follow just behind him, floating left into the living room as he's carried away somewhere else.

The weirdest thing is this: everything looks totally normal. There's a long blue couch, an afghan spread out on one of the cushions like someone's just taken a nap there, a glass with a dark lipstick rim on the little wooden folding tray next to it still half filled with water, a Chinese-style dragon rug just a little askew across the wooden floor, a pair of black flats in front of the TV set.

My body floats me over to the card table, to the glass with the lipstick rim. Her lips. I reach my fingers to it, expecting wax and warmth, as though she's just taken a drink and gone to find something in another part of the house. I expect her to flood back into the room any second and catch me—a total stranger—standing in the middle of her living room.

But then I remember that she won't. She can't.

She never will again.

And her lipstick print on the rim of the glass isn't warm and waxy; it's cold.

Creeeak. I jump, my hand fluttering to my chest. *Creeeak. Creeeak*—more and more, farther down the hall. My heart races faster.

"Flynt?" I call out. There's no answer.

My stomach: a sick knot, full of razor blades. Squeezing. Sharp. A humming sound now. A voice. *Sapphire? Are you here?*

"Heading upstairs, Lo!" Flynt's voice drifts down to me.

I exhale, but the panic lingers as the waves of darkness gather, push me out of this room and into the next.

The bathroom: behind her mirror, five samples of different perfumes in delicate glass bottles. I picture her standing in here, dabbing each one onto a different spot of her neck, her wrists. I grab one—the middle one—from the row, slide it into my pocket. More of her—I want more of her.

A small, framed drawing of a bird above the toilet catches my eye. I like the drawing—it reminds me of the one that was taped into her locker at Tens. I wonder if it's from the same person. *Bird.* There are two photographs of Sapphire tacked above the light switch—one where she is standing with Marnie, obviously at a bar, half turned away from the camera; one with a girl I don't recognize.

I float forward again. The kitchen: yellow walls, dried flowers in mason jars, boxes of Corn Flakes and Cheerios lined on top of the refrigerator. Magnets advertising local businesses, a Post-it note that says, *Laundry!!* in a girl's handwriting, more photos of Sapphire with her friends. I run my flashlight across each of them. In every one she's wearing that blue-black lipstick. I feel momentarily troubled by that detail. Where is her lipstick?

From upstairs, there's a clattering sound, as though Flynt has just knocked something over. A second later, his voice, distant, watery: "Nothing doing up here. A lot of cool crap, though."

I'm swept back out to the hallway and double back down the hall, toward what must be her bedroom—toward the room where she was killed, and the window that was blown outward by the bullet that missed my head by inches. I've been avoiding it. The door is just slightly ajar. I angle my flashlight inside.

Standing just outside the doorway for a moment, paralyzed, I take in the same blue walls, carpeting, furniture I saw through the window in the grainy, pixelated cell phone pictures that were posted to the crime blog. The plastic shades over her window are only halfway down, letting in a thin stream of light from the streetlamp outside. The wind blows through the shattered window, now crisscrossed with police tape, causing the shades to sway lightly, tapping against the wall.

Tap tap tap, banana.

The air is heavy, tense; the smell metallic. There is a vibrating feeling between the walls. This is exactly how it feels to walk by Oren's room. We can feel the particles of him, swimming around. Parts of him that will never equal the whole.

That's why we never go into his room anymore. If we did, we'd run around, frantic, trying to collect the pieces, hoping we could pull him together again. And we'd say, *We'll never let you go again. Stay here. Stay here. Stay here.*

But then he'd disappear. And we'd be alone again. Staring at the maroon comforter drawn across his empty bed.

I feel Sapphire draw together around me now, like if she could, she'd reach out and take my hand, pull me in for a long hug and say, *Go for it.* Because that's the kind of person I know, in my bones, that she was.

Six deep breaths. Two stuffed bears on her bed. Three pillows. One Rorschach spatter of blood against her wall. Sapphire's blood. Sapphire's face—it flashes before me—the gunshot—the cat—Oren—one bursting, terrible fist rising from the carpeting, holding all of them in its grip.

I close my eyes and open them again. Take another six breaths, three seconds each.

The first thing that catches my eye is her closet, to the left of her bed. It is a dark little cavern, brimming with colorful clothes. I step inside of it, sweep my flashlight across the dense wall of fabric—glittery, sparkly, scandalous-looking—skirts and dresses and shirts with complicated hooks and zippers up the center. I find a velvety black, rhinestone-encrusted bustier and run my fingers over its surfaces—different extremes of hard and soft. I'm filled with a growing urge to take it, different from my urge to lift three little plaster frogs from her desk—which I do, my heartbeat quickening, my face flushing with a familiar mixture of shame and elation—but my feeling about the bustier is a slower, more sober urge.

She wore this bustier. She moved in it, and sweated and ate and lived. That's what it means. *That's what I'll think of when I touch it, Sapphire, when it's mine.* I unzip my backpack and shove it, and the frogs, inside. Mine.

Ours.

So much to look through: but who knows how much time we've got before someone, a neighbor or a passerby, sees flashlights beaming on and off in different parts of the house and calls the police.

I pass the bloodstain near her bed on the way to the desk. It's still there, a hardened, ghostly shape on the carpet. Suck in my cheeks nine times as I pass. In and out. In and out. In. Dimly, I'm aware of footsteps. Flynt must have come downstairs again.

Her desk is a mess: stacks of old Moleskine notebooks and edge-crumbled day planners and funny hand-drawn calendars. I open one up and flip through; little scraps of dislodged paper flutter out and onto the carpet. They're disorganized, dates on the loose, fallen papers from different years, even. I can hardly breathe I'm so excited. She's led me here, to this treasure. I know it. She sent the wave that carried me here, afloat. She meant for me to find these, I can *feel* it.

I'm squeezing the last of the notebooks in my bag, about to call out to Flynt, when I notice one final, large, wrinkled piece of paper. I flatten it out with my palm: an ink sketch. I squint, look at it more closely—oval face, dark eyes, dark lips—it's her. It's Sapphire.

I pan my flashlight all along the image. It's beautiful. Graceful. Stark lines, lots of shadow. And in the left corner, in messy, loopy script, there's a signature.

Flynt.

My blood turns to ice: deep freeze, organs like trapped rocks.

He said he didn't know her, but he lied. Lied lied lied. He drew her picture. Knew how to get in—knew where the kitchen was, I suddenly realize—has been here before.

Oh my God. Everything burning in and out of focus, solar-eclipse-style.

A voice echoes from behind me, reaching my ears in slow, hollow waves: "Find anything good?"

CHAPTER 13

I turn around slowly, still clutching the sketch in one trembling hand.

Flynt's standing in the doorway.

Flynt sees the sketch in my hand. His face goes full-white.

Terror pulses through me, rising up from my feet and into my skull.

I'm shaking. I think: *Run*, but I can't.

He's coming toward me, reaching for me.

I stumble backward, stepping into a small nightstand with a porcelain lamp on it and knocking it over. The lamp crashes to the floor. Small painted bits of it shatter across the ground. My chest feels tight, so tight, the words sticking painfully in my throat.

"You said—you said you d-didn't know her. . . ." My voice comes out stuttering, a gasp.

"What are you talking about, Lo?" He reaches for me, and I twist away.

"You lied," I croak. "What did you do to her?"

"What are you talking about? What the hell are you trying to say?" His eyebrows knit together as he focuses on the paper trembling in my hands before pulling it from me.

"Jesus," Flynt whispers after a few seconds, so agitated that he whips off his bear hat and runs a hand over the top of his head. It's the first time I've seen his head exposed. "Okay, Lo. Look," he says, sighing deeply, shakily, "I didn't want you to know this, but—she was a friend of mine. I mean, not a close friend, but . . . I knew her."

My chest feels tight—I rock forward on my toes—I try to form words. "But—but if you *knew* her, why—why didn't you tell me? Why did you lie?"

"I didn't want to get involved, okay! I mean, you get that, right? She was killed. This is a big deal, Lo. It isn't a game."

"I know it's not a game," I spit out. "You're the one playing games. You're the one who lied—"

"You lied to me, too, when you said that you knew her." Flynt sighs and rubs the top of his head. "Look. I decided to help because I saw how much you cared, and, Lo, it inspired me. *You* inspire me, to be a better person. To do something worthwhile." He pauses, taking another deep breath. "But this is why we shouldn't be messing around with this stuff in the first place. You're clearly freaked out," he rushes on, "and *I'm* clearly freaked out, and I think we need to just . . . call it a day. Get out while we still can."

I look at his face, his bee-stung lips, his green-blue-gold eyes: there's something in them I don't understand—a despairing, pleading ache.

I still don't completely trust him, but for now, I have to let myself believe that what he's saying is true. I can't lose him.

He's the only friend I've got.

Flynt lays the sketch back on Sapphire's desk carefully, running his hand over her penned form, over the outline of the girl that floated through his fingers. I hug my book bag into my chest.

"Okay," I say, nodding, my voice raw.

"Okay what?" he says.

"Okay, let's get out of here," I say.

The cold rises around us and we draw closer together, as if magnetized by body heat. Flynt pulls my hand to his and squeezes, and I have an urge to pull away but another urge to melt right into him, to let him carry me somewhere and make me solid again.

He tugs me gently forward. I let him.

*   *   *   *

When I get back to Lakewood, I still feel like I'm moving underwater—wavy and slow and deep-sea. I pass beneath the interwoven arms of quaking aspens and river birches and slippery elms. I remember when we'd first moved to Cleveland and Bob Solomon, our kooky, tree-hugging hippy neighbor—as Dad liked to put it—went around putting classification labels on every tree within a six-block radius. Even after they'd all fallen off, Oren could still point to every kind and tell me what they were. He was surprising like that: what he noticed, what he cared about.

The memories flow through the liquid: sitting beneath the giant shellbark hickory on our front lawn; Oren sketching the

grain of the wood in microscopic detail, his face a map of blissful concentration; climbing up Mrs. Hawthorne's silky dogwood
three houses down, hooting like a monkey as he pretended to eat
leaves. I'm so lost in thoughts of the past that I almost miss the
very recognizable hulking man puffing steadily on a cigarette,
huddled half hidden in a doorway on the corner of Maplebrook
and Oak.

It's the bouncer from Tens. The one Gordon Jones called Vin.
I recognize the smashed tomato nose, the neck robed in gristle.
It's definitely him.

And he's one block from my house.

I duck into the shadow of two dark blue SUVs parked end to
end. Heart thumping rapidly, bally green sweater clinging to my
skin beneath my coat, I watch him. He stands there, no more than
fifteen feet from me, flicking his tongue like a snake between the
gap in the two front teeth, smoking, eyes flitting back and forth.
Like he's waiting for something. My heartbeat goes wild; something tells me he's waiting for *me*.

I watch him puff and release, puff and release, the smoke
winding wildly from his lips. I'm 99.9 percent positive that I've
never seen him around here before—his being here now can't
be a coincidence.

Pffft. My hand accidentally slides down the side of the Ford
Explorer I'm leaning against. The bouncer's head whips in the
direction of the car, his fingers fanning out against his giant
thighs. He starts to inch closer to me when the phone in his
pocket begins to buzz loudly. He answers.

"Yeah," he answers in a low voice, nodding vigorously. "Nope.

Yeah, I'm sure. Okay." He gives one last look around from his post before throwing the cigarette he's smoking to the ground and hurrying, head down, into a black sedan that pulls up to collect him, headlights cutting sharply through the dark.

I stay still. Watching, listening, trying to make myself invisible, crouched low to the ground as the car door slams shut, a hard hollow sound. I feel breathless again. The bouncer: he's the one who's been watching me. Could he have killed Sapphire? But why?

I think of those words, violently scrawled: *Now you know what curiosity did. Be careful. . . .*

The words spin and slur around me, twisting blood-red between the leafless branches of the trees. *Be careful be careful be careful.*

I tap my feet against the gravel. Nine times. Again. Eighteen. Again. Twenty-seven.

I pull myself up from between the cars and count the cracks in the sidewalk as I walk the final block home. Every few seconds I whip around, terrified that I'll see the sedan racing toward me again, the bouncer looming out from the shadows. My head is still whirring as I approach my house, climb up the clean white porch stairs. *Tap tap tap, banana,* open the door and walk inside, triple bolt it.

In my room, I thud my book bag to the ground and unzip it quickly. The three frogs I took from Sapphire's room. The three frogs will make me feel better, safer. *Mom would have liked these, when she still liked things.*

I place them in a small triangle, noses touching, at the foot of my ceramic daisy collection—which forces me to move my twenty-four metal skeleton keys beside my soft-bellied jester dolls and my bejeweled combs one foot's length closer to my Pennsylvania license plates, which, I decide, can stand mild shadowing via the comb tines. By the time I finish rearranging and ordering and restructuring, I only feel a little better. Which distresses me even more—if the order can't make things right, nothing will, which means I'm stuck like this, paralyzed within my own skull, forever.

I pull the other salvaged things from my bag to my bed: Sapphire's bustier, the thick stack of her journals. I slide my fingers over the velvet and rhinestones of the bustier. I *must* put it on. It will protect me. I need to be wearing it. Now. Shivering, I pull the bustier gently over my head, wriggling into it. It fits me perfectly: snug around my boobs, pushing them together, cinching my waist and making my nothing, narrow hips appear fuller. It feels right, holding me together, safe. Protected.

I curl onto my bed and pick up the first journal on the stack, heart pounding as I devour every word—searching for any mention of the bouncer. He's *got* to be somewhere in these pages. Maybe they were friends. Maybe they dated.

But, he's not mentioned anywhere, and I think back to what one of the girls said at Tens: *She never did extra to a guy for a hundred bucks, never went out with the guys from the club, not even the regulars. Not even the* bouncers.

I read pages and pages about Bird. She never calls Bird her boyfriend, even in her own private writings, but it's clear that whoever he is to her, he's very important. A very close friend, at least, and probably more from the things she describes that they do together:

Bird and I raided the Goodwill today. He said the goal was that we both look like "circus freaks" for our traditional Thursday "fancy dancing night." We dug through the $1 bins and found all sorts of crazy stuff—I found a floor-length spider-pattern dress and he found a jester hat with bells on it and a giant pair of silver pants. We snuck into the basement of this old red brick building on Meyers Street through the window and jumped around like lunatics. . . .

In another entry (September 8), she talks about midnight picnics on construction scaffolding: *Giant Eagle is the greatest—I swear. Bird has this obsession with Driscoll's strawberries (which are freakishly huge, btw). He hand-feeds me and calls me "Baby Bird." (Isn't he so romantic?? Ha-ha.) Sometimes the things that he wants to do—and when he wants to do something, we do it all the way—make me laugh so hard I come dangerously close to peeing in my pants. Wonder if he'd still find me sexy if I did. . . .*

I flip through each book with urgency. Interspersed between entries are funny little to do lists—*wheat bread, peanut butter, eggs, bobby pins, latex, smaller feathers, computer programmer, laundry*—in addition to dirty limericks and doodles (lots of hands and feet and flowers) and telephone numbers and dislocated thoughts and musings. Sapphire's a good writer, and the girls at Tens were right—she's funny. I keep reading.

I keep farting really loudly in my sleep and waking myself up because of it, she writes in one entry (April 29). *Is this normal? Does Bird hear it and just pretend that he doesn't to spare me the embarrassment, or does he really just sleep like a total rock?*

In another entry (October 16): *A regular pulled me aside tonight and told me he'd pay me a grand if I let him worship my feet for an hour. I said no, of course. But now, when he comes into the club, I swear I smell feet on him all the time (is it possible he just invests in foot-scented cologne?), and I can't help but look around at my coworkers and wonder which ones have taken him up on his offer. Nasty. I had to tell Bird about Mr. Foot Fetish. He laughed so hard he snarfed Dr Pepper all over me. I've been calling him Dr Pepper for two days.*

And another, near the end of her journal, one of the last entries (no date): *We've decided: for our anniversary, we're going to tell each other our real names. It's funny how in this place, it's the scariest thing you can share with a person—your real name. In normal places, you find that out the first time you meet someone. But, for us, it's our anniversary present to each other. And the best anniversary present I could want. To know something about him that I didn't know before. . . . Hope it's not something terrible, like . . . Bob. I hate the name Bob. Every day, I make a new guess, and he just shakes his head and says, "Not telling." I can't wait . . . four more months.*

In her later entries—over a year ago, according to the dates— Bird is still the primary subject, but something major has shifted: she writes a lot about him "flying away," getting sick. In one entry, she writes: *When I tried to come close to him the other day, he snarled at me like an angry dog. Maybe he's just hungry—I don't know if I've seen him eat anything in a week. I miss our late-night Giant Eagle raids, our picnics on other people's roofs . . .*

I wonder if the worst he ever did was snarl at her, or if it ever got seriously bad—maybe those are the things she wouldn't write

about. Or *couldn't* write about. Maybe he found one of her journals and read it, and then he got angry and hurt her. Could Bird be
connected to the bouncer somehow?

In another entry, she writes about her mother: *It's been 437
days since I came to Cleveland. I keep the number in a little book.
Every day, I cross the old one out and write the new one in. Today is the
437th day. And so now I'll always know: the day my mother died is
the 437th day since I've escaped from Dayton and the 437th day since
we've spoken a word to each other. And now there will only be more
days, but no more days to change it. I thought she wouldn't care if I
disappeared, and, turns out, I was right. She didn't care. She didn't
even try to find me. So, we're lost to each other for good now, I guess.
I'll have to start a new book of numbers. Today is Day 1. Day 1 of my
mother being dead. Tomorrow, it will be Day 2.*

I wonder what day she would have marked into her book today,
if she was still alive to do it. Staring at the cluster of scrawl on the
page, a jumble of numbers and letters, it hits me how young she
really was when she was killed: nineteen. So, she was just seventeen when she wrote these entries—my age—and only fifteen when
she ran away from home. Fifteen. She hadn't seen or spoken with
her mother since she was fifteen years old.

It's difficult for me to imagine her that young—in every picture
I've seen, she looks so much older. It's the makeup, of course.
But, it's something else, too. Something about her eyes.

I fall asleep sideways, face squashed onto the page I was in the
middle of reading—something about Bird, drifting, drifting away.

Sapphire's dark eyes peer out at me from between letters, numbers, unfinished scratches in the pit of my dreams. Blackness;

a cracking sound, and then: I'm pressed into a muddled crowd of people whose faces are being torn clean from their skulls by crows, swooping down from the sky. Black feathers float through the air like New Year's confetti.

I lift my hands to protect my face, but my hands have already been taken.

I try to scream, but my mouth is just a gaping hole between bones and bones and bones.

CHAPTER 14

Beepbeepbeepbeepbeep—my eyes snap open in bed, stare in disbelief at the alarm clock: 7:15. *Shit.*

Shit shit shit shit. I have to be at school in fifteen minutes. *SHIT.* My dreams were so deafening that they managed to drown out my alarm, which has been banshee-blaring for the past half hour.

The bustier is still wrapped tightly around me, pinching uncomfortably in places. I pull the first thing I can find over it (hunter green flannel), slip into a pair of crumpled black jeans from off my floor, lace up my Chucks, shove one of the journals into my book bag, *tap tap tap, banana*, and sprint like mad out of the house and to the bus stop. The bus has already left by the time I get there—but just barely—and I race to it, flagging it down several blocks ahead, panting as I step inside and slide into a window seat.

I watch my breath fog up the window in big, cloudy Os, unable to get a phrase from Sapphire's journal to stop turning through my mind: *I thought she wouldn't care if I disappeared, and I was right.*

I make faces in the window fog with my finger; squiggly mouths, turned-down eyebrows, post-electrocution hair. I erase them with the crease of my fist and start again. Six circles. Eighteen deep-fried hairs per circle. Unibrows: three. A giant planetary O that contains them all. Another circle around the first. And then another. Three giant circles, holding everything in.

I wonder if Oren thought we didn't care. It's probably why he didn't come back, why he ended up rotted away in some abandoned building somewhere. He didn't think we bothered to look for him. He didn't know that we were convinced, each of us, every second of every day, that he *would* come back. You set free the things you love, even if you don't mean to, and they come back to you. That's the reward; the Universal Cycle; the Law. By sheer logic: he would come back. Even when he folded into himself and looking at him became as painful as staring wide-eyed into a very bright sun, he was still ours. My bright, painful brother.

All that time, he was so close. Just a couple miles away. And we sat, waiting, doing nothing, while he fell apart, disintegrated.

We thought he would come back.

Maybe that's what Sapphire's mother thought, too, and that's why she didn't look. Maybe the things we think we have to believe are the things that end up killing us in the end, when we figure out we were wrong, about everything.

I make it through homeroom (though Weir does seem to look directly at me as he tells us in his familiar tone of grim: "*Please* try not to have *too* miserable of a day, kids.") I know Weir thinks I'm a depressive, a freak. He always looks directly at me when making his more defeatist comments, as though I'm clearly the one to whom they most apply.

The school day shuffles on.

Within the first few minutes of English class, as Ms. Manning drones in her post-nasal-drip voice about various Shakespearean renderings of doomed love, I reach into my bag and slip Sapphire's journal in the middle of *Romeo and Juliet*: Act Two, Scene Three (that old trick), flipping to a spot near the page that I'd drooled all over last night:

June 18: Bird was supposed to come over last night, but he showed up four hours late, pounding on the door like he was being chased. I didn't even want to let him in—I was pissed. He could have at least called. But he wouldn't stop pounding until I opened the door, so I gave in. He had this look in his eyes, I can't it explain it, but it freaked me out. He wouldn't talk about it when I asked what was wrong, he wouldn't say anything. But that's the curse, I guess, when you love someone . . . you'll take anything, even though they've made you feel like shit for two months straight. You'd open up one of your veins with a pocket knife if they needed your blood. . . . I don't think I'll ever be able to stop myself from wanting him. Sometimes I hate myself because of it.

I flip to another entry, earlier in the journal:

February 3: I don't know about doing it in the shower, but Bird loves it. . . . Marnie says she agrees that it's kind of sucky, but that she reads a lot of Savage Love and that it's all about being "Good, Giving, and Game." Now, I just need to figure out something that he won't like to do and make him do it, anyway . . . but I can't really figure out what—

"Penelope." A voice interrupts Sapphire's plotting. Ms. Manning's voice. I lift my head. "Yes, I am, in fact, speaking to *you*, Ms. Marin." I slam my book shut—the journal inside of it—folding my hands on top of my desk.

"I'm *so* interested, Ms. Marin," Ms. Manning wheedles in her rusted-spoke whine, "can you tell us what's just happened in the world of our *doomed* young lovers?"

My mind is a blank, and without thinking, I blurt out: "He wants to take showers with her, but she's doesn't like it."

The class goes apeshit. Ms. Manning stands there, cocking her head forward and furrowing her eyebrows into the bridge of her nose like she can't *believe* I just said that.

Oh. Shit. "I just mean—he wants to . . . shower her . . . with . . . love, but she won't let him. . . ."

The class laughs even harder; Ms. Manning's eyes are about to pop out of her face. I consider what might be my easiest escape route out of the room, but, looking around, I realize that no one's laughing *at* me. Tony Matthews is actually pumping his football-size fist into the air and banging his head like he's at a death metal concert, and Brigitte Crank and Sidney Lourie are both smiling at me so their teeth show. Brigitte gives me a little thumbs-up.

"Awesome," she mouths to me.

I sit up taller at my desk, looking forward, straight ahead, unable to suppress a smile.

"Okay, guys . . . that's enough. Interesting interpretation, Ms. Marin." She shoots me a glare and heads back toward the front of the room. "Moving on . . . In act three, scene five of the play, we find our lovers in what position?"

Another eruption; Ms. Manning must realize what she's setting herself up for. And, for once, I'm actually in on the joke.

*   *   *   *

After gym class, in the locker room, I stare at myself in the mirror by the lockers and, for the first time in a while, don't hate what I see. I run my hand up my shirt and feel the hardness of Sapphire's bustier against my palm. A happy shiver runs through my whole body. I lift my fingers to the top of my flannel and unbutton the first three buttons, sliding down one of the arms to expose the dark, glittery strap of the bustier against the pale skin of my shoulder. I like it. I feel good. Even though breathing is a little tougher than usual, I like how the bustier keeps me contained—like how I feel in my room, surrounded by all of my objects. Protected. Held up by something.

I consider the beautiful people at school: Keri and Camille and Sidney and Mara Turner and Annica Steele. Straight, silky hair, little minor ski-slope noses, a kind of effortless haughty beauty that pierces through you when you pass them like the sound crystal makes when you *tink* it with a fork—a reverberation of beauty, a high song that perks your ears, makes you smell fresh grass through the snow. Could my face ever do that, I wonder. Could I be . . . pretty? I shade the bump in my nose with my finger, push my bangs to the side.

As I emerge from the locker room and make my way to the science wing, a tall blond boy with sleepy eyes—he's just a sophomore, but still—turns his head to look at me as I pass.

I turn my head, too, to look at him back, when I collide with someone.

Jeremy. The second our eyes meet, his cheeks flame up. "Wow. Lo. You look, like, a little different, right? Is that a new shirt or something?" He tucks a strand of thick hair behind his ear.

"I've had it for a while, actually," I say, tugging on the hem. "But, thank you. I . . . like your T-shirt. It looks really . . . comfortable."

"It is! Dad got it at a Neil Young concert in the seventies." Jeremy looks briefly at his feet and back up at me. "I can't believe my 'rents were ever cool enough to stay out past like, eight P.M. I just wish I could build a time machine and catch them smoking a bowl together as fifteen-year-olds. They could use it now—they seriously need to chill. You know?"

I don't, not really, but I nod, anyway, force a smile. "Yeah, definitely. A time machine." I could use one, too.

"So—hey! We're still on for studying, right?"

"Yeah, um . . . about that." I inhale, then exhale in a rush. "I totally forgot I have to take my mom to the doctor today. Remember how she's sick?"

He deflates just like a balloon when it's popped. "That's all right," he says.

"But definitely some other time," I jump in. I can't stand to see him look like that, like a kicked puppy. "Maybe next week? I can buy you pizza or something."

Instantly, his face perks up again. "Yeah. Yeah, that would be great."

"Cool." I pulse my fists three times. I have a whole week to figure out a new excuse.

"Actually, there was something else I was, um, wondering about," Jeremy says, his voice inching just a little bit higher. "Do you, I mean, would you like to . . . gotopromwithme? He says the last part very fast, stringing the words together into one word that doesn't make any sense.

"*What* did you just say?" I ask, genuinely confused.

"Prom." He repeats, more slowly this time. "I want to know if you'll go to the prom with me." I hear each word, but they still make as little sense to me as the first time.

I count tiles in the floor (*sixteen, seventeen, eighteen, nineteen . . .*)

"Jeremy . . . I don't—"

"Just think about it, okay?" Jeremy sounds more confident than I've heard him sound before; his lopsided smile inches its way up his right cheek. "Just, like, take some time and *ponder*. See ya later, Lo!"

And before I can protest, he strides away, hands in his skinny-jean pockets.

*   *   *   *

I *ponder* prom as I wind through the science wing toward my locker.

The awkwardly short limo-ride to the school auditorium, the train of shimmering designer dresses and rigor-mortis-stiff diamond-studded updos, the sweat and heave of the gym beneath a ceiling laden with "Midnight in the Amazon" themed décor, the blinding, rising disco ball.

Finally, the last slow dance of the night: the snaking pattern of couples whispering—and then Jeremy's arms, wrapping unsteadily around my waist. I close my eyes and let it happen.

His lips hit mine and the fantasy shifts: Jeremy's breath becomes pine and snow and clove and grass and his arms wrap more firmly around my waist and his lips part against mine and I like the smoothness of his tongue and when I open my eyes: it's Flynt kissing me.

Flynt's eyes. Flynt's fingers. Flynt's tongue.

I don't want it to stop.

I'm so lost in the fantasy of him, of his warm, rough hands moving down my back, that by the time I reach my locker, prepared to *tap tap tap, banana*, I almost don't notice it: the locker door. My face. Everywhere. Eight missing eyes.

Four gaping mouths.

My locker: covered in a pattern of Xeroxed, blown-up photos; my school picture from last year. From the yearbook. Eight of them, stuck to the door in a sick square. My face slowly tapering away in each—consumed by something ravenous until it's gone entirely. And I'm burned away.

Scrawled across my lips in black ink like stitches, keeping my mouth shut, the warning: *Back off, bitch.*

It's acid. I recognize its effects from experiments in chemistry class. Litmus paper. Binder paper. Ink. How it licks everything up like flames.

Eight. Eight squares. Eight warnings. The number spins through my head, I stumble to the floor; the hall feels suddenly like it's tilting. Or maybe it's the whole world. I steady myself, try to focus my eyes, stand back on my feet: is this really happening?

I stare hard at my locker as my head begins spinning out of focus. It's real.

The bouncer. Again. Warning me.

He knows where I go to school. He's *been* here. He must have been here only minutes ago. Which means he could be watching me right now. He could be watching me all the time—he must know how often I'm alone—and how easy it would be to kill me. I spin around. People walk by. Some whispering. Some laughing.

My face—my eight faces—are dissolved entirely now. Slips of curled paper wave, tendril-like, from the locker door. I throw myself at them, scraping them off, shredding what's left. Six times torn. Again. Again. I try to stuff all the shreds of paper into my pockets, but they don't all fit. I'm cramming them in, shoving them now down my jacket, anywhere to hide them.

I should call the cops. But I can't. Not after last time.

"Get away!" I scream, pieces of torn paper falling from my fists.

People disburse. No one helps. No one tries.

I'm shaking, trying not to cry. My chest feels like it's collapsing. I lean against the wall for support, fumbling toward the exit.

"Lo!" My name rings through the hall. "Hey! Lo!"

Through a haze, I see Keri Ram on my right at the end of the hall perched with her celestially flowing auburn hair at a folded-out card table with a big sign that swirls into focus: PROM TIX!! $25.00 ADVANCE!! 2.5 WEEKS TO GO!! GET 'EM NOW OR YOU'RE NOT GOING TO GET SCREWED!

Her lips are pursing toward me, as are her long silky eyelashes, her cheekbones, her perfect china-white teeth. "Whoa. Are you okay?" She's handing me a tissue. In her other hand, she's still holding a stack of prom tickets—pink, green, red. "Is this about Jeremy?"

"Wha—what?" I thud down into a squat. I can't stay on my feet anymore. Bits of paper spill from my hands: I spread them out in front of her. Some of them are no more than that single line of writing. *Back off, bitch.*

Keri moves into a crouch next to me and puts a hand on my back. "Want to talk about it?"

"Someone's after me," I blubber. "I don't know what to do. I don't know who to tell."

Keri sighs. "Look, whoever it is, I'm *sure* they're just jealous." She helps me up to my feet.

"Yeah right," I mumble.

"Seriously, Lo. You're *so* pretty—in this totally unique way. You kind of look old and young at the same time." She's tilting her head to one side, nose squinched up, examining me. I open my mouth to protest, but she rushes on, "Like non*conventional* or whatever. Have you ever noticed how on *Top Model*, all the girls who win are kind of different-looking? It's so a thing! Seriously, a lot of people wish they could be like you. You know . . . special."

I want to say: I'm tired of being special. I want to say: I want to be normal. But no words come.

Keri squints at me, obviously worried. "You live off of Maplebrook, right?" I nod, weakly. "Just wait a sec for me to close up the booth, and I'll drive you home. It's on my way."

I don't feel strong enough, or safe enough to resist, so I wait, and I let her weave her arm through mine and lead me through the halls, counting lockers as we pass, *nine, ten, eleven*; my other arm begins to feel very, very uneven. I keep counting, pushing away the panic. *Sixteen, seventeen, eighteen.* "Later, Allen," Keri calls as we pass Camille, examining her hair in her locker mirror.

"I thought we were hanging after school today . . . ," Camille replies, a sour tug in her voice as she stares at me. *Twenty-one, twenty-two, twenty-three.*

"I'll text you in, like, twenty, okay?" Keri calls over her shoulder; I *tap tap tap, banana* before she turns back around, and we push out the door and into the front parking lot. Keri leads us to her car; BMW; shiny red. Front row center. A warm breeze rushes around us; Keri removes her arm from mine and pulls her hair into a low ponytail before we settle into the chilly leather seats of her car. I can't stop seeing my eight faces; peeling away into ash.

Keri's talking to me about prom as we drive, but all I catch are snippets, intercepting my own thoughts about the bouncer: about how—how in the hell he found me, found my locker, and why—why he would have killed Sapphire in the first place. I'm missing something massive, and I have a feeling I'm about to run out of strikes.

"*Lo.*" Keri's voice cuts through my thoughts. I raise my head to look at her. "You're, like, *hitting* your legs. Over and over again."

I stare at a collection of dark stones in the middle of the side-walk. *Four, five, six.* "I—I didn't realize," I answer, honestly, as we drive past the doorway where I'd spotted the bouncer yesterday.

I pull my coat up around my chin and push my head farther down into it.

"Well, I'm just right up here, so . . ."

Keri pulls over a few houses away from my own. "Here?"

I nod. "Thank you . . . for helping." The words feel unnatural, difficult to say. "Really."

Keri hugs me, squeezing tightly as she says: "Don't stress, Lo. For real."

Being hugged is bewildering, overwhelming. Tears prick my eyes; I get out of her car quickly, embarrassed, turning toward my actual house. I have no idea why Keri is being so nice to me. She doesn't even know me.

"See you later," I call over my shoulder, already walking. Needing to walk. Needing to tap. Needing to count cracks.

Seventeen, eighteen, nineteen.

If she knew me, maybe she wouldn't be so nice anymore.

Twenty-four, twenty-five, twenty-six. Twenty-seven to make it perfect. Start again.

CHAPTER 15

"Lo," my mother's voice creaks through the dark slit of her door-frame as I pass on the way to my room. She's sitting up in bed, her eyes clear in the bluish television glow. The TV announcer says: *"Congratulations, Peggy! You've won a brand-new stainless-steel washer. And. Dryyyyer."* The crowd goes wild.

My mother smiles: "Come over here." Her voice is unusually calm.

"With a retail value of over two thousand dollaaaars!"

"What's up, Mom?"

I inch closer to the bed and she pulls my hand to hers. It's cold. And bony. She hasn't done this—hasn't wanted anyone to touch her, or to touch anyone else—since she cast anchor into the dark, stale-smelling harbor of her room over a year ago.

I remember when she used to make dinner. She'd always make sure my plate was even on both sides, make sure that my chicken was cut into the right number of pieces. That she gave me the right number of vegetables. Otherwise I wouldn't eat. Dad never got it; he just got angry with me for repeating things over and over again, for counting cracks in the sidewalk when I walk, for having to start over when I mess up.

"Look at that smile, folks. Peggy, from North Carolina! Is your family here in the audience today?"

Mom looks up at me. "Your father told me what happened the other day, Lo, at dinner." She pulses my hand in hers. "He says you seem stressed. That you've been coming home late."

I clap my hand against my thigh, six times; start counting hairs in her left eyebrow (*sixteen, seventeen, eighteen . . .*). "I—I've just been studying. I've been going to the library a lot—"

"Is this about a boy?" she interrupts, before I have a chance to finish.

"What? Mom—no." It's like she and Keri Ram share the same brain. "I mean—"

"Lo, it's okay," she interrupts again. "I understand. I certainly had my fair share of boyfriends before I decided to settle down with your father."

"No," I say, a little more emphatically. I try to draw my hand from hers, but she won't let me.

"So, what is it?" she continues, a weird half smile crossing her face. "You've been sneaking out to see him? You don't want to bring him around? You're embarrassed by us?"

"That's not it *at all.*"

"Well, then, what is it?" she says, her voice starting to become shrill. "Something bad? Are you involved with bad people, Lo?

Drugs? What? Are you doing drugs now? After everything we've been through?"

I try to make my voice soothing. "Mom, No. I'm *not* doing drugs. I swear. I'm not hanging out with *anyone*."

"Don't lie to me, Penelope," she says, small flags of spit flying off her lips. She is gone, drifting away from stable ground. "I know you've been sneaking out all week. I hear you. Creeping, creeping. After what happened last year, how dare you disappear on me and then lie about it? How dare you?" She wraps her arms around her stomach. "No," she says, "no, no, no, no, no. Not again."

"Mom, please." I want to touch her. I want to say something to make her stop, but I can't.

Suddenly, she's sobbing, her whole body curled into itself like a leaf wrapped around a twig, her voice coming through in blubbery wails, in short-breathed spurts. "I—I didn't know. You believe me, don't you? I didn't know. Oh *God*. My baby. My baby." She lifts her fingers to her face, digging her nails down her cheeks.

"I'm going to get you some water, Mom." I whisper the words. I back away toward the door, squeezing my fists against my thighs, filled with a feathery feeling, as though I am breaking apart.

In the kitchen, I fill a glass with cold water from the tap and dump it out. I fill it again, dump it out. I fill it a final time, without dumping it, and pull myself away from the sink. The rituals are in overdrive. They slow me down, but I can't stop them. I take three steps up the staircase and have to go back one—up three, down one, up three, down one—until I reach the top.

By the time I come back into her room, my mother has stopped crying. She has collapsed backward on the bed, eyes glazed, and every so often a muted whimper makes its way out of her throat.

"Come on, Mom." I sit gingerly down on the bed with her. "Drink this, okay? Here. Let me help you." She's limp as a doll as I prop her head up with one hand, angle the glass toward her lips with the other.

Behind me, the TV is still blaring. News time, now. *"Thanks, Tom. I'm here at the Westwood Center where Dumpsters are finally being reinstalled after nearly a four-month removal due to a bomb threat in late December."*

I place the now-empty glass on the bedside table and swivel around, toward a picture of a happy-shiny broadcaster standing in the wind-whipped parking lot in front of the mall. Westwood Center: I remember hearing something about Westwood Center . . . something important . . .

"Police confirmed shortly after the threat that it was, in fact, a false-alarm, but decided to remove Dumpsters in the vicinity, anyway, as a precautionary measure. For the past four months, the city has been forced to hire private waste and sanitation contractors, hiking up rents for all tenants by nearly twenty percent to cover the costs. Local business owners Glenn, Donn, and Joe Weinberg protested, saying no businesses at Westwood Center should be forced to pay so exorbitantly for services that should by reasonable standards be included in rent, and other business owners agreed. After a protest in front of the Twenty-third Street station on Friday, finally, Cleveland police have cleaned up their act for everyone involved."

My mother's breathing slows, and her eyelids flutter shut. My throat feels tight, my head like a balloon ready to burst.

Why can't I remember?

I creep quietly, swiftly, from Mom's room, making sure not to wake her.

Back in my room, I stare at my objects and my objects stare back at me.

Suddenly—a ringing sound from my book bag. It takes me a few seconds to piece it together: my cell phone.

CHAPTER 16

I dig furiously around until I locate the phone. My cell *never* rings. I stare at the screen: I don't recognize the number.

"Hel-*lo*?"

A car horn blares in the background. A confetti-throw of static. "Queen Penelope?" the voice at the other end says. "Can it be she?"

I bite hard into my bottom lip, flooded with relief. "Flynt! You finally got a cell phone?"

"Never! Pay phone, baby. Miraculously, they still exist. . . ."

"But . . . how did you get this number?"

"You gave it to me, L! First day we met!" I hear his breath through the line, soft and steady. He's right—I did. An image from my stupid prom fantasy pops into my head. His mouth. His big straight teeth. I put my tongue to the roof of my mouth nine times and then swallow another three; it's not real. It'll never be real.

"So, did you hear about Vinnie?"

"Vinnie?" I ask, confused.

"The bouncer at Tens. He was arrested for killing Sapphire today. It's the talk of the town over here in Neverland. So, it's all over. We're free, Queen Penelope!"

I quickly remove a pile of stuff from my computer, cradling the phone with my shoulder. New search: Cleveland Neverland Crime. B. Hornet's Neverland Crime Blog pops up: a new headline in bold red: "An Arrest for the Shooting of Area Girl: Sapphire, 19."

Click. The article loads; I hold my breath.

4:10 P.M.: CST, April 8th

By: Mark Stanton, the Plain Dealer

CLEVELAND—*Police arrested a man this afternoon for the murder of an area girl, Sapphire (last name unknown). The victim was a dancer at Tens, a Neverland club in the 2100 block of East 119th Street, where the suspect, Vincent Navarro, 43, worked as a bouncer.*

Officers apprehended Navarro around 3:00 P.M. at work after uncovering conclusive DNA evidence at the victim's home—the scene of the crime.

Navarro served two of a five-year prison sentence that began in 1998, for armed robbery and assault with a deadly weapon. He was released on parole in 2000 and has been employed at Tens ever since.

So, it was him—the bouncer—and now he's gone. In prison,

where he belongs. And I have nothing left to worry about. I should feel light. I should feel *free*.

Except, why don't I? Why can't I shake the feeling that something's still not right? When I saw him, a block away from my house, he was talking to someone on the phone. Who, at that moment, would he have *needed* to speak to?

"Hello, Lo? You still there? Shit, did my change run out? Hello?"

"I'm here, I'm here. I'm just . . . I can't believe it. I—"

"Come meet me in, like, two hours. By the birdbath?"

I hesitate, listening to the minor static on the other end of the phone, a rush of traffic. The prospect of the bus ride into Neverland, alone, as it's starting to get dark, doesn't exactly seem appealing and it's beginning to annoy me that I've always got to go to him.

"Come here. To Lakewood now," I finally tell him.

"No," he says abruptly. "I told you. I don't leave Neverland. Ever. And I need to take care of a few things first, so, two hours." He pauses. "Just come here, okay? I'll meet you at the bus stop."

I hesitate. But no matter what I do now, every time I close my eyes and every time I open them, too, I see it all—the cat, my burning face, the bouncer huddled in the seamy dark, Sapphire's dark blue lips—and Flynt's the *only* person I can talk to about it.

"Fine. Two hours," I tell him, and hang up.

The bouncer. Vincent Navarro. I wait for my heart to lift, for my head to stop pounding. But, for some reason, it doesn't.

I brush my bangs out of my face, three times, and glance

quickly into the mirror. Sapphire's bustier still peeks out beneath my hunter-green flannel, dark against my pale skin. Her face flits across my face and once again, and just for a second, we're the same person. Wrapped in each other. Breathing together. Alive.

*　　*　　*　　*

"Your Highness," Flynt says, standing up from the gum-studded bus stop bench to bow. His bear ears look slightly off-center and more threadbare in the orb of the streetlight. *Tap tap tap, banana.* I want to bow back and say something witty, but my bangs are bugging me. So, I put my fingers to work in lieu of words, combing and flattening, combing and flattening as I walk to him.

"I think we should talk somewhere more private, Lady Lo," he says to me, folding his real ears into his hat. "I'd take us to my crash pad—it's the basement of this barbershop on the corner of Grover and Miles, a few blocks that-a-way—but, I'm actually kinda hungry. And there's a diner nearby we can walk to."

A breeze folds through the trees, six more streetlamps click on in a row. "Okay." I'm eager to keep moving, curious about what he's got to say, what he knows. We turn onto Egret Street. "Flynt, I—"

"Shhh," Flynt says, pointing.

Standing a few feet away, beneath a flickering streetlamp near the end of the block, is a man wearing what look to be at least seven coats. A tweed hat is upturned between his red rain-booted feet, and he is swaying back and forth with his tiny arms in the air and singing, Louis Armstrong–style: "Mah Bay-bee. Ohhh. Mah

Bay-bee, left me so-o-o-o-o saaaayyyd. S-o-o-o saaayyyd. Have you seeeeen huh, have you seeeeen huh, Oooo, won't you tell huh that I miss huh. S-o-o-o baaaayyyd."

He looks too small for his whale-bellied voice. As he sings, he seems to pinwheel around himself, revolving on his own hilt, shining like a celestial body burning light through deep space.

And then I remember him—the homeless man, wailing and swaying as I ran from Sapphire's house the day she was murdered.

Flynt stops beside me, says into my ear: "The Prophet."

"That's his name?"

"That's what everyone calls him." Flynt drops his voice low, like an old southern man before a campfire: "Legend has it, he's been coming to this corner, every single night for forty years, to busk. You know—sing for money. And everyone calls him The Prophet because he knows everything about everyone in Neverland. He's like our own little almanac."

My heart does jumping jacks as he says: "He knows everything about everyone." Exactly the person I need to talk to.

"I'm going to go ask him about something," I tell Flynt.

I practically leap forward, planting myself a foot or so away from the tiny swaying Prophet.

He smiles at me as he sings, his eyes a wide, pasty violet color. I stand there nervously, waiting for a break in song, watching his mouth open and close—several of his teeth are gone, and the rest look stuck into his gums like Chicklets. I look quickly away, pulse quickening, reaching into my purse for money.

Three dollar bills. One by one. Three seconds before each new bill.

"Bless you," he says.

"Excuse me, but I was wondering if you know—" I begin.

"What I know is. Wonder. What I know is. Light," he sing-speaks, still swaying his head between his shoulders, his coats floating and dropping to the ground each time he lifts his arms.

"Okay. But, do you also know—did you also know—a Bird?" I take a deep breath—Oren waves to me inside my head, only half a body, floating down Butt Creek.

He gazes at me with shocking violet-blue eyes. "The light is falling. The sky takes us all." He moans softly, "Ohhhh *yes*."

He angles his face downward, a darkness coming over his expression. "Oh yes. I know a Bird. Funny name. A unicorn all the time. And a nightingale when it suited him."

I shake my head, confused. "But—do you know where I can find him?"

He cuts me off again, singing, "Fly, fly away. Fly away with my baaaaby. . . ."

I turn on my heels, counting my steps back to Flynt. I've got to take a giant one at the end to make it twelve instead of thirteen. He's standing in the same spot with a crooked smile on his face, shaking his head.

"You're funny, Lo . . . all those little things you do. Your Queenly Gestures. I like them."

My body goes hot all over, as it always does. When I'm caught.

"I should have added," he continues, clearing his throat, "that nothing the Prophet says makes any sense." He weaves his arm through mine. "Come on." Flynt says, pulling me forward. "It's cold out here."

*   *   *   *

Rabbit's Diner is mostly empty when we get there—a time-warped place lined with filmy aqua booths, little jukeboxes at each table, checkered floor dappled in grease. We order a plate of curly fries from the soggy-faced waitress, who knows Flynt—of course—and brings us Cokes for free.

Flynt bends forward over the plate of fries and lifts one into the air. A bead of grease drips from it, splatting onto the table. "That's what I'm *talkin'* about!" he says, popping the fry into his mouth, smiling as he meets my eye. He keeps looking at me—a few long, warm seconds, his eyes widening, sparkling gold and blue and green.

"So . . . ," I begin, dropping my eyes again to the plate, grabbing the ketchup bottle and squeezing a dollop onto my napkin, and then another, and another, evenly spaced, "on the phone you mentioned the bouncer . . . at Tens. What do you know about him?"

I raise my eyes to him, and he's still looking at me, in that same, intense way, like he wants to . . . kiss me or something. I look away again, feeling myself blush; I reach for another fry.

"Not much, really; he was pretty rough, I know that," he says, dancing his fingers across the table until they almost meet mine. I quiver. "I just wanted to make sure you were okay. And I thought we should celebrate, all of this, finally being over."

"Right. Yeah," I say, trying to force a smile. My jaw tightens, I dip a fry into each of my three little puddles of ketchup, three times. It's not over. I know it. But Flynt seems so certain, so ready to believe, to step away. The bouncer. Vincent Navarro. Vinnie.

His arrest happened before the end of the school day. . . . There's no way he could have left the warning flyers on my locker. And, who was he talking to, who picked him up that day . . . in the black sedan? He can't have been working alone. No way. I finish ketchup-ing my fry, eat it in three bites, trying to push the spinning thoughts from my head.

"That's a good look for you," Flynt says, laughing, staring at my mouth.

My face burns, I scan my outfit for stains, holes in embarrassing places. "What? What are you talking about?"

He leans over the table and brushes my lips with his thumb. "Ketchup," he answers softly, showing me the evidence on his finger. My body goes hot. "Maybe I should have left it . . . you looked pretty cute, covered in ketchup."

I feel a smile spread across my face and I clap my hand over it; I don't want him to know, to know that he can do that to me.

His hand is back on the table and so is mine, and they're nearly touching; there's a band of heat between us, magnetic. "I think," he begins, "we should do a little Dumpster diving, Queen P . . . to celebrate the good news." He slides his hand slightly forward; our fingertips touch. *Dumpster-diving. Dumpsters. Dumpsters . . .* Something starts turning in my brain as soon as he mentions it; something important.

"The Westwood Center . . . ," I say aloud, staring at the three flattened pools of ketchup on my napkin. "Why can't I . . ." And then my blood turns to ice. "Mario." My fingertips fly away from his. My hands press hard against the battered edge of the table. "Flynt!"

He turns to me, a worried look on his face.

"This guy Mario," I begin, speaking rapidly, "he was—he was selling things that belonged to Sapphire. That day. At the flea." My hands fly to my thighs, begin tapping beneath the table.

"Yeah . . . so what?" Flynt tugs on his bear ears, reaches for a fry.

"So . . . he told me he got everything from the Dumpsters outside of the Westwood Center. But he couldn't have! Right? They weren't there. There was a news report today. Business owners—they were protesting; all the Dumpsters were removed, months ago. He knows something—he definitely knows something—we have to—we have to find him."

Flynt leans forward, blinking. "Lo—I really think we've got to let it go now. They already arrested the bouncer—he did it."

"But why would Mario have lied?" I protest. "He's got to be connected to this somehow. Maybe he *knows* something." I pull a five-dollar bill from my purse and plunk it down on the table, scooting quickly out of the booth. Flynt follows, catching my hand before I can bolt out the door, boring his eyes into me. "What? Are you not coming?"

"Lo. Listen to me." He rests his hands on my shoulders; his face is stark and serious. "You have to leave it alone. The bouncer is in prison. They wouldn't put someone in prison if they didn't have a really good reason to think he belonged there."

"Right . . . of course, because cops are *never* wrong." I wriggle out from under his hands. "*First* you tell me to stay out of it, and then you say you want to help me, and then you tell me to stop again! I'm so sick of this—of your secrets!" I burst out, ignoring the stares of other customers. "Why don't you just tell me the *truth* for once?"

He puts his hands back on my shoulders, pressing into me harder. "Lo, I *care* about you. I just want you to be safe, okay? That's the truth. That's all I want. And," he continues, gently, "do you think that *maybe* you've just become obsessed with this case, with Sapphire, because it gives you a way to avoid dealing with your own shit?"

I wrench myself, again, from his grasp. "My shit?" I parrot back. "What the hell do you know about *my* shit? You don't even know me. You don't know anything!"

Flynt's shaking his head; he looks like he might cry. "Lo—I didn't mean—I'm—"

"You're a liar," I spit out, nostrils flaring. "That's all you ever do—all you've *ever* done. You said you hadn't been to Tens in forever, but you had; you said you had no idea who Sapphire was, but you did. Everything. Everything you say is untrue." I stare for a second, blindly furious, into his eyes—the eyes of another person who doesn't think I'm good enough or strong enough.

I'm filled with a violent urge to spit—some raging shoot of saliva that would come out fiery, speed past our heads like a comet—but I don't. My feet are pulsing, screaming at the rest of my body, at my blood. *Go. GO.*

Now, Sapphire whispers, fluttering to me through every tiny jukebox speaker. *Now.* I have twenty-seven seconds to leave—twenty-seven, the mother number, the protector, the number that sees, that knows, that transmutes its knowledge through every part of your body. Twenty-seven seconds to leave this place and get to the street. Twenty-seven seconds, or it's all over.

Or I'm dead. *(Five, six, seven.)*

I don't look back *(ten, eleven, twelve)* as I run past the beat-up booths and through the old diner door that's got bells on it. *(Seventeen, eighteen, nineteen.)* The *urge* flashes through my fingers—no choice—and I swipe the bells before I leave. They sound like the choked hymn of out-of-practice angels, knocking into each other in my pocket as I run *(twenty-five, twenty-six, twenty-seven)* farther from the warm light of the diner, farther into the ramshackle, farther into the mess.

CHAPTER 17

I run the whole way from the diner to the flea, and by the time I arrive, I'm heaving, back and ribs and chest moving up and down like a scatter graph as I pause to catch my breath. It isn't Saturday. I've never been here on a day that isn't Saturday. I don't know what it will be like—what it will feel like—if he'll even be here—if the world will spontaneously combust. All I know is: I had to get here before it closed—before it was too late to find him.

I need to find out why he lied.

Tap tap tap, banana. Almost every vendor is in a state of partial-pack-up by the time I enter.

"Mario. Mario. Mario," I say aloud, clapping the syllables against my thigh, the diner bells jangling in my pocket as I do. Nine. A good sign, even though I know it'll be hard to find him here, in this maze: fewer vendors than I'm used to, but still, hundreds, in a wayward mass of curtained off tables and booths and stands, hooked together with metal and rope, strung with starry lanterns and cords of tiny lights, the landscape even more blinding and intoxicating and scattered and impossible at night. I squeeze Sapphire's butterfly in my pocket hard. *Help me.* I feel her fingers lock around mine for a second inside my pocket. *I'm here,* she's saying.

I weave madly through stalls in no particular sequence or order; it makes my head spin to violate my rules. I don't see him. I tap the syllables of his name again against my thigh—*Ma-ri-o* (break) *Ma-ri-o* (break) *Ma-ri-o.* Maybe he already packed up, went home. Maybe, like me, he only comes on days with three syllables.

I can't hold on to this weaving—every six steps I have to stop and put first my right hand to the ground, and then my left, and then my right again. I try to pull my collar up so that it conceals my face, so that people can't see me. Nine, nine, six. Nine nine, six until—finally—I arrive back in the spot where I first saw Mario, where he gave me Sapphire's butterfly as payment for my reticence, where I swiped the horse-pendant necklace, where Flynt blurred past me, sending me shooting into Mario's table in the first place.

A jagged pain arrows through me when I think of him.

I touch the ground—right, left, right—and walk up to the booth where Mario's should have been, approaching the new man behind the table. He is loading records into milk crates, his goatee like too-stiff cotton, thick black eyeglasses, a red bowtie clipped to the top of his button-up.

I clear my throat. "Excuse me." *Ma-ri-o, Ma-ri-o, Ma-ri-o.* No time to waste.

The new vendor looks up at me over his glasses, dumping an armload of records onto the table. "Closing up now. But I'll still take your money, if that's what you're wondering." He flashes me a warm grin as he stacks and rearranges.

"No. I'm wondering—" Mario's sick, cherry-red hair flashes through my head for a second. "I'm trying to find this vendor who was here last Saturday—Mario."

He thinks for a second. "You mean Marty? Big hairy guy who sells baseball bats?" He motions with his thumb to the left. "He's about ten booths that way."

I shake my head no, pumping my hands in my coat pockets. Nine times. Nine times. Then six. "No. Not Marty. Mario. Dyed red hair? He sells vintage stuff."

"Hmm. No. I don't know about anyone named Mario. But I'm only here every other week and never on Saturdays." He flashes me a tight-lipped *sorry*, and I bow out of the booth, breathing quickly. I see the clouds part, a spine of red-gray sky. Sapphire's butterfly grows warmer against my skin: *keep looking.*

I go down the line, booth by booth, ground-touching, nine-nine-six, interrupting whoever I have to—sidling between conversations, box-packing, cigarette-smoking, whatever—to ask about Mario. No one knows anything. Some people, like the record-booth guy, have never even heard of him, and the people who have say that he wasn't a regular at the flea—if they remember him at all, it's that he'd set up shop maybe three days total the whole year—and so they never had the chance to find out anything about him: who he was, where he lived, what he did otherwise with his time.

I'm starting to feel sick, when an older lady, packing up her eyeglasses display with intense concentration, calls to me as I pass her.

"I heard you down there," she says. "You're looking for Mario, right?"

"Yes." I say. My heart skips a beat. *Ma-ri-o, Ma-ri-o, Ma-ri-o.* "I—I need to ask him about something he sold me last week. It's important."

"His booth was next to mine a few Saturdays ago," she tells me, lifting a pair of studded specs, rubbing the glass with a soft yellow cloth. "Nice man . . . said saying something about how he was only selling here to earn some extra money, so that he could move out of The Juniper. You know, over on Euclid Street, all the way at the end? I hear nasty stuff about that place."

My heart starts pounding faster. *The Juniper.*

I grip Sapphire's butterfly in my pocket, pulse it three times. She pulses back: *yes yes yes.*

"Hope that helps." She sighs, turning away to grab a new box. Her back to me, the *urge* wages its full-scale attack—two pairs of silver glitter-framed cat-eye glasses sing to me on the edge of the table—my fingers fill with heat and speed. But, as my hand starts to shoot forward to grab them, I pull back, jam it hard into my pocket, and squeeze the butterfly instead. She turns back to me, lifts another pair of glasses, begins to clean them.

"It does," I say, breathless, realizing for the first time, maybe ever, I did it. I resisted the *urge.* "A lot."

*   *   *   *

The evening darkens around me as I head to Euclid Street. I remember where it is because I'd passed it, running from Sapphire's house; only three blocks from Lourraine Street. I'm not worried right now about what I'll do when I find Mario. *Just get there*, Sapphire whispers through me. *Just keep going.*

I put Oren beside me, too, as I run. I give him the *let's race* eye. And I go, torpedoing through streets that seem to narrow into each other, so thin.

Power lines zigzag above me—hanging dangerously low and giving off little sparks every so often that have, at some point, probably set most of the trees on fire—their bark now charred and chapped and raw. The houses spring up in seemingly random tufts, some leaning into each other for lack of alternative support, big holes gnawed through the brick and concrete.

By the time I angle a sharp right turn onto Euclid Street, Oren has disappeared, vanished behind me; I'm alone again.

"I won," I pant out, into the freezing air, slowing to a walk. My lungs are burning and tears prick up at the corners of my eyes.

The cracks in the pavement are getting wider and the wind is howling wilder as I walk, my heart banging around in my chest. I pause at a deep hole in the street to let an enclave of rats complete their apparent exodus to a different alleyway. Looking up, I see it: The Juniper. Number 222 Euclid Street, next to a pillared highway bridge at the end of the street.

Two—terrible. A split-apart ghost of a number.

The Juniper is a squat, run-down building, eerily isolated but with the appearance of being almost squeezed to the point of suffocation. It has sliced-up, painted-chipped wood for a face and half-boarded-up windows for eyes.

My blood goes cold; I tap: *Ma-ri-o, Ma-ri-o, Ma-ri-o, Ma-ri-o, Ma-ri-o, Ma-ri-o.*

I practice what I'll say in my head: *Tell me the* truth *or I'm calling the cops this time.*

The sky is steel-wool gray as I climb the stairs, legs like hot lead, diner bells jangling with each ascending step and the butterfly biting jaggedly into my fist. I consider my obstacles: no working streetlights, a murderer inside, no one around but rats to hear me cry for help. *Tap tap tap, banana.*

The door clicks open. Easy. It wasn't even locked. Of course: the lock is broken.

There's a directory inside. Tenant's names, listed by first initial and surname. I don't know his last name.

Two different tenants whose first names start with *M*.

M. Vecchio; 103

M. Egorin; 212

Tap tap tap, banana. I walk through the open entranceway, beneath the sagging plaster in the ceiling, beige carpeting rife with stains, walls darkened by deep gashes and holes. Everything reeks of cigarettes, of the sweet, dull, stale tongue of liquor.

My body floats, underwater again, to the first door. I stare at it. Everything feels wrong; bad; I should leave.

But my body is starting to twitch. I need in, need to know. The crazy feeling is blooming, the storm-type thing in my torso, climbing into my throat and down my arms and legs and into my eyes, even. If I don't knock on this door I'll hear Oren in my dreams for weeks, demanding, *Why why why. Why didn't you try, Lo? Why didn't you just do something for once, something important?* Even when he doesn't say it—when it's just his face, staring at me from some dark, distant place—I know it's what he means. Why didn't I *do* something?

Why do I let things slip away?

I knock on the door. Nothing happens. No answer. I knock again.

Seconds and seconds and bleeding seconds of the creeping, silent stuff.

I'm turning away from the door, ready to try the next one— M. Egorin; 212—when I hear something like feet, scuffling quickly along a splintered floor. The knots in my stomach pull tighter. He's in there. I just know it.

Things are fluttering up into my mouth—butterflies—stretching their wings between my cheeks, teeth-tickling, pressing against my lips. I open my mouth to let them out, but nothing comes.

I turn back and knock again. No answer, but, still: the feet, scratching, scraping. If I don't do this, something bad will happen, anyway—to my family, to Flynt, to someone I care about. If I don't put my hand on the doorknob in six—no, in twelve seconds—it'll happen. Something so awful I can't even imagine it yet. I count to twelve and my hand shoots to the doorknob and I turn it.

It opens.

Tap tap tap, banana. I step inside to inky blackness, a wall of thick, cold air. The darkness of this place wraps straitjacket tight; it's the sensation of having stumbled directly into a coffin.

An invisible avalanche of mud, kicked down from the living

world above, is rising, filling the room, rising choke-high. I'm struggling to breathe. I can't find the light. I reach my hands out and walk zombie-like, slow, until I find the wall, run my fingers along the drywall and insulation.

The earth's still rising around me, but it's just the blackness, a fist gripping tighter and tighter. I really might die here. In the dark, with no one, like Sapphire. They'd museum my room, judge it. I'd be the freak who stole things, who tapped and counted, who couldn't walk in a straight path to her bed. *Tap tap tap, banana*.

The wall is an endless, pocked valley.

This is what death is like, right here.

I feel something.

The light switch on the wall.

Something against my leg.

I'm screaming, huge, as the lights click on.

A black cat curls its tail around me, claws at the rip in my tights. Relief almost doubles me over. Just a cat. A cat, scratching around the empty apartment. I kneel, grateful, take its face into my hands.

"You're all wet, kitty." I remove my hands slowly, look down at them. They are coated in red. Blood. They're covered in blood.

I stand up dizzily, stomach heaving, take two stumbling steps forward. There, in the center of the room, I finally find Mario: wormy mass of his intestines pouring onto the linoleum floor; wings of browning blood pooled slimy and spread around him, eyes open wide, terrified. Mouth half open. Trying to breathe. A weak, barely audible sucking sound. Throat—spilling. Three more cats circle around him; skeletal, hungry.

Pipes exposed. Cut. Lacerated. *Oh God.*

Like the cat. Like the cat. *Now you know what curiosity did.*

But Mario isn't dead. Yet.

I turn away. My head spins.

I don't know how I get outside, but, suddenly, I am—shaking, choking. I fall into the cold wet grass and dirt and dark, door swinging closed behind me. The world is swinging, loose and wild.

Moon huge. Breath heavy.

CHAPTER 18

I stare at my hands. They're shaking, red-palmed. I collapse onto my knees, rubbing them into the grass and dirt. Full of death—full of blood—*his* blood. I need them clean.

I need help.

Somehow, I manage to dial 911. Somehow, I speak the address, speak the facts: "There's a man. . . . He's dying. Please. Come." They tell me they're on their way.

I hang up the phone. No noise. Stillness all around me. A few minutes later, two pairs of headlights wind through the dark toward me. The cops. An ambulance.

My breath comes in uneven hiccups. Two officers slam their car doors shut, an insect-like buzz coming through their walkie-talkies. I struggle to stand, but it's like I'm sinking—unsure right now where my body ends and the muddled ground begins.

The insects buzz: "Ten-four. Possible homicide at the corner of Euclid. No. We got a bus already." A swathe of static.

Two EMTs leap from an ambulance, carrying a stretcher; one of them is a woman with very, very short hair and the other is a man wearing a dark blue jacket and carrying what looks like a defibrillator and some other equipment. They run across the dying lawn to the run-down building, push inside.

A female officer starts scouring the grounds, aiming her flashlight beam into the dark. A fourth officer—tall and thin, pointy-chin, bird-beak nose—extends a hand to help me up. "Ms. Marin?"

I nod, facing him, six breaths in, six breaths out. Can't stop seeing Mario's dying body. His eyes wide open, corneas rolled back, every part of him shivering its life away. Six breaths in, six breaths out.

"I'm Officer Flack. And that's my partner, Officer Menken." Officer Menken—pug-nosed, button-eyed, a woman teetering on the verge of fatness—looks briefly up and then returns to her notepad to scrawl something. "So," he continues, eyeing me carefully, "you called 911, right? Do you live in the neighborhood?"

"No," I answer with difficulty—my throat feels full of choking thickness. "Just visiting." I repeat under my breath, "Just visiting. Just visiting."

"What was that?"

"Nothing. It was nothing." One more time, too soft to hear: "Nothing." My face is burning. I tap: nine, nine, six on the right leg; nine, nine, six on the left; nine, nine, six on the right again.

He looks confused. "So, how did you end up over here? Is the man inside a friend of yours? Relative?"

"No, not really," I say. "I—I bought something from him at

the flea market a couple of weeks ago, and I wanted to see if he had anything else like it. I was already in the neighborhood, on my way to the bus, so I thought I'd—" I hiccup twice. *Bad.* Blood. Stomach turning. My head feels like it is being squeezed between two dark planes. I don't even know if I am making make sense "I went inside to—to see, and the door was, was open—"

Officer Menken comes to stand beside Officer Flack. "Reynolds radioed for backup. Davis and Frank will be here in under five." She eyes me warily, still scribbling things into her notepad.

"What bus?" she asks me abruptly.

"Bus?"

"Yes. Bus line. You said you were on your way to the bus." Her voice is curt. It makes my stomach hurt even more, the edge of this voice. Like a paper cut.

"The ninety-six." I answer—the bus where onion-sack girl led me, the day Sapphire was killed in the daisy-yellow house.

Bullet. Glass everywhere, spidery, sharp.

It wasn't him. It wasn't him.

"Hmm," Menken says, disbelief curling from her voice like steam. She scribbles more information into her pad. "And what were you doing in the neighborhood in the first place, Ms. Marin, before you decided it would be a good idea to stop here for a visit?"

I dig my nails into my palms. *Don't wince. Don't scream.* "I was visiting my friend"—I have to stop myself from saying Sapphire—"Flynt." The pain arrows through me again, just saying his name. "And I passed by here on the way back to the bus. I live in Lakewood." The pain in my palms pierces through me.

"You shouldn't be walking around here," says Flack sternly.

"This area is dangerous. You're a young woman, alone. You're a walking target." He shoots me a disappointed-father look. "Still in school, I hope?"

"I'm a junior, at George Washington Carver Senior High." The words sound funny leaving my mouth. Like they're not mine. My eyes move to a piece of lint on Flack's right breast pocket. It taunts, pierces every cell in my body—it's off-kilter—demands to be removed, so the jacket will be clean again. Better.

My right hand shoots forward to capture the lint but before I reach it, Flack's got a grip on my hand and I can't. Can't reach it. Frustration swells in my chest, in my hands; I let out a cry, begin to shake. The lint is still there. It needs to be removed.

"Whoa. Whoa," he says softly, slowly releasing his grip of my hand, placing it back by my side. He tries to meet my eye; I focus on the laces on my shoes: six *X*s. They relax me a little. "I know you've just been through a trauma, but I need you to try and stay calm for me, okay?"

"I just—I needed to fix it," I try to explain. "I couldn't—it didn't belong there—I couldn't not fix it."

He gives a strained little chuckle, pulls the bit of lint off his jacket himself and holds it up as though it's a gun he's planning on dropping, as though he's trying to prove it won't hurt me. When he releases it, it spins through the air, falling into darkness. "Let's everybody stay calm, okay? No quick movements."

"And keep your hands where we can see them," Menken says. She cocks her head a bit, narrows her eyes. "Funny that you'd end up all the way down here, by the train tracks. Not the first place *I* would look if I was trying to find the bus."

"I got lost," I repeat. I'm starting to shake again now as I pull at the frayed bits of my own jacket. "I didn't know where I was going."

Just then, the door to Mario's building whooshes open; two EMTs walk slowly down the steps, across the lawn to the ambulance. The stretcher is still between them, heavier this time. Heavy with a body. Covered in a white sheet. The blood rushes from my head straight down to my feet. Everything feels unreal.

Flack puts one arm on my back and begins shepherding me toward one of the police cars. "I'll get a car to drive you home. Your parents are probably worried sick; I'm going to take a wild guess that you missed dinner two hours ago and never called. Trust me," he says gently, "I've got two kids around your age—I'd ground them for a year if I found out they were out here, in this part of the city, alone."

I almost tell him. I almost confess: *No one's looking for me.* "Yeah, okay," I whisper instead, balling my hands into my coat. I look back over my shoulder, to where Menken is standing, tapping her scuff-less black boots in the tall, cold grass. I look up at her; she's gritting her teeth, staring me down.

"Oh, and"—he moves his hands off of my back, reaches into the pocket of his starchy-white uniform shirt and hands me a small white card: *Lieutenant Leif M. Flack: Cleveland PD*—"make sure you get in touch if you think of anything else, anything you might have forgotten. Anything and everything helps. And give me your John Hancock, will you? Name and a phone number should do it." He extends his notepad out to me, shrugging his shoulders up to his ears, zipping his coat up a little higher. "Cold out here tonight."

Penelope Marin, I write. I grit my teeth, but I can't stop from writing it again. *Penelope Marin.* And again. *Penelope Marin.*

"Just once should do it," he says, sounding wary now.

I bite the tip of my tongue three times and manage to write my phone number only once.

More cops have arrived, now, and everything is red and white spinning. I close my eyes. My head hurts.

"Hey, Flack!" That's Menken, calling to him from the porch. "Come over here for a second, will you?"

"Hold tight, okay? I'm going to get an officer to take you home. Just give me a second." Flack jogs over to Menken, and both of them disappear inside. As soon as the door is closed I *tap tap tap tap tap tap*, not waiting for my promised ride—can't wait—and start walking quickly away in the other direction, burying my face into my coat, a new hopelessness jogging around my chest.

The bouncer couldn't have killed Mario, obviously. Mario knew something, and someone was after him to make sure he didn't speak. He had a *reason* to lie to me—he knew something he wasn't supposed to know or he had something he wasn't supposed to have. No way it was coincidence. Mario was wrapped up in this whole thing somehow, just like the bouncer was wrapped up in it, and now they're both out of the picture.

I'm wrapped up in it, too.

I zip my coat all the way to my chin, pull my cell phone out of my pocket: 11:30 P.M.

No missed calls—Mom and Dad haven't even realized that I'm gone.

*   *   *   *

Back in my room, I move my Limoges porcelain boxes up one shelf, arranging them in new groups of three, evenly lined, one inch between each. Then the paperweights—all glass, tiny universes frozen inside, planets the size of fingernails—all need to move to the opposite wall. Six on one shelf, six on the other. Directly above or beneath the others, respectively. Which means the copper daisies need to move from the left of my desk to my right and the bejeweled turtle combs to the left and my state-embroidered pennants (still missing: Delaware, Nevada, Nebraska, North Dakota, South Dakota, West Virginia) three inches down the wall and two to the right.

No. Everything's still off somehow. Tilted. Asymmetrical.

I'm so tired I can hardly stay on my feet. I stretch out—just for a minute—across three silk and pearl peacock cushions on the floor, and the ground starts to take me between all the fistfuls of sixes and nines and twelves, bordering each other, never touching, the wall clocks ticking together in a steady pulse: four thirty A.M. *Just a minute*—I decide, letting my eyes close—*and then I'll figure it out. Then I'll make it right.*

CHAPTER 19

Our old basement in Charles Village, in Baltimore: Oren, Sapphire, Mario, and I are sprawled out on our ancient yellow-and-green tweed pull-out couch, watching TV. Sapphire gets on top of Mario, and they start rocking back and forth. Oren leans over to whisper into my ear, a gibberish language I don't understand, and when he pulls away, we're all lying on the carpet, which is now thick with blood, our heads pressed together in the middle. Mario, Sapphire, and Oren float up to the ceiling; Oren says, *Get up here, Lo.* Oren says, *Hurry, we're going to lift away soon.* But I'm paralyzed, I can't reach him; they float away, they're gone.

I wake up gasping, my phone buzzing violently on my night-stand. I grab it. My voice comes out shaky: "Hello? Flynt?"

There's a pulse in the background, a steady, pumping beat. "Uh. No. It's Howard—the manager at Tens. I'm looking for Juliet?" A tinkling of glasses, a woman's voice shouting from a distance: "So, should I just get up there *with* her, then?"

I shoot up in bed, smooth down my hair—*Tens*—Mustache: "Yes. This is Juliet. Hi. Hello."

"Hi, Juliet. I've passed your application around to some of the other managers. There's an amateur night tonight; if you'd like to come by, we can see about an audition. That work for you?"

"Yes," I answer immediately. I had completely forgotten about the application, and the questions I didn't have time to ask.

"Good. Just make sure you bring a non-see-through thong, high heels, and a dress to dance in, okay?"

"Okay."

"Bye now."

Click.

I sit on my feet on my bed for another minute, staring at the time on my phone. 11:45 A.M. I've missed the first five periods already. No point in going to school now. A mixture of terror and excitement courses through me. I can't wait until tonight. I need answers now.

Now that Mario and the bouncer are out of the question, I realize I *have* to find Bird. Someone must have set up Vinnie to take the fall for the murderer, and someone killed Mario to keep him from speaking.

Mario, Sapphire, the bouncer. They were all linked together somehow—by something, by somebody.

Head pounding, I rock back onto my pillows. I'm missing something, I know it. Something important, a piece of information, hidden away—elusive. A shiver runs up the whole length of my spine, standing me upright: Sapphire's journals.

She vibrates around me, through my ears, through my head: *keep looking.*

June 5: Bird might be the only person I have left, and he's driving me crazy.

June 12: Bird slept over all week. Even when I left him to go to work, I'd come home and he'd be in the same place on the couch or in my bed where I'd left him. I always ask if he wants to talk about it, but he shakes his head and starts kissing me so that I forget all about it. I think he's manic or something. But I like the second part, the kissing part. It works.

I flip ahead farther, heart pounding.

February 11: Fuck. I love him. I fucking love him. Why can't I just pull it out of me? I just want it gone. He wants to torture me. That's why he hasn't called in four days. I have to work tonight and pretend that everything's okay because no one's going to tip a stripper who's sobbing all over their four-hundred-dollar suits and whiskey sours. Bird. You're killing me.

He's all she wrote about. He was responsible for her greatest joys and her most howling awfulnesses—aside from her mother, maybe, who remains only a scattered ghost, here and there, throughout the entries.

Bird. Of course.

I close Sapphire's journal and stare at the dusty red cover, a feather scrawled into the top left corner with a black felt tip pen, working something out.

Bird is the key to everything I don't yet know. He is the missing link.

I throw off my blankets and get out of bed, then lift Sapphire's bustier from the chair by my vanity and slide it over my body, feel it press and hug across every inch. It will protect me—Sapphire will protect me—I'll be ready. For anything. I have to be—tonight, I am putting this all to rest.

I find the same jean skirt and crocheted shrug I'd worn the first time I went to Tens, and throw them on over the bustier. I don't have any high heels besides Mom's, from the eighties, or a non-see-through thong. I don't have *any* thong. I wonder if all normal girls wear thongs, and if I'd been born normal, I'd have one, too.

Before I leave, I touch each of Sapphire's three frogs, lightly, on their heads; feel for the butterfly in my coat pocket, the soft piece of paper nestled into the sole of my left shoe; flip the light switch on and off six times.

Downstairs on the kitchen counter, there is a glass of orange juice and a bagel, untoasted, cut in thirds, the way I've always liked it. A note next to the coffee machine reads: *Had to get to work early. Big meeting. Have a good day at school. —Dad.*

I pour the orange juice down the drain and eat two of the three bagel segments as I walk toward the bus stop. The final third I shred into small pieces and scatter behind me. The air is full of fluttering and dark motion as the birds descend, swooping, crowing triumphantly, on the feast.

*   *   *   *

In the weak early spring thaw of daylight, Tens is duller and squatter and less frightening than I remember it being in the dark. Still, my breath catches in my throat and my heart starts pounding as I push through the door into the cigarette-smog of the club: *Tap tap tap, banana.*

A man is waiting for his jacket in the vestibule, tapping an elegant leather shoe against the ground as he checks the watch on his wrist with mounting frustration. My stomach flips. It's Gordon Jones.

"You got it back," I say abruptly, standing in the darkened doorway.

He glances up, looking completely startled. I feel my whole body blush. He probably doesn't even remember—our time together in the booth, the clumsy girl who tumbled onto his lap.

"What?" he says.

"Your watch," I blurt out, wishing I could drop through the floor. My body is burning. "You got it back."

His jaw drops slightly. He squints at me. *He doesn't remember.* I bite hard into my lip and push past him into the club, ducking behind a pillar to pause and collect myself. I squeeze the butterfly eighteen times in my fist. *I'm so stupid. Why would he have remembered* me? *He sees a million girls all the time. I'm nobody to him.*

Still, I can't get the feeling out of my head—the drunk rush I'd felt as he stared at me like I was beautiful, desirable. Like I was someone he would want to get to know. Disappointment creeps through my chest. *Was none of that real, either?*

The club is mostly empty at this hour. Three middle-aged guys sit at three separate points in the room, each wrapped in his own solitary bubble as he watches the girl onstage—the small, curly haired girl I saw being escorted upstairs just before I tripped into Gordon's booth. She crawls up the pole like a squirrel. Her rib cage is strikingly slender, highlighted by the amber stage lights. She slides weightless, like silk. I can't take my eyes off her.

One of the men—weak, graying hair cropped around the sides of his head, shiny as a peeled onion on top—leans forward, closer to her as he sways his hand in the air for another drink. A waitress swoops in from the hidden place to the left. I recognize her face as she comes closer—Lacey.

I wait until she walks in my direction to step out from behind the pillar and call her name. I don't even know what to say next. She whips around, pulling the empty drink tray sharply into her chest and wrinkling her nose. I've seen Camille do exactly this at school with her books when an undesirable sophomore approaches her from behind.

She squints at me, shows the slim gaps in her teeth through her red lips. "Oh. Hey. Julie, right?"

I don't correct her. "Right."

"You get hired yet?"

"Not sure . . . ," I say. She shifts her tray to the other hand and smacks her gum. "I'm supposed to audition later."

"Oh yeah. Amateur night," she says, gum clicking. "Well, good luck. At least it doesn't cost anything to audition. The managers are a bunch of horny assholes, but they like to think of themselves as businessmen." She glances back at the three men in the audience, fiddling with their ties. "Then again . . . I guess there's not much difference really." She blows a bubble with her gum and turns to walk toward the bar, bumping her hips a little to the techno coming through the speakers. I stop her.

"Do you—do you know a guy named Mario?"

She whips back around. "Mario?" She wrinkles her nose, thinking for a second, shaking her head; "I don't think so. . . . Should I? He a customer here or something?"

"I don't know. I mean, maybe. He's got this . . . creepy bright red hair, and he's pretty short, probably in his forties. Kind of sounds like he's high when he talks . . .?"

"Nope. Definitely don't know that guy."

I tug at my shirt, bite my bottom lip, three times on each side. "Well, do you know if Sapphire ever shopped at the Cleveland Flea, then?"

Another girl walks past then, whacking Lacey on the butt with her tray.

"You're in trouble, Donna!" Lacey calls after her, turning back to me, tapping her foot, sighing broadly. "About the Cleveland *what*? What's this about, girl? You have a lesbian crush on Sapphire or something? I hate to tell you this, but you're a little too late. Besides, she wasn't a switch-hitter." Lacey laughs at her own joke. "Anyway, Sapphire never shopped at no flea market. She didn't *have* to shop. People just gave her things. Flea market . . . ," she mutters, shaking her head as she walks past me and to the bar, drink tray pressed against her hip.

I stand there as Lacey saunters away, still shaking her head, in the hazy bar light. Seconds later, the waitress who'd swatted Lacey's butt with a tray, comes over to me.

"You were asking about Sapphire, right?" She flips her drink tray over and slides it under her arm.

"Yeah," I answer, breathless. "Yes. I was."

"Sorry for listening," Donna says flatly, as though she isn't sorry at all. Then she drops her voice to a whisper and says with sudden viciousness, "You know, she wasn't the sweetheart everybody thought she was. No way she made that much money above board, you feel me? I mean, some nights she was walking out with six or seven hundred, and the rest of us barely made house." Donna curls her lips back as my head spins, trying to guess what it even means to "barely make house." It probably has to do with some kind of fees that the girls have to pay, but I can't help imagining them playing house like little kids, except in sparkly stilettos and fishnet thongs.

Donna goes on. "You ask me, she was definitely hooked up. *Someone* was paying those bills, and I'd bet my ass she was paying him back, if you know what I mean. Nobody gets that many gifts for doing nothing."

"Gifts? What kind of gifts?"

Donna snorts. "You know, love notes and shit. And jewelry, handbags, necklaces . . ."

Love notes—the words perk my ears, my memory: the bird drawing—in her locker, in her bathroom. "She had a boyfriend, didn't she? Bird?" I press.

"If she did, he was loaded. Some of that shit was *costly*. And some was just . . . creepy." She looks back to the audience; Onion Head has his arm raised, another empty drink in his fist. "Shit. That's my cue," she says, peeling sleekly away, tray balanced on her right palm.

I start walking toward the exit. Somehow, I have to track down Bird.

As I reach the vestibule where I'd spotted Gordon earlier,

collecting his coat, a man in a valet uniform, a knit cap pulled low over his eyes, is standing in the way, blocking it off.

"Excuse me," I say, trying to push past him.

"No, Mees," he says in heavily accented Spanish. "Exeet theese way, theese way." He ushers me back inside the club, and points to a dim, glowing sign at the back of the club, marked EMERGENCY EXIT.

"What's wrong with that exit?" I ask, turning over my shoulder to look at it.

But he doesn't understand. He just keeps saying the same thing. "Theese way, theese way, Mees." We reach the back of the club, to the door sandwiched between the VIP booths and one of the prep bars, and he opens it for me, pointing a hairy finger down the long hallway. The hat is shading his eyes almost entirely, but I can see that they're a flat brown color; heavy purple circles beneath. "Exeet theese way, please."

"Okay!" I tell him. "I get it."

Tap tap tap, banana. The door clicks shut behind me as I walk down the creepy hospital-white hallway, my stomach knotting up. It even *smells* like a hospital in here. I run my hand along the wall, lifting it at every crack, staring, too, at the white linoleum tiles, dodging the cracks between tiles. *Ten, eleven, twelve, thirteen, fourt—*

In a flash: one of the plain white doors to my left flies open.

My stomach drops to my toes.

A figure all in black, wearing a distorted, rubbery black mask, lunges for me. Before I can run, I'm pulled into the room behind the door. I have no time to tap. He has broken the rules. *Please*

please please. I struggle to move my arms out of his grip—have to—have to tap. No—*oh God oh God oh God*—can't move—too tight. Pitch black. Hands twist my arms behind my back. They burn. They're burning. I try to pull one more time, to *tap tap tap, banana.* It's scratching through me—the *urge,* the need—it's ripping at my skin, at every single cell. I start to shake, to cry, try to scream, but the man—must be, he's giant like a man, rough like a man—claps his hand over my mouth, hard. His hands taste like tobacco.

Oh God. Oh no. I feel sick, stomach roiling, turning, high-diving into the jelly pool of my legs.

His arm wraps around my throat, pulling tighter, breath against my ear. "Whatever little game you think you're playing," he growls, as I gasp in all the air I can, "you'd better lay off, or you'll end up like your friends. And trust me, if you think what we did to that nosy freak Mario was bad . . ."

I can't breathe. He's going to kill me. I'm going to die here, in this little room, where no one will find me. I see my mother's face when she used to wake me up in the morning with the softest kiss on each of my cheeks. Right one, then left. Afterward I would always ask her to kiss them again: first the right, then left, then right again. Three kisses. Safe. I feel her bend over me, smell her lavender.

He blows his hot cigarette breath into my ear again: "This was your final warning. There won't be another one." He shifts his other arm back to my wrists, tightening his grip, tugging, twisting. Someone's moaning. It must be me. "Now I'm going to give you one chance to run. On the count of three," he says, like a clown at a children's birthday party, leading a game of hide-and-seek in a graveyard. "Ready?" He tugs again, like I'm made of rope.

"One." Swings my arms, madly, ripping them from their sockets.

"Two." Digs his nails in.

"THREE."

The door swings open. I run, pain everywhere, ignoring it, pushing through the exit door at the end of the hallway. Running—through the hazy light of the sun, its peaks and dips piercing through the buildings and the arms of dead trees.

CHAPTER 20

My breath cuts through the cold air in tinny, wheezing gasps. My knees ache. But I can't stop running. I feel eyes on my back, everywhere. Eyes, scraping my skin, wind—squeezing itself around my neck tighter and tighter and tighter.

A car scrapes with a high *whinnnny* around the corner and I leap—skirting behind a bush in another person's lawn. I try to *tap tap tap, banana*, but my feet are lead and my mouth doesn't work. I bite my tongue nine times. Nine times, again. Pulse my shaky right hand around Sapphire's butterfly, six times. Do it all again, and again—it's weird how you can feel like you're sinking and floating at the same time, how not even your body in space makes any sense.

This was your final warning. There won't be another one. The words ring again and again in my mind. My stomach won't stop heaving, like I need to puke. But nothing will come out.

I can't go home. I can never go home again—he'll find me

there too easily. I feel in my pocket for the butterfly and brush past something else: a small rectangular card. *Lieutenant Leif M. Flack: Cleveland PD.* On the back of the card is an address: the police station.

I abruptly change directions, head for the bus that runs downtown. The butterfly grows warm in my fist, and I know it's Sapphire, telling me she's here, telling me, *There's no other way.*

*   *   *   *

"Lieutenant Flack's not in today," a thin, long-nosed, redheaded cop says, glancing briefly up at me over her stack of papers. A gold pin on her lapel reads: GRAHAM.

"But I—I need to talk to him. Now," I choke out. Fire is running down my throat. I hate the cops. I hate looking at their starchy blue uniforms and their smug, tired faces.

I know cops are supposed to help, but ever since that day— when they came, when they told us about Oren, and the world unraveled and fell apart and they just said, *Sorry to be the bearer of bad news*—seeing a cop gives me an itchy feeling. A twitchy, not-right, off-balance feeling.

Bad news is a cancelled picnic. Bad news is a credit card bill. Bad news is not my brother, my only, beautiful brother, gone forever.

"Your name?"

My hands curl into fists beside my legs when I finish tapping, trying my hardest to muffle the word *banana*. But she hears me. I can tell. My face radiates heat.

Graham says: "Uh—sorry. Didn't get that," like she thinks I'm crazy. Totally nuts.

"Penelope Marin," I say, and then two more times, under my breath as I squint: *Pen-el-o-pe-Ma-rin Pen-el-o-pe-Ma-rin.*

"Well, Penelope, Officer Graham and I are on duty right now. If this is pressing, I suggest you tell us," says the man beside her. His nameplate reads: PIKE. He's slightly rumpled-looking, with little button eyes.

"It's about Sapphire, the girl who was"—I tap quickly nine times, right palm against my thigh so that the word will bounce, not stick—"killed. In Neverland."

"That case is closed, Penelope," Graham pipes up. "Did you hear? We've arrested a man in connection—"

"No." I shake my head. "No. No. Not closed."

Pike eyes me wearily, then looks at Graham, and rises from his desk. "Okay." He crosses to the front of the desk with a legal pad, pen, and a Snoopy mug full of dark brown coffee until he's standing, towering, beside me. "Let's go somewhere more private, and you can tell us what you know."

The Cleveland Police Department is square and beige and mauve. It is itself a kind of prison cell: painted-over brick and linoleum floors with touches of metal and glass, and filled with nonstop ringing and beeping and buzzing. Pike leads me, humming something under his breath, through a halogen-bright hallway to a room with a slide-in plastic panel marked: OFFICER MITCHELL PIKE.

Tap tap tap, banana. I whisper it, pulse quickening, praying his humming will be loud enough to cover my *banana.* He says nothing.

Inside is sparsely furnished: a long, solid wooden table, more blank mauve walls, four plastic gray chairs, one wooden picture frame (happy family), Christmas tree, big furry dog. We sit, and Graham follows right behind, a mug of steaming tea in her right hand, a folder in her other. She places it in front of me. "Hope you like Lipton black. It's all we've got."

Pike sits back in his flimsy chair, crossing his legs. Graham leans forward, resting her elbows upon the table. Pike clears his throat. "Try to relax, okay?" He uncrosses his legs, crosses them again, left leg on top this time. "We're here to listen," he continues, taking a sip of his coffee, fiddling with his pen. "Whenever you're ready."

I pull the mug of tea to my lips, taking a cautious sip. Still too hot. They both scoot forward, closer to me, waiting. They brought me tea. They want to listen. The walls blend into each other, the corners smoothing around us in this blank, static-less room, and so I tell them—about being pulled into a room in the back of the club by the bouncer, threatened—the cat, the acid. About Mario, the Westwood Center. All of it.

Graham looks at Pike and back at me, fingers smoothing the surface of the manila folder on the table in front of her. "What I'd like to know is—what were you doing in the strip club in the first place?" She rubs her chin, raises her eyebrows. "Do you work there?"

"No, I don't. I don't work there." I tug my coat more tightly over my amateur night outfit. "I told you, I went to try and find out—"

"Listen. Unless you're under eighteen, it's really none of our business," says Pike, folding a piece of paper from his legal pad four times. It makes me cringe, four. Four means double-bad. "We've seen more of you Neverland kids than you can know—getting caught up in that lifestyle—doing things to support . . . certain habits." He shakes his head, whistles softly. "You're all so young, you think you'll live forever. And then . . ." He snaps his fingers.

I imagine what I must look like—garish makeup smeared across my face.

Graham opens the folder in front of her carefully and produces a handful of pamphlets, sets them on the desk between us, her eyes pitying. I don't look at her; I don't look at the paper folded in fourths. I count scuff marks on the first six tiles of the floor to the left and right of me, to the back and front—eleven; better than eight, but still not good.

"There are *many* treatment programs in the Cleveland area," she tells me in a feathery voice. I feel my body start to go numb, my knees knobbing in toward each other; "NA, AA, not to mention a whole host of smaller groups that we can help connect you to if you'd like. They work. It just takes time."

I grip the front of the desk to stay upright in my chair. "I *don't* do drugs," I burst out, and then, trying to stay calm, "I don't even *live* in Neverland." In the front room, everything buzzes and *riiiiiiiinnnngs* and statics and *nine-one-one, what-is-your-emergency?*s.

"We're not judging you here. Okay? Can I make that extra clear?" says Pike. "But you're the *only* one who can save *your* life, and so you've got to learn to help yourself. You've got to *want* to help yourself, or, and I'm sorry to say this, but"—he picks up his Snoopy mug and blows into it. Twice. *Bad*—"you'll end up just like her."

I scratch my arms. Nine times. *Scratch scratch scratch scratch scratch scratch scratch scratch scratch.* Again. Nine times. Again. It'll only be worse if I don't, I know this, and screaming in the middle of this blank, soulless office full of dumpy plastic furniture would be a whole lot worse than the embarrassment of scratching my arms in front of two don't-give-a-shit cops.

"No," I say, my voice raw. "You're wrong. About Sapphire. She wasn't a drug addict, either. She wasn't like what everyone thinks. This wasn't—this shouldn't have happened to her. It's wrong. It's wrong. *Wrong.*" And then another three times—*wrong wrong wrong*—because six is even better.

"Miss, *please* calm down," Pike says, extending the *please* far too long. "Of course it shouldn't have happened, but, around here . . . these things—"

"No," I sputter. "I—I think your *story* is wrong. I—I know that the vendor at the flea had Sapphire's stuff, and I know he lied to me about where he found it. And now he's dead, too. He's dead because he knew something, and somebody wanted him dead. And now *I'm* in danger."

The phones buzz and whir, reverberating through the hallway, pressing into the room like a hoard of angry bees. Graham puts her chin in her hands and stares at me pointedly. "Look, I have no *doubt* that this guy—Martin?"

"Mario."

"Right, Mario—I have no doubt he was lying. He probably got

the goods illegally. But that by no means indicates that his death and this girl's murder are at all connected. That's not exactly how it works."

Pike fiddles with the Bic ballpoint pen. "Besides, your word alone isn't sufficient. You might have thought about calling us when you first *discovered* these stolen goods." The way he says "discovered" makes it seem like somehow *I'm* a criminal. He moves the pen around in his hands, back and forth. "And as we told you earlier, we've already arrested someone in connection with Sapphire's death."

"The bouncer. I know. But he didn't do it. Or if he did—he was hired by someone. Mario's death proves it. And I think—I think I know who it is."

Graham heaves a deep sigh, meeting Pike's eye and looking back at me. "Okay, Miss Marin. So, what's your theory? Who's responsible for this death?"

"Deaths," I correct her. "Mario's *and* Sapphire's."

Graham twirls a pen in her hand. "Right. Deaths. So," she says, raising her eyebrows, "what is this person's name?"

"I—I don't really—I'm not sure exactly. What his name is. But Sapphire, she called him Bird."

"Bird?" Graham leans back in her chair, crossing her arms, like I've just told a joke that isn't funny.

Pike rubs his face. "Uh-huh. Got it. Should we send some officers into the trees to scout out murder weapons?"

My hands move to the table, tapping—right, left, right—three times. They're making fun of me. They don't believe me. "I know, it sounds ridiculous," I plead. "I know that, but—he's after me,

now, too, because he *knows.* He knows I'm on to him or something, and so he's been threatening me. Stalking me. I swear.
He—he wants to kill me."

"I think you're being slightly paranoid." Graham exchanges a
look with Pike. I see her hands move again to the pamphlets, inch
them slightly forward. "Have you ever experienced delusions?
Hallucinations of any kind?" She pauses, asks in the gentle sing-
song voice of principals and priests. "Have you ever heard any
voices?"

"No—no!" The words push forth, my fists pound the table.
"I'm *not* paranoid. I need your help. You—you have to help me."

"Well, Miss Marin," Graham says, curtly, "we've been trying
to help you this whole time, but if you don't want our help, then I
think this meeting is over."

Pike takes a sip of coffee, swishes it around his mouth, clicking
the edge of his legal pad against the table and lounging backward
in his chair with the kind of calculated gusto that says: *We're done
here. You can go.*

I get up from the table, dig my nails into my thighs, a desperate, lonely feeling sinking through me. The tea, the expressions
of concern: it's all an act. I feel Sapphire's butterfly like a leaden
weight within my pocket. Failed. I've failed her.

"Did she—" I pause; desperate; a shot in the dark. "Did she have
any lipstick in her pockets when they found her? Blue lipstick?"

Graham looks up sharply. "Excuse me?"

"Blue lipstick," I repeat. "I know she had blue lipstick. She
wore it all the time. She would have had to have it on her. I know
it. I know her."

Graham looks at Pike, leaning forward again in his chair, and back at me. She blinks slowly, eyebrows knitted together. "You *knew* her?"

My breath is short and fast. Wrong. Again. Idiots. "No," I respond, quickly, my throat tight and sharp. "I didn't *know* her, I just . . ."

Pike's fake smile is now mingled with a look of disappointment. Graham's frown has deepened. It's official: they think I'm completely and utterly insane, or a drug addict, or both. One of the lost children of Neverland.

"Okay, Miss Marin. I think we've heard all we need to hear. You've wasted enough of our time around here." She stands from her chair, tenting both hands on the large manila envelope full of pamphlets. "I've got to inform you that if we catch you messing around in this business any more, you *will* be charged with obstruction."

Pike ushers me to the door and through the stark, cold hallway, the buzzing and ringing and thick gurgle of voices, back to the front of the station, straight to the front doors. "We better not see you here again," he says. "Be good and stay off the streets, okay?"

I don't answer—just turn away; *tap tap tap, banana* as I push out the door. I try not to scream. I try not to pound my fist into the glass until it breaks, shatters in flying shards toward them. I stand there on the front steps for another minute—too angry to move, even.

I stare up into the sky, into the light cutting through the trees. It's the same with Mario as with Sapphire: they'll put his case at the bottom of a ten-foot stack. *Sorry to be the bearer of bad news.*

I feel a pulse, a growing storm shooting through my body as I stand there on the cold concrete steps and stare through the tinted glass.

If the cops won't take care of this, then I'll have to. Somehow.

CHAPTER 21

My crash pad—the basement of this barbershop—corner of Grover and Miles . . . Flynt's mumbled words from yesterday swim through my head as I wander the streets of Neverland, certain I'll never find the place, never make it back out of Neverland alive. It has started to pour and I'm soaked. My clothes hang on me like heavy skin, my hair is streaming, dripping into my eyes.

And then, I round a corner onto Grover Street, and there it is. An old sign says T. MERONI'S: BARBER.

I pound on the door three times. Fifteen seconds later—not the worst number but also not the best—Flynt opens it, eyes wide, mouth falling open when he sees me. "Lo—holy crap."

I can't speak. I tug on my hair six times.

"Well, get in here," he says, reaching for my hand and pulling it gently; his skin is warm, soft; his big hands, his long fingers, his right palm streaked with yellow paint. I *tap tap tap*, hiccuping through my *banana* and step inside into a wide, cold room full of mirrors and old swivel chairs, a checkered tile floor, counters lined with a few cloudy Barbicide jars, an old radiator in the corner. I let him lead me downstairs. His hands are so warm.

A thin orange cat meows as we hit the landing, rubs his head against my legs, purring. "Moby," Flynt says, clicking his tongue, motioning to the cat. He opens a door at the other end of the raw, drafty basement—there's a big unplugged refrigerator inside, insulation and piping peeking out of the half-stuccoed walls. "My wardrobe," he explains, opening it and pulling a T-shirt from within a pile of clothes. He walks back to me, his feet padding softly on the tapestry of carpet samples spread over the concrete floor, and hands me the shirt. "You're soaked," he says. "Put this on."

He turns away and goes to the bally mustard-colored couch, clearing space among the tubes of paint and discarded clothing. Paintings line every wall—nudes—women, some with animal bodies, made of tree branches, leaves, flower petals, gesso, tar.

I rip off my cold, wet sweater and the bustier beneath it, and put the T-shirt over my head. It's big and soft and smells like him—like pine and grass and snow and cloves. There are three tiny holes on the right sleeve—good. A good sign.

"Lo," Flynt says, softly. "Talk to me. What happened?"

My feet take me to the couch, and Moby leaps up into my lap and I pet him and start to talk. About Mario. About Tens, and being pulled into the pitch-black room and nearly strangled.

Flynt leans forward on the couch, staring at me, eyes burning. "Wait," he says, voice tight. "Did you see who it was? Could you describe him, I mean?"

I wrap my arms around my knees, tenting his big, soft T-shirt over them. "No. It was dark." I gulp, stare at the crease in my arm. "But whoever he is, I think he's working for someone. Sapphire— she wrote about her ex-boyfriend, Bird. I think—I think maybe he got violent with her." Flynt opens his mouth, but I rush on. "I can't find him. I don't know anything about him. No one knows anything about him. But I *know* he's involved somehow. I can *feel* it."

"Jesus," he says, standing from the couch and making a full circle around it, landing back in front of me, sitting down again. He rubs his hands up and down his thighs. "Jesus, Lo. This is serious." His eyebrows are knit, his face is gray. "You know that, right? You know how serious this is?"

"I *know* it's serious," I tell him, meeting his eye and then retreating, hugging my knees again, so tight. "That's why I went to the police."

"You did?" Flynt goes very still. "What did you tell them?"

"All of it. I told them everything, from the beginning." Anger floods my limbs thinking about it; my nails dig into my knees, I'm shaking with it. My head, my hands. "They thought I was a drug addict. They gave me *pamphlets*. They didn't care. They've never cared."

"What do you mean *never*?"

I run my fingers across the white circle on Moby's forehead: nine, nine, six; nine, nine, six; nine, nine, six. My mouth feels like cement.

"You can tell me, Lo." Flynt sits back down on the couch, reaches out and touches my right knee, then my left. Perfect. Even. "Please tell me."

I look for a sign, for some kind of change to indicate that it's right to tell him. But there's nothing. A great, wide hollowness; a white silence. Everything blank, open, waiting.

"My brother," I manage to croak out. "Oren." His name feels like a thousand paper cuts all over my body. Nine, nine, six—circles around Moby's white spot with my fingers. "He died last year."

I look up at Flynt quickly, then back down. "His senior year of high school. He—he got into drugs. Heavy stuff. Maybe he was into it before—I don't know. He started just leaving, for weeks. When Mom and Dad tried to question him, he'd get angry. Start screaming. And . . . he wouldn't come back for a long time, and every time he looked skinnier and was just mean. He wasn't . . . he wasn't *him* anymore, you know?"

I take a deep breath. It hurts to talk. But it hurts more not to—the words are pushing on the back of my throat, struggling to get out. "He dropped out, you know? My parents put him in rehab, but it didn't work—he left as soon as he turned eighteen." I try to breathe. "Then he would sneak into the house and steal Mom's jewelry to sell it, but once she figured it out she put it all in the safe and he stopped . . . he stopped. He stopped coming by at all." My face is wet and I'm shaking; I've started crying without knowing it.

Moby leaps from my lap and onto Flynt's—I must be pressing his white spot too hard. I wipe my face and nose. "Six months later the police showed up at our door"—breathe breathe breathe—"they'd found him. In an abandoned apartment building. Mill Street. He'd been dead for a week. A week." My vision is completely blurred now, but I can't stop, even though I'm speaking in a whisper, barely choking out the words. "A neighbor called to complain about the smell. They had to identify him from—from his dental records." I pulse my hands into new tight, round fists, a cry peeling from my throat.

For a moment, there's just the sound of my huffing and sniffing. Flynt is silent. He's waiting. "And—it's my fault. It's my *fault*. I could have done something to help, but I didn't. I did *nothing*."

I'm shaking, heaving. Flynt slides closer to me on the couch, bends his head down to speak to me, softly, easing out his words. "Lo—listen to me—there was *nothing* you could have done. You're not responsible."

I look up at him, his face a watercolor blur. The hollowness gathers me up and moves me from the couch, like a zombie, to my shoes. With trembling fingers, I pull the crumbling piece of paper that I never leave home without from the left heel and hand it to him. He unfolds it, confused.

It had words on it once, in ink, but they're indecipherable now. I've looked at it too much, held it too much, let it slide beneath my heel for too long, thought about it so hard I've burned holes into it with my brain.

"I—I don't know what this is," Flynt says.

"It's from Oren," I say, gasping in tight fistfuls of air. "He wrote me nineteen days before he died. He needed money. He wanted help. And I ignored it." Flynt tries to say something, but I shake my head and push on. He needs to know the truth. "I told him not to contact me. Not until he was sober. I could have done something. I could have saved him. But instead I—I let him die. I killed him."

There it is: my secret—my darkest secret. My body feels like it's breaking. I start pulling at my hair. Pulling pulling pulling. But the feeling won't go away, the feeling of imbalance. Everything is dissolving.

Flynt puts his arms around me. His touch feels like fire, but I don't have the energy to shake him off. "Lo," he says, "it's okay. It's going to be okay."

"No," I croak out, and now I'm sobbing. My lungs are full of knives—my ribs, too, and my throat. "It's not okay. It will *never* be okay."

Flynt grabs me tightly between his arms, presses me into him, and I'm shivering and crying and shaking and everything is dark, like I'm being pressed between the walls of a collapsing tunnel. I let him gather me into his warm chest. His chin touches the crown of my head, and he's whispering, "Shh, shh, shh," and I'm making his shirt wet with my tears, but he doesn't seem to mind. He leans gently backward, pulling me down onto his chest.

His long warm fingers brush the hair out of my face as I deep breathe into his chest for what feels like hours. At first I am burrowing into the silk-soft of his flannel, his grass and clove and snow and pine smells rising around me as though I am in the middle of a wide, dense field. And then I am in a field—and then I am nowhere—and then I am drifting, drifting somewhere new.

Sapphire's sitting on my bed with the dead cat on her lap. She keeps petting it, and saying, "Four thirty-seven," over and over.

She reaches into the air and opens her palm: she's holding a tube of lipstick. She opens it and rubs some onto my lips. The cat's getting blood all over my bed, and when the blood drops from its neck and onto the carpet it becomes a butterfly in midair—*the* butterfly—glittering, wings folded back, head bowed; I swoop down to try to catch one before it flutters away, out of reach, but when I look back up, I'm with Oren, and we're in our basement in Gary, Indiana.

We're digging through our costume chest next to the big sliding-glass door, looking for the best wizard clothes we can find; we're about to put on a Thanksgiving play for the whole family. It's starting to snow outside and we're off from school tomorrow. Oren smiles—he's lost two teeth up top and one on the bottom—and pulls out a long purple dress covered in tiny white stars that used to be Mom's. "I found yours, Lo! The *best* Ruby Rainbow Wizard costume *ever*!" He rushes over to me and he smells like soap and dirt and chocolate—like Oren—and I raise my arms and he slides it over my footie pajamas and hugs me. "I knew it. You look like a *real* wizard now, Lo." And then he hugs me tighter and the snow falls and it smells like turkey and fireplace and the adults are making clicking sounds with their heels on the floor and I hear Mom laughing really loudly. Everything is warm.

CHAPTER 22

I wake up some time later with an eerie feeling—I'm being watched. I lift my eyelids open a fraction.

Flynt has drawn a chair up next to the couch and is looking at me, intensely, as he moves a thin piece of charcoal back and forth over a piece of paper. Even though I'm embarrassed that he was watching me while I slept, no one else in the world has ever looked at me like he's looking at me right now—like he could stare at me forever and never get bored, like I'm the most interesting thing he's ever seen. The top of his flannel is unbuttoned and hangs, like his dreads, loose over his shoulders. I lift my arm to my head, scratching three times at my left ear.

"Lo—don't move," he says, seriously, his eyes like honey in the basement light—warm and amber and shining. "I'm still working."

"I had an itch."

"Let me know next time, and I'll scratch it for you. Before the terrible itching incident ruined everything, I was about to start on the dark shadow of your elbow crease. Now I'll have to re-create that perfect, dark, little cityscape from memory." He grins. "I'll be done soon, I promise."

I sink an inch deeper into Flynt's lumpy couch and watch him draw. Our eyes meet, and I shiver a little and push my bangs back and forth over my forehead, three times, out of habit.

"Hey!" he says.

"Sorry—sorry—it won't happen again, really!"

He lifts his charcoal and blows on the piece of paper, black dust flying onto the legs of his patched jeans. His eyes move across my face, my forehead; he keeps drawing. My horrible bangs. I want to comb them out, but I've already promised that I won't. My throat feels raw when I swallow. I remember crying, telling him everything, but it feels faraway, like I dreamed that, too.

"So, how'd you get that scar over your eye?" Flynt asks, resting his charcoaled hands for a second on his knees, eyeing it.

"I fell into a creek, by our old house in Minnesota"—I pause for a second, remembering Oren's arms, wrapping around me, pulling me up, putting his warm ear to my chest, testing my heartbeat—"but my brother saved me." Flynt's eyes move down the left side of my face, his hand moving with them, bent to the side and shading in something furiously. "Can I ask *you* something now?"

"'Course you can, Lope."

"What's your real name?"

I watch the breath catch for a second in his chest. Moby wakes and leaps onto the couch in that instant, stretching his paws languidly over my midriff. Flynt reaches his arm out and shoos him away. "He's such a diva." Flynt laughs "Thinks he's handsome enough to be in *every* drawing."

I meet his eyes, and he lowers them to his sketchpad.

"You can tell me. I won't tell anyone. Really," I say. I want to tap, but I can't so I bite my lip instead, six times.

"Can't. I'm sorry. Sworn to secrecy." He winks, trying to make a joke out of it.

"Why not? You can say it once and you'll never have to say it again. I mean, it can't be *that* bad—we had a neighbor in Detroit named Richard Krotchtangel. *Dick* Krotchtangel. Really. I'm not making that up."

He laughs, but it's halfhearted. "It's not like that. It's not a bad name, it's just that . . . it's all tied up in my old life, and I don't like thinking about my old life anymore. Which is why I'm Flynt now." His face darkens for a moment. "People can only kick you so many times before you just have to walk away, you know?"

My dream comes screaming back to me—Sapphire—*four thirty-seven*.

"What kind of people?" I ask, quietly.

"People," he says abruptly, his face hard and still. Then he looks down at his sketch and continues drawing. "My stepfather, for example."

I wait in the silence, afraid even to breathe, for him to say more.

He focuses on the sketch in his lap; then goes on. "I think that's why I like drawing so much." He starts moving the charcoal over the page again so quickly, it's like it's dancing. "You get to see a side of people . . . you get to see past the bullshit. You get to see beyond that. Being a kid doesn't last, right? That innocence doesn't last. But it never totally goes away, either—we all keep it, stored up. In our eyes, or something. You know?"

He pauses and looks right at me: right into my eyes, like he wants to jump inside of them. He puts his sketchpad down on the floor and his charcoal next to it. He comes to me on the couch. I watch as he reaches his fingers to my face and brushes my bangs away with his hand, as he brushes them away, three times, running his finger over the scar above my eye.

Something catches in my throat as he touches my scar so tenderly, like he's never touched another person's skin before—and I look up at him and I'm shivering because I've never been touched by a boy like this before and I don't know what to do, or think, and I can't remember how to breathe.

And then, slowly, he leans forward and I lean forward and our lips are touching—gently at first, hesitantly—before I press into him and his hands meet my neck, my back, gliding across me, over me, around me and we're kissing hungrily, greedily. My first kiss.

And, then, I *do* know what to do, and I've never wanted anything so badly before—all of it, every single part—Flynt's warm lips against my lips in the syrupy basement light, Flynt's skin against my skin and the lumps of the couch, pressing like small fists into my back, Flynt's big hands staving off the chill pressing through thin walls, the tips of his fingers, grazing over every part of me beneath the gaze of his hundred painted nudes. I feel possessed by my wanting.

We keep kissing as he wraps his hands around my waist and

flips me beneath him; dimples like crescent moons; teeth like rows of stars. I pull back, gasping slightly as he tugs me into him again. My skin burns as he inches his fingers under the borrowed shirt, toward my belly button, tracing a circle around it—a perfect circle—softly pressing into my belly, moving his lips to my face, kissing it all over, emitting halos of soft, warm air. And then I want this so badly it fills my whole body, pure heat rising up from the soles of my feet.

I let myself kiss him, too; moving my mouth to his, our lips press together, soft and slow, his tongue tracing an arch across my lower lip. I can't stop being amazed by it all, how it feels to kiss another person, how it feels to kiss Flynt.

I move into his hands; they move farther up my belly, to my rib cage, to my chest, finally lifting the shirt over my head as I shiver between his hands. My heart leaps and trips between his palms. For a second I worry that he'll notice my misshapen boobs beneath my bra, and I pull away a fraction.

But he doesn't seem to notice my hesitation, my asymmetries and flaws. He's staring into my eyes. He takes my hands, moves them under his own shirt. I feel the long muscles of his stomach, his chest, his own heart, skipping wildly. His mouth moves to my ear, biting it very gently. It tickles. The basement light settles on our shoulders; Moby meows suddenly in the corner, a loud yowl, and we both laugh. It feels good to laugh.

I move my fingers farther into his shirt, pulling it slowly, cautiously off him as he lifts me, a firm, quick pull, closer to him. Our bodies press into each other, our heartbeats touch. He kisses my forehead; my scar; my nose, lips, chin, neck—nuzzling in, scruffy, his tongue running over my teeth, his breath against my skin—my belly; my chest; my thick, dark, now-wild hair.

"God, Lo," he mutters softly. He runs his hands up and down my legs.

I want to kiss him everywhere and so I do: his face, all over, every single inch of his lips and his neck, his collarbones and the little divot in between them. His mouth tastes earthy, warm, like grass and sunlight and salt. His skin smells like the T-shirt he gave me to wear; pine and cloves and something new I can't identify—something that I could smell forever, though. Raw and wood and sweet.

I start to move my finger over his smooth chest, tracing shapes, figures, patterns in threes and sixes and nines. Perfect circles. As I trace, my heart begins to slow, and I let my nose fall to his warm sternum. I draw three straight, even lines down to his navel—when I see something that makes my heart stop.

I shoot upright, push away from him.

"What's wrong?" Flynt says. His voice is raw.

There's a tattoo above the waistband of his torn moose-patterned boxers.

"Lo?" Red has crept into his cheeks, his eyes wide.

A tattoo of a bright blue bird.

Everything slows down, gets loud and wobbly, begins to fall apart. "It's you." I whisper, unable to pull my eyes away, so stunned I can hardly breathe.

Bird.

"What?" Flynt says, squatting on the couch, stabilizing himself with his palms on the lumpy threadbare cushion between us, shaking his head furiously. "What are you . . .? Lo—come back here. Talk to me." He tries to grab me and pull me to him, but my ears are full of fire and my legs are full of fire and the number *four thirty-seven* is pushing itself through my head over and over again and then just *four* and four is a horrible number and it means *go. Get out. Now.* Sapphire: calling to me from a different universe: warning me.

I leap away from him, arms outstretched toward me on the couch—*liar liar LIAR*—the words beat through me, hard, sharp—grab my still-wet clothes from where I left them; throw them over my body; tripping. Trying to keep the sob out of my chest.

Four four four: up the stairs, the number looming and heavy. I hear him, calling my name as I run: "Lo! *Lo!* Please come back here."

Tap tap tap, banana. Body burning, heaving as I push out into the street, still dewy in the predawn gray.

Birds are chirping, signaling the dawn.

Flynt is Bird.

CHAPTER 23

One week later. Seven days. A rough, terrible number. A number that seethes and moans. I have hardly left my bed. I have missed five days of school. Now I'm not sure how I'll ever go back. Dad is away on business. I told Mom I was sick. This is the truth. I *am* sick. And hungry.

In the grocery store: I flick my eyes back and forth down aisle nine. Household items. Rows of toilet paper and paper towels and cleaning products and scouring pads in rows. Colors that don't go together.

A bin in front of me full of pink and yellow sponges: A small neon sign: 50% OFF!!! The tingle starts in my feet and shoots through me like a current, all at once. My eyes swim in my skull. An old lady across the aisle puts a twenty-four pack of Fluffy Dream brand toilet paper into her cart. The voice in my brain clicks on: *NOW*.

I reach into the sale bin. Pull out three sponges. Stuff them into my pockets—the pressure in my chest breaking up—before I pay for my other groceries. Dad's the designated grocery buyer, but he's been on a business trip to San Francisco. With him gone, there's nothing left in the house.

Loaf of multigrain bread. Off-brand apple juice. Jar of Nelly's Nutty creamy peanut butter. Twizzlers. That should last me for the next couple of weeks.

It has been a week since I saw the tattoo. Since I figured out Flynt was Bird. Every time I've tried to leave my room this week, I've been assaulted by the realization that everything is in the wrong place and then I'm forced to rearrange, and, eventually, the hours whittle themselves away to nothing, to darkness.

Today: only the miniature wooden rocking chairs, only a switch, from the southwest corner of my room to the northeast—not an incredibly time-consuming process. And then the pangs in my stomach wouldn't quit, and I realized that if I ever wanted to eat again, I had no other choice. I'd have to go outside and buy myself groceries.

Outside, on the way back home, the Bigtooth Aspen and the Buckeye and Northern Catalpa are all beginning to flower and re-leaf. The pavement has more cracks in it than I remember. I have to be careful about when I look up into the trees—if I miss one, I have to go all the way back to the grocery store, and I think if I don't eat something soon I'll collapse.

Cracks in the pavement: *twenty-six, twenty-seven, twenty-eight.* I kick at twigs on the street, push them off of the sidewalk so that everything's clear. *Twenty-nine, thirty, thirty-one.* Can't walk with twigs. Twigs at my feet. Twigs in my eyes. Twigs in my hair. Filling up all the space in the universe. Why is everything suddenly so crowded?

This is why it's not a good idea to go outside. A person could suffocate outside.

Flynt's a liar. I knew it. From the beginning I knew it, but I pushed it away. Liar liar liar. I can't believe I fell for him, for his creepy sketching and his stupid bear-eared hat and his patchy-quirky-art-boy act.

I *tap tap tap, banana* until my wrists and tongue are sore as I walk to the 48 bus on Eutaw Street.

The bus shows up, glinting with sunlight. *Tap tap tap, banana* on each side of my body. The bus driver shoots me a disgusted look.

"Just counting my change," I announce to her too loudly. "Making sure I have enough."

She doesn't say anything, just rolls her eyes. "Sit down so we can get moving."

The bus is crowded. The lady I have to sit next to is old and smells like cabbage. She scoots over in her seat an inch or two. "No school today?" she asks as I sit down. She's got one of those duck-headed umbrellas poking out of her big woven purse even though the sky is cotton-candy blue and cloudless. Her hands rest on top of each other in her lap like balls of pizza dough.

"I don't know," I answer, staring at her chubby, wrinkly, little hands.

How could I be so stupid? He wouldn't even tell me his real name. I stare through the window past cabbage-breath lady, watch the trees skating by. Imagine Oren monkeying through each one to the next, a long-armed chain of him.

Flash: the man's fist in my mouth. My throat constricting around it, trying to scream in that very dark room, the *urge* pulsing through me like fire—like acid.

The old woman shifts beside me, turning back to me for a second. She continues to frown, pity radiating from her eyes. I turn my face sharply away.

Flash: Flynt's warm skin, fingers brushing against my collarbones, over my lips. His lips. The weight of his body over mine. Our fingers intertwined. The rush in my belly. Our legs braided together on the couch.

I never meant anything to him. Nothing at all.

Flash: the last time I saw Oren. So skinny—he was already so skinny, his eyes ringed with purplish disks, his hands shaking. He tried to hide them in his pockets. *Catch you on the flip side, Lope.* Last words I ever heard him say. *Flip side.* Did he know already? Did he know he was leaving me forever?

Catch you on the flip side. Sorry to be the bearer of bad news.
Poof.

I feel the *urge* shake through me again—the duck umbrella. It noses lazily out of the old woman's purse, seeming to glimmer and shine in that familiar, needy way. Her eyes are fixed again on the window. I reach my fingers down, brush the smooth wooden head, the hard black eye—*now*—I have no choice.

I grab it, push it under my coat. Her head spins around, hands flying immediately to her purse.

"What on earth . . . ?" Her lips curve into a horrified little O as she tries to form words. "That's my *umbrella*. What are you . . . ?"

Her hand moves to her chest, flutters against the space above her heart.

I jump out of my seat. Tug hard on the chord, two stops from where I need to get off—*bad*. She rises next to me, putting her hand out as if to pull me back, but she's slow, arthritic. Shame is beating through my chest, hot and poisonous. I weave my way quickly to the front of the bus as it shudders to a stop, doors swinging open.

Tap tap tap, banana. And I'm out on the street as the bus closes its doors. The old woman's face is huge in the window, amplified—shaking her head, lips pruned together. I hug her umbrella to my rib cage, watch the sun glare of the bus windows disappear down Gresham Street as the sick feelings swirl around in my belly.

Back home I shove a piece of peanut-buttered bread in my mouth, refrigerate the perishables, lining them up by size and shape.

As soon as I return to the attic, I realize I never should have left. My room looks stricken, sick. Each of the antique brass wall clocks need to be moved. Next: the short wire trees currently residing beside the floor lamp by the window must be moved beneath the printer's drawer full of thimbles, and then the thimbles must be placed in three even rows on the desk in front of the teal Olivetti typewriter, but not too close to the partially rusted maroon Smith Corona.

As I'm placing the first thimble at the foot of the Olivetti, the doorbell rings. I drop the thimble, and it skitters beneath my desk, between several stacks of newspaper.

It's the old lady—she's traced me. *Diiiing-donnnnng.*

I hear my mother's muffled voice, wailing to me from within her room: "Looo."

When I get downstairs, I see it's not the old lady.

It's Jeremy. He waves from behind the glass panels of the front door, a folder dangling from one gloved hand. I open the door, *tap tap tap, banana* quickly, dead quietly, stepping halfway outside to meet him.

"I brought you your homework," he says. He hands me the folder. His nose and cheeks are tinged red, like his hair. The folder hangs there between us—I don't want it. I don't want to think about school right now. After a few seconds, he drops it back by his side. "So, what's going on? Are you dying of the flu?" He cocks his head and shrugs. "You don't *look* sick."

I reach out and grab the folder from him. "Thanks," I mumble. I start to turn and head back into the house, but he keeps talking.

"There's this super confusing lit stuff we have to read for English; you might need me to explain it to you," he says, taking a small step into the hallway. "I had to ask Manning about it like eight times." *Eight.* I cringe. Tap six times on each side to reverse it, ears burning, looking away from him, willing him to leave.

"Also," he continues, softly, "I wanted to come by and make sure you were okay and everything since you didn't show, you know, for our study date this week. You rain-checked on the rain check. I mean, it's totally fine," he rushes to say, when I open my mouth, "but I'm glad you're not dead, because I still have a bunch of snacks. So, whenever you get better . . ." He pauses, briefly. "I guess we'll have to make a new date." He grins, his blue eyes get even bluer. "You know, so they don't go to waste or anything. . . ."

"Lo." Mom's voice interrupts from the top of the stairs. I turn; she's standing there, watching from the landing, hands planted on her jutting hips, still wearing the velour sweats she had on last week. "What's going on down there? Who's that?" She coughs, and it makes her whole body shake.

"Someone from school, Mom," I answer. "Don't worry about it."

She comes down a couple of stairs, anyway, narrows her hazy eyes at Jeremy, who is still half in and half out of the house, shivering in the open door.

"Penelope." She inhales sharply. "Don't make your friend stand outside like that. It's cold."

I turn away from her and back to Jeremy, anger burning through my chest. I *tap tap tap, banana* under my breath, disguising the *banana* as a kind of grumbly cough before I invite Jeremy in and close the door behind him, knocking my teeth into each other—nine, nine, six—until I feel a dull pain in my gums. Mom continues to stand there, eyeing us.

Jeremy looks to my mother at the top of the stairs. "Hi, Mrs. Marin. I'm Jeremy, Lo's, um, study partner." He lifts the folder in his hands toward her. "I brought her work over."

"Hmmm." Her eyes are thin slits. "Come up here," Mom says to me, mouth twitching. I walk up the stairs, remembering the on-sale sponges in my coat pocket, the duck umbrella lying on my bedroom floor; they haven't been placed yet. That's why everything is going wrong, spinning out of control. I'm suddenly so overwhelmed that I hardly notice Jeremy has followed behind me up the stairs, still clutching the folder of homework in his hands.

I don't want him to see Mom, her eternally coffee-stained, sick smelling pajamas; her stringy, greasy, wild hair. I don't want him to know how we've all let ourselves die here, how we've been buried.

"Mom—Jeremy. Jeremy—Mom." I say it again, twice, beneath my breath: *Mom-Jeremy-Jeremy-Mom; Mom-Jeremy-Jeremy-Mom*, horrified that he might hear but pleased by its symmetry.

"Does your friend know about all your little habits, Lo?" Mom asks. I look away, burning all over, feel a lump growing in my throat. "Well, it's just who you are, honey, and I don't see how anyone could miss them, right?" She laughs a little; she somehow thinks she's being funny.

I shoot a fast glance at Jeremy. His face is burning right alongside mine.

She smiles. "So, *this* is who you've been sneaking around with, Lo?" Her voice is playful, gossipy.

My head is burning so hot, I think I might burst into flame. "No, Mom," I say—when, suddenly, her eyebrows slip back downward, curving inward like a collapsed drawbridge, and I know she's crossed over, back into nowhere land.

"Well, you didn't have to lie about it. That's the worst part, Lo. All the lying." She forces a streak of wild hair behind her ear and turns abruptly, floating back into her room. The TV turns back on: *"One hundred percent of mothers agree, Dew-Gone is better than other mildew removers!"*

I click my tongue against the roof of my mouth, nine times, nine times, six times. "I'm sorry about that," I say, forcing my hands to remain still. "Thanks for the homework. That was really nice of you, Jeremy. I didn't think anyone ever noticed when I missed school. . . ."

Looking up briefly, I examine his face: he doesn't look freaked out by Mom at all. Instead, he looks serious, determined, kind; I imagine this is how he looks when he's running, as he wins, like, every meet. I wonder how often Keri watches him. I wonder if he's ever noticed her in the crowd as the track stretches before him, long and dark and endless. "Lo," he says, huskily, interrupting my thought. "I . . . always notice when you miss school. You were gone for almost a month last year. I was worried you weren't ever coming back." His big blue Vans are pigeon-toed into each other, the right knocking softly into the left. He clears his throat. "And, to be honest, the homework stuff was just an excuse, to come see you." He rocks forward in his Vans, catching my eyes. His are wide, crystal blue. "I think you already know this, but, I . . . I don't know anyone else like you."

"Jeremy—" I step back. I tug at a loose thread on my left sleeve, search for one on the right. "I think you're great. I think you're really, really nice."

"I think *you're* really great, I've thought that since—"

I cut him off. "But, Jeremy—you're cool. And I'm, I'm. . . . not right. For you."

I find a new thread on the left, pull it free. Search for another on the right. And one more, left and right, to make it three on each side. Better. Jeremy frowns, puts his hands in the pockets of his gray skinny jeans and rocks back on his heels.

"I think . . . you should try and date someone more . . ." I clear my throat. "Someone like Keri Ram. That type. Someone who's good at things and pretty and, you know, *normal*."

He looks at me, totally confused. "Lo—but I like *y*—"

I interrupt him again. "Someone more your *speed*. Someone who's excited about things. Someone who wears nice clothes and—and has a professional haircut." The more *I* think about it—the two of them, side by side, his red hair and her auburn; their straight, little ski-slope button noses; his calm alongside her cool—the better I feel, the more I know it just makes *sense*. Like seeing the Olivetti beside the Smith Corona. They match. They belong together.

"A professional haircut?" Jeremy shakes his head. "Look, I don't even know Keri Ram—"

"I'm not saying it has to be her. It could be anyone. Anyone besides . . . me." My fingers fly to my thigh, start tapping.

"Does this mean . ." Jeremy inhales. "Is that a no to prom, then?" There's a genuine ache in his voice.

My stomach sinks.

"I—I need to go to the bathroom. Stay here, okay?" I need to wash my hands. I need to be alone.

Jeremy runs a hand through his hair, so it sticks up in spikes. "Yeah. Yeah, sure. Okay."

I wash my face, three times. The gurgle of the sink, the water pounding against the pewter basin, comforts me. Wash my hands nine times. Nine seconds per wash. Flip my bangs back and forth across my forehead.

When I open the door, calm enough to emerge again, Jeremy's not in the hallway. I glance to Mom's door—still shut, her mutterings a muffled soundtrack from within. An awful feeling starts knotting at my stomach, and I whip my head around to the other side of the hall. To Oren's room. The door is wide open.

My whole body goes cold.

My feet draw me forward. The rest of my body is stone. Jeremy turns to me from inside, holding a record in his hands. Oren's record. I stand shaking at the threshold—can't go in—not enough *tap tap tap, banana*s in the world. Not allowed in. Oren hasn't said I could come in, and never will again.

Jeremy's voice rings, tinny, from within. "Rust Never Sleeps! *So* awesome. Is this your brother's room? Man. I didn't even know you *had* a brother."

Jeremy's hands. All over his things. All over my brother's things.

My organs drop straight to my feet. My head is dark. My jaw rocks open.

I'm frozen, shaking. "Get out," I manage to whisper.

"What?" Jeremy says, eyes crinkling, looking suddenly uncertain. He puts the record back—stacks it haphazardly in the wrong place. *Oren will freak.* "What—what's wrong?"

"*Leave.*" I might fall. I might melt. I might spontaneously combust. "Please."

"What's—what's wrong?" He steps cautiously toward me. "Was I not supposed to be in here or something? Your brother's weird about that stuff?"

No. No. No. He doesn't *get* it.

"Get out." Now my voice is strangled, a moan. "You have to get out." I can't speak; my body shakes; I'm swallowing back tears so hard my throat starts to clench and unclench. I curl against the wall, trying to steady myself, trying to keep down the scream inside my body.

"Oh God. Look, I'm sorry. I—I had no idea. . . . I'm leaving, okay?" He pushes past me into the hall. He hesitates next to me, but I can't look at him, can't even feel him next to me.

"Sorry," he whispers again. Then, he pounds down the stairs, and a second later I hear the front door click shut.

CHAPTER 24

Oren's open doorway gapes at me like a wound as I dash past it, unable to look in again. I take the stairs to the attic two at a time, missing once, going back to the landing and starting again. Back in my room, everything is wrong again.

He knows. He knows everything—about my house, my habits, my not-family. Soon other people will know. I'll never be able to go to school again.

I pull everything from the north wall. Three inches higher. Three inches more.

Oren's face emerges between the keys of the Olivetti. His teeth: the only thing left after his skin melted off in that apartment where he died, all alone.

I grab Sapphire's journals from the stack beside my bed, stuff them with her bustier into a box in my closet, already overflowing with things, bury that beneath a stack of other, heavier boxes.

One final thing: the butterfly. Eternal anchor of my left coat pocket, unrelenting imbalancer. I squeeze my fingers around it like I might snuff out its life in the hot crease of my palm.

I place her butterfly figurine and its folded wings high above me to float upon the uppermost shelf in my room. The shelf full of dust, the shelf of lost, the shelf of surrender. Where I'll never have to see it again.

Where it will flutter away, disappear, disintegrate. Alone.

Diiiing-donnnnng The doorbell rings again.

It must be Jeremy. He left something, or he's returned, demanding an explanation.

Diiiing-donnnnng Mom will start howling for me if I don't get it.

I crawl away, down all those steps, shuddering when I pass Oren's room, holding my breath, the way we used to do when we passed the graveyard.

I plant myself at the landing of the stairs, call to the door: "Go away, Jeremy. *Please!*"

A slight pause, and then: "Ms. Marin—this is Officer Gardner, from the Cleveland Police Department." A woman's voice, gentle, un-cop-like.

I freeze.

"Hello? Ms. Marin?" She knocks again, lightly. My breath catches in my throat; I creep to the door, open it tentatively.

Officer Gardner smiles softly at me. She's prettier than cops are supposed to be, with wavy black hair pulled into a messy bun and big, round eyes, so dark brown they almost look black. "Penelope?" she asks, pulling out her badge, blowing a loose wave of hair from her face. "I'm Officer Gardner. You can call me Lucile, though, if you'd like." Her cheeks are round like apples.

My jaw goes tight, chest rigid. "Is there—is there a problem?" I squeak out. My tongue feels loose and hot in my mouth. They've figured it out: the stealing. The fact that I broke into Sapphire's house.

"Are your parents home?"

"No," I lie, staring at the rip in my right sock. "At work."

"Well," she says, scratching at her right ear which makes me need to scratch at my left, and then my right, and then both, two more times, quickly, wishing the *urge* away. "Would it still be alright if I asked you some questions?"

I stand there dumbly for a second.

"Don't worry, Penelope," she says softly. "You're not in trouble. I just have a few questions about Sapphire, okay?"

I turn around quickly, pretending to be checking on something, and *tap tap tap, banana* before uttering a relieved yes and motioning her inside. I pray that Mom is asleep by now, or has been sucked in by the television.

I lead Officer Lucile Gardner through the sepia-lit hallway and into the living room. I sit in the middle of the couch so she won't try to sit next to me, and she takes a seat in the big overstuffed leather chair, the one Oren made Dad buy one Christmas.

Officer Lucile Gardner folds her hands over her knees, uncrossed, planted firmly on the carpeted floor. "I overheard some of your conversation with Officers Pike and Graham, and I also heard how they dismissed you, and why." She tries to catch my eye, but I avoid looking at her. "As you know, we've already arrested someone in connection with the murder, but I'm not convinced . . . I'm not convinced."

"Why not?" My head feels numb; my words sound loose and echoey.

"Sometimes . . . how do I put this? Cleveland sees a lot of homicides. And there's a lot of pressure on the department to get someone booked, to sign, seal, and deliver. Do you see what I'm saying?"

I don't respond. She rubs her forehead. "Let me start over. Look, everybody likes an open-and-shut case. It makes everyone happy. And some cases are open-and-shut. But in this case . . ." She clears her throat, slides her hands down to her knees. "I think that some significant details have been ignored. You asked something at the station that piqued my interest. You asked if anyone had found any lipstick on her when she died. Why did that detail in particular jump out at you?"

I shrug, settle deeper into the couch. "Don't know."

Her brown-black eyes widen. She leans forward slightly in Oren's favorite chair. "Penelope, I think there's something you're not telling me."

I stare back at her dully. I feel nothing. A great swathe of gray. "Look, I don't remember what I said," I lie. "She's dead. I don't really see the point in trying to figure out why anymore. Nothing we do is going to bring her back."

Officer Lucile Gardner's round cheeks seem to deflate. "If you think like that, then, no," she says, "Nothing will happen. Nothing will change." She straightens up, balancing her palms flat on her knees, her arms twin straight lines. "But I'd still like to know *why* you asked about the lipstick. I'd like to know how you knew about it."

I count the loose threads hanging from both of her sleeves—two on the left, one on the right. Separately—bad, but together, *good, right, safe*. Still, I can't exactly explain to her that I was unable to *locate* the lipstick after breaking into Sapphire's house and rifling through her things because that would involve divulging to a police officer that I'd broken into a murder victim's house and rifled through her things. So, I shrug my shoulders up to my ears for three long seconds before saying: "I just thought she might have it on her, since it was apparently, like, her favorite possession."

I can't explain to her this, either: that I have all her favorite possessions; that I don't want to part with them, that I *can't* part with them. I cannot explain that what once was Sapphire, now belongs to us both. I can't explain to her that if I did not have her butterfly, her horse pendant, she would be fully silenced, gone forever.

Officer Lucile Gardner steeples her hands upon the bridge of her thighs. "It *was* on her," she begins. "But not in the way you think."

Despite everything, my heart jumps in my chest. "What do you mean, not in the way I think?"

"When we found her body, there was a word written across her torso in lipstick." She sighs heavily. "The detail was never released to the papers. That's why I was so startled by what you said."

All the hairs on my arms tingle, perk upright. And very faintly, Sapphire's ghost rises around me.

"What word?" I ask. My voice sounds tinny, as though I'm hearing it from far away.

Officer Lucile Gardner's cider-sweet voice rafts toward me, she clears her throat. "Slut." She lowers her eyes briefly before raising them again to meet mine, searching. "Do you know anything about the people in Sapphire's life . . . ? Anything that might have happened . . . ? Any enemies she might have had?

Sapphire wavers, slides from my skin, pooling like electric eels at my feet, stretching all along the carpet and infecting everything with their surprising sting.

I think of Flynt: how easily he got into her house, how he knew where everything was—the sketch he'd made—her near-bare body, the shadows penciled into her chest and ribs—how he'd lied about her. About everything. About the journals—about *Bird*—how she'd written of his violent streak, his blow-ups.

But I can't. Part of me doesn't want to say it aloud. Once I do that, it makes it true. And despite everything, I still don't want it to be true. "I don't—I really don't know," I say. I think of Sapphire's face disintegrating into ash beside me.

"Penelope?" Officer Lucile Gardner stands from Oren's Christmas chair. "Are you all right?"

I'm pulling, hard, at my scalp. Nine pulls per side. Officer Gardner tries to put her hands on my shoulders, and I back away. No. Interference means I have to start again. I don't want to start again.

"I'm fine," I finally respond once I finish all eighteen pulls, gasping a little. "I had, um, a bad itch." I stare at the floor. "Lots of homework to do. I'm pretty stressed right now."

"It's okay," she says gently. "I've got a lot of work to do myself; I remember how much homework they give you in high school. Too much, I think." She laughs a little, awkwardly, making her way to the front door. "Penelope, I know how easy it is to get frustrated by the way things work, but sometimes all it takes is someone who cares. Someone who forces other people to care." She reaches the door, resting her hand on the knob. "I'm not ready to give up just yet." She lets herself out, leaving me standing in the hallway.

Just my luck: Dad's Accord pulls into the driveway, as Lucile gets into her white Cleveland PD car. The trees are quiet outside, the wind is slow.

Their doors slam at the same time; her wheels crunch over the gravel and spin gently away; his footsteps plunk through the garage and the door whooshes open and shut.

"Lo?" He's already almost yelling as he barges inside. "What was a policeman doing here?"

"Police*woman*," I respond flatly.

He peels his coat from his shoulders, his fingers going white as he clutches it, and his suitcase and his briefcase. "Don't be smart with me, Lo. Answer the question."

"It was *nothing*, Dad. Not important. Routine." The word *slut* is skidding through my brain. So. Jealousy. A jealous boyfriend–type.

Bird. It's the only explanation. I think I'm going to be sick.

"Routine?" he growls at me, resting his suitcase against the wall, clunking his briefcase to the floor. He steps closer to me. "Do you think I'm that stupid, Lo? That I don't know when you're lying to me?"

I don't respond. I rub my hand on my right leg. Then my left. Then my right. Nine, nine, six.

"Stop doing that *shit* and answer me." I see the muscles strain in his neck, the vein in the center of his forehead bulge. "What did you do? Huh? Are you stealing again?"

He interrupted my count. Have to start again. This time, I count out loud. It's the only way to make sure I'm doing it right.

"PENELOPE. MARIN. *STOP*." He lunges toward me, ripping my hand away from my right thigh. I struggle with him, pushing my other hand into his hard-gripping arm, pushing him away from me with every ounce of my strength.

"Let go of me!" I cry out, fighting my hand toward the wall. Need to tap. Need to pull.

"Stop, Penelope! Just stop and listen to me!"

"Let me *go*!" I wrench away from him.

Something shifts: he gives up sagging a little into himself, defeated, small. Liberated, I rub my hand against my corduroy— nine, nine, six, and then the other side, and then the first side again. He watches me wearily, in silence. As soon as I finish, I push past him, grab my coat, and run out the door. *Tap tap tap, banana; tap tap tap, banana; tap tap tap, banana.* I don't even know where I'm going. I don't have anywhere to go. But I want out and away.

Waiting, alone, on the cold bus stop bench, I swallow the taste of salt before I realize I've started crying again.

I remember the time I went with Dad to a movie when I was probably five or six. I'd fallen asleep in the car on the way home and he'd carried me inside, my hair long and bubble-gum-shampoo clean down his back. He thought I was asleep but was singing anyway, lullabying softly into my ear. "Riders on the

Storm" by The Doors. He used to sing it to me every night before bed. Never missed a night. I couldn't sleep without it.

The bus arrives. The doors swing open to swallow me, then creak shut. The suburbs twist and wind around me, and before I know it, the streets have transformed into a puzzle of dips and cracks, the buildings: cobbled board-ups, boxy creatures with knocked-in heads.

I'm back in Neverland.

I wander aimlessly, and somehow find my way to Lourraine Street. Back to Sapphire's house—puke-yellow, daisies shining and stagnant in the limp late-afternoon sunlight. *Slut slut slut*—the word tattoos itself into my mind. *Wrong*, I want to scream, *you got it all wrong.*

A moving company's here, packing all of her things away into boxes, piling them sloppily onto the curb for tomorrow's haul. I reach instinctively into my pocket for the butterfly. Not there. I took it out; I placed it high on a shelf. I thought I could get rid of her that way.

I creep closer to the sad stack of boxes.

My own life, too, will one day amount to this. Sad little boxes of things. Garbage to be taken out.

The *urge* peaks through me. I reach into a box, pull out the first thing my fingers find: a nail clipper. I'll save it. I brush my fingers against its rusted silver. I'll make it important, even just this one tiny thing that she probably kept in her medicine cabinet or in her bedside table, used once every two weeks or whenever she remembered to. A new grief swells in my chest as I walk away without paying any attention to where I am going.

The sun folds itself below the hollow trees and spine-shrunk buildings of Neverland as I finger the nail clipper in my pocket, turning down a random narrow street sandwiched between two gray concrete warehouses. I think of the men who packed Sapphire's belongings away into cardboard boxes—men hired by the city, men who never knew her and will never think of her again after today, when they slink home to their own small, tired lives.

For a *slut*—the word, the word again—there will be no grieving. I run my palm against the metal, feeling its teeth sink into my skin. Sapphire's teeth.

Screeeeeeeek—the sound of tires scraping pavement close by.

Very close by.

Gravel hits my back, a few tiny rocks ricocheting off the wool of my coat, a beam of heat—a new light reflecting off the sleeves of my jacket, burning, too hot.

I turn. The breath sticks in my chest.

I try to scream, but my throat is like steel wool; the sound gets trapped, strangled.

I try to see, but twin beams of a vehicle are barreling toward me through the narrow alley, blindingly bright. The walls close in, cinch up, trapping me here.

There's nowhere for me to go—no space on either side.

I wave my arms frantically in the middle of the street, back and forth, hoping the driver will see me and slow down.

But I quickly realize: the car isn't going to slow down.

It's coming for me.

It's going to hit me.

CHAPTER 25

The engine revs behind me, speeds up, lights bore into my back. My shoes rip across the uneven brick as I run.

Closer, it's coming closer—I have nowhere to go—my heart leapfrogs through my chest. I'm not fast enough.

Bird wants me dead. *Flynt* wants me dead, so I won't talk. Roadkill. They want to crush me, flatten me, bury me.

Closer. I trip, barely manage to right myself. *SCREEEEEEEEE.* My legs start to give way.

No time. No time. No time to scream.

And then, suddenly—the wall ends—an empty space—*an entrance.* An alleyway. I *tap tap tap, banana* and throw myself desperately into its dark mouth as the car passes me, missing by inches—seconds, milliseconds—and careens away. I pant as I run, mad, through the narrow alleyway, sliver of sky shivering above me.

I stop running at the opposite end of the alleyway, plant my head against the brick wall, and try to catch my breath, next to a stitch of graffiti that reads *Lil' Dev* in loose, loopy scrawl, red and green. I hear voices ahead of me and tense up. But it's just two older men, pushing their way out of a grimy bar.

I *tap tap tap, banana*, right and left, then step inside.

It's dim in the bar, and it takes my eyes a few seconds to adjust.

"You got ID, little lady?" the bartender asks me. His thin, ropey arms are covered in tattoos, blending into his dark skin. The left displays a large-breasted Pegasus-girl surrounded by birds, banners between their twin beaks; the right, three lithe polar bears, one with a can of Coca-Cola in its paw like in those old commercials.

"No, I—" I stammer, breath catching in my throat. I shake my head, three times; my bangs slide back and forth, my face hot with shame, still trembling from my very near-escape. "I just need—"

"I'm sorry, but I can't letcha stay here unless you're twenty-one." He balloons his bony cheeks for a second, pounding his fist lightly against the bar; the large-breasted Pegasus-girl dances. "Not my rule, but I got to—"

"Followed—I think I'm being followed," I blurt loudly. One of the customers—tweed cap, crooked teeth—swivels in his seat to look at me. "I—I just need to make a phone call." Of course I don't have my cell phone—the one time I truly need it. "Please."

His brows curve downward. "You okay?" he asks, his voice low and serious. "You having some kind of problem with a boyfriend? Need me to call the fuzz?" The bony cage of his chest is visible through his Alice in Chains T-shirt. "I mean—I'll do it. They know me *pree-tty* well over there."

The other customer—electric gray hair, excessively droopy

eyelids, massive-bellied, and toothpick-legged—laughs loudly. "Yah. They sure do, Joey. Sure do." He looks at me. "Joe did eight years. Armed robbery." He smiles. One tooth missing; right cuspid. "It's no secret," he reassures me, leaning closer, his voice a raw bellow. "First thing he tells most people, really and truly. He's rehabilitated now, though, right? I'm not spilling no beans, am I, Joe?"

I look around: it's a dingy, scuffed-up place; a dirt-and-old-cigarette scent has burrowed itself into every surface. A sign on the mirror reads CLEMENTINE'S.

I step closer to the sticky bar, closer to Joe, tugging on both sides of my coat as I count the Kentucky Gentleman bottles lining the back wall: eighteen. Dad drinks Glenlivet. He told me once that it tasted like caramel, which prompted me to sneak some from his glass when he wasn't looking. It was *nothing* like caramel. "No," I say too quickly. "Don't call the police. Please. I just—I need to make a call."

There are no other options. I have no one else.

Joe squats and reaches for something on a shelf close to the ground. When he stands back up, there's an old rotary phone in his hands; he sets it gently onto the far end of the bar.

"All yours," he tells me, stepping away, grabbing a half-full bottle of Kentucky Gentleman and refilling both customers' glasses.

I pluck my fingers through the number holes, winding them around and around. It rings. I wait, hold my breath.

Click.

"Hello?" Dad's voice.

"Dad?" my voice creaks through the line.

"Lo?" His voice snags. He clears his throat. "Penelope—what's going on? Where are you?"

I cup my palm around the receiver, trying to muffle the swiveling of chairs and *tink tink* of glasses and the *thunk* as they hit the bar. What if he's so mad when I tell him, that he refuses to come? "I got lost," I say. "I'm using the phone at a bar." My throat feels very tight. "Can you come pick me up?"

I can imagine the vein, pulsing deep blue in the center of his forehead. "Where *are* you, Lo?"

I put my hand over the receiver, turn to Joe, who's fixated on a tiny elevated TV in the corner: Monday Night Football. Browns versus Bears. "What's the address here?"

"One-Six Hayes," replies Joe, eyes not leaving the game.

I whisper the address to Dad and he curses. "I'm on my way."

Click.

The bar is low-lit, a strand of half-broken Christmas lights casting a dull glow onto the rows of liquor bottles. I sit shakily down on a swivel seat at the bar and lower my eyes to count glass-stain rings—*twelve, thirteen, fourteen, fifteen, fifteen-and-a-half.* . . .

A door at the other end of the room swings open, and a long-haired, stoop-backed man comes rattling out, broom between his hands. He whistles ear-splittingly off-key, as he starts to sweep, gathering up the clots of crumpled napkin, split shells of peanut, all of the other crap on the floor. I start my count again. *Nine, ten, eleven, twelve* . . .

Joe pulls his eyes off the TV screen to holler at him: "Jesus, Paul. Lay off it, okay?"

"Hey—Joey," he says, the man croaks. He has the voice of a bullfrog. "Put some music on in here, and I won't have to make my own."

Joe laughs, resting his bony elbows on the bar, his T-shirt sagging so that Alice in Chains tents off his ribs. "Hearing you just makes me wish we had Bird back, you know?"

My heart stops. I grip the raised ridge of the bar hard as the words fly out: "You know Bird?"

"Yeah, sure," Joe says, shaking his head. "He used to help out around here for cash. Man, oh man, that kid could whistle like a frigging *nightingale*."

The other men nod in agreement.

I slide halfway off the stool. My body feels wobbly and loose: Flynt can't whistle. I know for a *fact* he can't—that he wasn't *blessed with the whistling gene*—he told me himself the first time I met him; we'd laughed together about it. My throat is being squeezed by a million fingers, but I manage to choke out: "Do you—do you know where I could find him?"

Joe cracks his knuckles. He and Paul exchange a look.

He shakes his head, cracks a small smile. "Why—he get you pregnant or something? He owe you some money? I'm just kidding, he was a good kid."

"Was?" I ask.

Joey shrugs. "He stopped coming by here a couple years ago."

"I just need to ask him something. That's all. I have something . . . I have something of his." This is true, in a way. I have Sapphire now. She floats all around me, all the time.

Joe shrugs. "Maybe we're not even talking about the same

Bird. Tall guy? Black hair down to about"—he cuts with the flat of
his hand to the center of his ear—"here? Mole in the center of his
forehead?"

My organs go soft, loose inside me. The description . . . the
height. The hair. He could whistle like a bird, had a mole in
the exact center of his forehead that he always hated. That he wore
baseball hats to try and cover up, every single day.

Everything in me drops, bursting—straight through the earth,
straight through to the molten, spinning center.

My brother. Oren.

Bird.

CHAPTER 26

"You know him?" Joe asks.

I nod slowly, wavering in the hazy overhead light as he stoops, pulling something from within a set of plastic drawers beneath the bar. "Then here, take this," he says, tossing me a navy baseball hat with a white *D* on it. "It's been behind the bar for ages."

Oren's favorite Detroit Tigers hat—the one he used to wear, every single day—in my hands. A prized part of his collection. My throat seems to cleave in two; a weird, mangled whimper escapes.

The echoey sounds of the bar, the football-game whooping and the *tink* of glasses and the *scuff* of shoe against linoleum melt away around me. I thud back into my seat.

Oren was Bird, which means Bird *couldn't* have had anything to do with Sapphire's murder, because Oren has been dead for over a year. My breath staccatos through my chest.

Another part of my brother's life we knew nothing about.

A shiver runs up my spine: Sapphire was . . . Oren's girlfriend.

Tweed Hat stands; I watch him wave limply from the corner of my eye, walk slowly out the door. Joe says, "See ya, Carl." I fold the baseball cap into itself, slide it carefully into the waistband of my jeans.

Suddenly, it makes sense—all the inexplicable ways I've felt drawn to her, how fate must have drawn me to her daisied driveway, to Mario's table and to her glittering, wing-drawn butterfly pendant. We both wanted the same thing: for him to live. When it didn't work out, we were both infected. By that gnawing, silent thing that crawls inside of you and hollows you. It's when her diary entries stopped: a little over a year ago.

It's why I can't rest, why I see her face between curtains and clouds and tiles on the floor: she found me. She chose me.

"Penelope." I whip my head toward the door. Dad. His face is red and exhausted.

His work shirt's undone, white undershirt in full view; neither are tucked in. This means he's upset. So upset he first had to loosen his collar to prevent himself from hyperventilating.

Flynt and Oren and Sapphire are butterflying through my head—a whirring, fizzy feeling—as Dad tornados over to me, grabs my arm, and pulls me with him into the oddly warm, alarmingly pee-scented alley before I even have the chance to thank Joe for the phone call—and for so much more.

"Come on," he practically growls. "We'll talk in the car."

Dad's grip is so strong on the left—and I tug away, pulling at my right arm to make it even. And then I have to do it again, because one time per arm, a total of two, is a crude, dislocating number, a number that will make me scream.

So many secrets. Oren could have told me. I would have known where to look for him, then. I could have helped him. I could have saved him. *Tug tug tug.*

Dad's watching me, shaking his head. I know he hates what I do; he's always hated it. Maybe he hates me in general at this point, since, ever since Oren died, I haven't seemed capable of stopping. "Neverland, Lo. Jesus, I just can't believe . . . after everything . . ."

He rubs his eyes. I don't respond. He hasn't asked a question, and, also: now, I have to bend down and stop and touch my feet. Six times right, six times left, six times right again, because they, too, feel completely off-kilter, sick.

"You know your brother was found not too far from here." I can hear his throat constricting as he speaks. "You know that, right? You want to end up like him?"

I have to start over before I can stand up and walk any farther. The bar is still close enough to smell: musk, sugar, tar.

"Holy Christ," he bursts out. "Holy *fucking* Christ; you're driving me crazy with that shit. I'm trying to have a conversation with you, and you are actually driving me *insane.*" I have to block him out. Have to keep going. He stoops down as I'm midway through, grunting as he wraps his forearm under my waist and forces me up. His forearm presses Oren's hat into my waist. The alcove is dark, lights from the street cutting in; disjointed angles, crude shapes spearing the black.

I wriggle fiercely back down to my feet, choking back expletives, tears sliding down my cheeks to finish my toe touches. I have to start over, though, because he's interrupted me, so angry I could choke or scream.

He stands feet away, breathing heavily; his back question-marking beneath the streetlights. A heavy minute of silence passes before he snaps again.

"All right. That's *it*." He bends to grab me again, the fabric of his sport coat whipping against my cheek, dragging me by my left arm through the narrow, brick-lined passageway to the car. I'm too exhausted now to resist. But I *tap tap tap, banana* loudly, not even trying to hide it, and when I get inside I have to pull on my right arm again to even it out, and then both sides, two more times. Six. Better.

I plug my eyes to the window as we drive, watching for signs—from Sapphire, maybe—folded into the stars, with Oren now, too. Maybe they're both whispering to me—through the Box Elder and the Kentucky Coffee Tree and the Black Chokecherry.

"You know, I get angry because I love you. You know that, right? Your mother and I, we both love you." We've pulled into the driveway, but he makes no move to get out of the car. He grips the gearshift with his fingers. "All I'm asking is for you to let us in."

But I can't focus. One of the two lamps is out on the porch, and the asymmetry makes my stomach hurt. "Lightbulbs," I say, turning to my dad, digging my nails into my scuffy black pants. "Where do we keep the lightbulbs?"

"Lightbulbs?" He shakes his head at me. "What are you *on*, Lo? Tell me what you've been doing." He is practically roaring. "Because if you don't, I'm going to do whatever it takes to find out for myself." He practically rips the keys from the ignition, letting himself out of the car. I follow, close behind, feeling horribly,

hideously off-kilter, panic snaking through my whole body like acid, like poison.

"*Please*, Dad," I say, trying to keep my voice low, calm. But the panic bubbles out. "I need a lightbulb."

But he won't turn around and he doesn't answer me. I run to the front door as he unlocks it and *tap tap tap, banana* as fast as I possibly can, slipping inside behind him as he throws his coat across a kitchen chair and begins jogging up the stairs. And then I realize—as I dig through the pantry for lightbulbs—he's not stopping at the second floor—where *his* room is. He's going farther up. He's going to the attic.

To my room.

The broken lightbulb is tugging, but I ignore it and barrel upstairs, everything suddenly very loud around me: my feet pounding against the stairs, heart jackhammering around my chest, brain crashing in my skull.

His back is a dark giant, an eclipse in the doorway to my room.

"Get out, Dad!" I scream. "This is my place. *Mine.*" I try to push him. He's boulder-heavy. Immovable.

He doesn't even fight back, just stands there, his mouth slightly open, gaping. "Jesus mother of God. Jesus," he finally whispers, swallowing hard, looking around my room. "What the hell *is* all this *shit*?" His voice is slightly hysterical; he runs a hand through his thinning hair. "What have you been *doing* up here? I can't even—I can't even *walk inside* your goddamn room." He's rubbing his face with his hands; eyes wide, full of terror. Full of disgust. "This is . . . this is *sick*. This is the kind of shit a *sick* person does—piles and piles of—garbage." Spit firecrackers from his lips and he's blinking now, rapidly. "I can't believe . . . how did we not . . . Jesus. *Jesus.*"

"Jesus," I whisper, one more time, to make it three. My whole body is hot, furious as he speaks. He steps out of the doorway, kicking into my room. Kicking into the nine soft-bellied jester dolls at his feet, disturbing them, breaking two of their soft, perfect china faces. I scream and lunge after him.

He bats me off, crossing his arms in front of his chest. Keeps shaking his head, voice frighteningly monotone. "We fix this. We fix this *now*." He tears out of the room and tears back in, thirty seconds later; I'm still clutching the jester dolls. Now he's got a giant black trash bag.

"No, Dad, *No!*" I sob as he starts going through my things, haphazardly, kicking at piles, pulling things off my walls, throwing them away: antique brass wall clocks. Minnesota. Baltimore. Cincinnati. All of them. Suddenly: smashed, scattered like dust. Like trash. My heart is ripping through my rib cage, shimmying up into my throat where it sticks, blocking off my air supply. I'm going to suffocate, right here. Right now.

"*Stop,*" I plead, trying to wrestle him away from my Smith Corona, my Olivetti—he's shoving them apart, letting them fall. Their keys come loose, tumble off, their undersides tremble away. He lifts parts into the gaping trash bag mouth, squeezing them between his fingers, his horrible fingers.

"Newspapers? Jesus, Lo. Why did you *save* all this shit?" He folds them up in his arms, dumps them away. I've saved every one, since Oren died. To document what he's missed, to have record of every day that has passed. In case he came back. He'd want to know. He'd want to see. "And old cigarettes? Half smoked . . . Oh *God*. Just *piled* up garbage . . . You could catch a disease. . . ."

He kicks over to my desk, plucking loose my pennants from their neat rows, flinging them to the ground. My whole body is a scream. I am being ripped to shreds from inside. But I can't move. Like how people must feel witnessing a natural disaster—totally helpless—houses, lives, people, everything—ripped away completely.

The drawers: he opens them, shaking through each and every paper, magazine clippings, a collection of crunchy, dried-up, russet-tinged leaves I'd started saving this spring, just as the season turned. He tosses them into the bag with everything else.

All I can do is cry: "*Dad*. Please, stop. Please stop. Please *stop*." But he's a hurricane. Blind. Hungry.

He slams a drawer shut so hard the whole desk slams into the wall behind it, knocking everything from both shelves to shatter on the ground with a loud *crash*—twelve glass horse figurines, three Limoges boxes shaped like top hats, three silver replications of sugar skulls I found buried beneath a forgotten pile in a dusty store in Detroit.

A pause. The clouds gather back their torrential rains; something in him shifts. He stands there, not moving, blinking, like he's been snapped out of a trance. And then, without another word, he shakes his head slowly and walks out of my room, dropping the fattened garbage bag.

My knees thud to the ground. Oren's hat comes loose from my

jeans, falls to the floor; my hands move to my shattered things. I pull them from the bag, pull them to me, feel them, sliced, raw-edged between my fingers. Glue. I need. Glue. Or tape. My insides will explode. I'll die. Everyone will die. The world will collapse.

The world *has* collapsed. It spins and slurs around me—my body is sinking, melting into the ground, splitting, writhing. I lift a jester doll in my hands, hold it to my chest—it shatters against me, falls apart. More, lift more. Everything, I hold everything and everything falls away, divides, separates into more parts, nothing whole, nothing fixed. So, I start to lick, barely even registering how disgusting this is, how pathetic I am. I don't care. I don't care. I need to fix this any way I can. Each piece, each crumbling section of a whole, stick them together, hold them together. My tongue tastes like caulking, plaster. Bits flake off into my mouth, slide down my throat; I gag. I hate myself. I have to keep trying. My stomach clenches. And nothing fits. Nothing stays. There's a blackness eating the edges of my vision.

I drag my hands through the rubble, when my fingers brush against studded edges, curved wings. I look down: Sapphire's butterfly, a new, dark cleft down its center. I stare down at it, eyes spilling, wishing I'd never put it up there on that shelf—all my fault. Again. For neglecting it, for wishing it away.

I lift it between my fingers and gasp as it splits neatly down the middle into my palm, revealing something small and thin and square tucked into the hidden space between its wings.

My heart skips a beat: a SIM card.

"Holy shit," I whisper out loud. The air crests around me,

sweeps away my fight with Dad and all of the beautiful, shattered things around me to a different, distant island. Out of sight.

I'm marooned in my own dry space. The only other thing in the room my nightstand, the cell phone on top of it. So, I grab it, and, trembling from toes to throat, unfasten the plastic back, slipping Sapphire's SIM card inside.

CHAPTER 27

The screen blinks on. Little black dots solder together to make words: *Please enter your three-digit security code.*

Shit shit shit. I try random combinations of numbers, bargaining silently with fate to guide my fingers to the right ones. *Give me this and I'll apologize to Dad; I'll take better care of Mom; I'll start fighting harder against all the weird, awful things my brain makes me do; I'll help the homeless—does Flynt count?*

Three-six-nine; nothing.

One-zero-one; nada.

Nine-nine-nine; nope.

Then—something hits me—a divine spit of inspiration: *four-three-seven*—the number Sapphire repeated to exhaustion in my dream. The number from her journal.

The screen blinks. *Loading.*

I kiss the screen six times, three seconds between each kiss, as a little computerized sand timer replaces the words, and computerized sand begins to sift slowly from one portal to the other beneath my lips. When I finish kissing, I look back to the screen—loaded. All of her contacts; all of her text messages. My fingers are shaking—my whole hand, in fact. My legs, too.

Tiny symbol of an envelope. *Click.*

With trembling fingers I search her contacts: *Bird.*

Old messages—loads of them, pages and pages.

I scroll to the first—the oldest—from over two years ago—when Oren still lived at home, just before he became a shaky, hollow-cheeked, zombie brother. And then I feel the *urge* to kiss the screen again, six times, three seconds between kisses; maybe he'll feel that, too. Maybe he'll feel how badly I miss him, all the time, every split-apart second of every jagged day.

I finish kissing, lift my eyes back to the screen. A series of texts, from almost three years ago, swims before me.

2/03 10:06 a.m.: You're sleeping next to me right now. You're all wrapped up in blankets, and you look like a delicious lady-sandwich. I might eat you before you wake up. Just wanted to let you know.

3/12; 2:36 p.m.: Yah. I'm at Clem's until,7 but Joe's not here so maybes I'll get to sneak out early for our pic-a-nic. And, yo girl, don't forget the S-berries! P.S. You're so pretty.

5/20; 5:11 P.M.: I love you like crazy. I was thinking . . . let's build a big nest in a tree and live there together!!! I'm SURious. K?!

I open the following message and a picture loads onto the screen, grainy and pixilated. I wrap my arms around my chest, feel my heart rise into my throat.

It's him—it's Oren and Sapphire. They are kneeling, holding hands beneath a giant bur oak. His face—my brother's—looks happy, happier than I remember it being for a long time, and sober; she looks so *young*, wearing a clean white T-shirt, jeans, no makeup—not even her signature lipstick. They look so in love.

So alive.

My stomach knots up as I read further through my tears—closer to when Oren disappeared, the months and weeks before he must have rotted away all alone on a flat of cold cement—and the passages in Sapphire's journals about Bird's *unhinging* begin to become clear.

I can't see you. I need to be alone. I'm about to rip my skin off.

And then: *I'm trying, baby. Nothing is working. Nothing will ever work. I think I'm going insane.*

And: *I can't tell you where I am I don't know where I am I'm sick.*

Finally: *I'm sorry I didn't show up for our anniversary name thing—I couldn't wake up. I can't do anything.*

He must have been going through heroin withdrawal. Mood swings—these were his flights, his unhinging, his mental slips. He was trying to stop using, and it wasn't working. It didn't work. But, still, he was trying. He wanted to get better. He wanted to live. I start shaking as I come to one of the last text messages he sent to her: *Sapphire, I will never not love you. That would be impossible. I think I will love you forever.*

At the bottom of all of Oren's messages is one—a solitary one, several years older than the rest—from a 937 number, no name. I open it: *Katherine, I finally tracked this number down from your friend Erin and have been calling and calling. Please let us know you're okay. Love, Mom.*

Katherine. Her name was Katherine—her real name.

It hits me, my body filled with a rush of ice: Oren never knew. Their anniversary never happened; he missed it; he was too sick, laid up in that cold window-cracked warehouse, beginning his slow rot. He never knew her real name, and she never knew his. And, it stands to reason, if she didn't know his name—she wouldn't have known who to look for in the papers, how to attend his funeral, how to visit his grave. He was Bird to her, and she, Sapphire. They never found out the truth.

Shaky, heartsick, I perform a cursory scroll through her other text messages: hundreds and hundreds from someone named *Anchor*, back several months.

1/17; 6:01 A.M.: I just had a dream about u.

1/17; 6:05 A.M.: U were naked. I was naked.

1/17; 6:11 A.M.: Now I'm horny; it's all ur fault.

Scroll forward, further, a little bit closer: *2/28; 3:18 A.M.: Where were u tonite??*

2/28; 3:21 A.M.: I needed to see ur body, and it wasn't there.

2/28; 3:22 A.M.: Do you understand what ur ass does to a man?

2/28; 6:05 A.M.: So . . . will I EVER get to see you outside of the club?

And further, still, closer to the present: *3/09; 4:06 A.M.: Ur a dirty whore.*

3/09; 4:16 A.M.: No, I'm not drunk. Don't u know what a piece of trash u r?

My heart burns as I read—closer; closer. I hear Dad rustling around downstairs; the front door slams shut. There's a brick lodged in my throat.

4/18; 1:07 A.M.: $5,000. One Night.

4/18; 1:10 A.M.: Well, how about I double it?

4/18; 1:14 A.M.: $15,000. Just a BJ.

I hear the whine of tire against gravel and pavement as Dad's car peels out of the driveway.

I scroll, shaking, to the top, to the last few texts from Anchor, hold my breath as I read from three weeks ago: *I'll rip u in 2. U know I can.*

Same night, *5:29 A.M.: I swear if u don't do what I say, I'll make u pay bitch.*

And the final text, *5:31 A.M.: Slutslutslutslutslutslutslutslut slutslutslutslutslutslut.*

Over and over again. Up and down, it fills the message, gets cut off at the end so it just says *Sl—* and my stomach starts to hurt thinking of the word, the same word, scrawled across Sapphire's dead body in lipstick: *slut.*

Whoever Anchor is, it's clear he was obsessed with Sapphire. He'd harassed her, threatened her, tried to bully her into having sex with him.

Could he have killed her, too?

It flows through me, hot blooded, that force she's radiated through me from the second I found her butterfly. I know who she was. I know she was loved. I know she loved back, even when it shredded her, dizzied her, drove her to madness. I know that my brother loved her till he crumbled away to teeth and bones, and that Sapphire—*Katherine*—and I found each other—connected through the air, through our cells, through some distant time-splitting, unknowable *force*—for a reason.

I can prove her life mattered.

I couldn't save my brother. I let him sift like sand through my open palm, let him get sucked away with the tide. This is my chance—maybe the only one I'll ever get—to do something. To change something. To reassemble, fix the leak, turn the shattered whole.

The grainy picture pops into my head: crisp white of her shirt, clear green of Oren's eyes, their coral lips.

They were kids. Now they're gone.

And as I move my eyes across the minefield of my room, her clean face seems to appear between the plaster and glass and broken things, rising from the debris to float there in the half-dark before settling back down in an arch of dust.

I see you, Katherine, I think to it—to the air and the floor and the shatter—*and, soon, everyone else will, too.*

CHAPTER 28

I stare at the cell phone in my hand, at the name I've scrolled to in Sapphire's contact list, now frozen on the screen: *Anchor*.

I need to know who Anchor is.

First I kiss the screen again, six times. Three breaths between kisses. Eighteen—wrapped around me, urging me forward in its calm, steady way.

Block my number; press SEND.

I hold my breath, shaky, as the *riiiiiiiiinnnng, riiiiiiiiiinnnnng* pierces through me. I wait, exhale quickly, swallowing up another shallow breath. *Riiiiiiiiiinnnng*—again. A subtle *click* before an automated voice pipes through: "The cellular caller you were trying to reach is unavailable, please try again later." I keep the phone pressed against my ear, waiting for someone's real voice to crackle through announcing his name, at least. It doesn't.

I return to Sapphire's contact list—have to kiss the phone six times again when I reach *Bird* to be able to move on at all;

eighteen means *go*, eighteen means *you will not meet harm*—and see the number for Tens tucked in with all the rest.

Her heart belonged to Bird. Maybe Anchor knew this. Maybe this drove him crazy.

I wonder if Anchor was one of Sapphire's "regulars" at the club. Based on the hundreds of creepy text messages he sent Sapphire, he must have met her there. The club was likely the site of the majority, if not all, of their interactions.

The other girls must know him—to at least recognize his name, have an idea of who he is.

I have to go back to Tens, one last time. I've got a lead now, a name.

Anchor.

But I'll need a disguise. I can't risk it otherwise—can't risk the narrow hallway, the stifling dark rooms, with doors that open like mouths to swallow me. The fist in my throat.

I'm all out of warnings—the man in the black mask told me so himself. I wonder if it was Anchor who practically strangled me in the dark.

I lift my book bag from the floor, retrieve Sapphire's bustier from the closet. Makeup. Skirt. It's all I've got—but it might not be good enough. I need to be unrecognizable.

I lift myself to my feet, wiping the wet from my eyes with equal force, three sweeps across each eye, stare at myself quickly in one of the mirrors on my wall—all nine still, mercifully, in tact. My bangs have shifted to the wrong side of my face revealing the white, hot dent above my left eye.

I start to brush them away but don't—a thought interrupts:

Flynt. Who isn't Bird. Whose lips I've felt—soft, smooth. Maybe he wasn't lying about any of it. Maybe he really did think I was *beautiful.*

I sniff, staring at my snowy skin; cheeks dappled strawberry-pink; dark, tangled sheet of hair; big eyes—green, more olive-y than Oren's. I haven't seen Flynt since the day we kissed and I ran away without explanation, without anything.

Flynt: he's the person I need. Flynt: the boy who likes me—scars, bruises, and all. The boy who will hold me together, the boy who means *home.* The basin of my belly goes warm, tingly. He's it.

And I owe him a very big apology.

*   *   *   *

On the bus ride into Neverland, I look through the window, watching signs whir by on the street. Pull the chord near the GEE WHIZ! CHEEZE WHIZ! billboard that means Flynt's makeshift home is close. The bus creaks to a stop.

I *tap, tap, tap, banana* quietly, ignoring the stares of the people close enough to hear me, walk the two blocks to his barbershop squat. I watch cracks in the pavement, count squares to keep images of my screaming, cut-up room at bay. It assaults me nonetheless: cracked, plaster doll faces, scattered typewriter keys—plucked out, empty sockets where once they were cradled—no patient, warming groups of nine and six and three—just a single mass grave.

I reach the crusty marble steps of the barbershop—fifty-one squares between the bus stop and here. A jittery, bubbly feeling fills my body after I knock on the door. Six times. Three sides per panel. I wonder what'll happen when he sees me: If he'll pull me into his chest. If we'll kiss. If I'll have to kiss him first since I'm the one who ran away in the first place. If I'll get to apologize. If he'll let me.

But he doesn't come to the door. I knock again. Nine, nine, six—I tap each of my legs between knocks on the door. *Cawww*—a bird shrieks behind me, three times. Three means *go; do something; you are protected.* I put my hand to the doorknob and twist it. It opens.

Tap tap tap, banana; tap tap tap, banana; tap tap tap, banana. It's dark, colder inside than it is out. I call his name, tentatively: "Flynt?"

Nothing.

I start down the curving, half-broken cement stairs. Everything's coated in dusky blue light, smelling of cement and dry wall, nothing human.

When I reach the bottom, my heart nose-dives straight to my toes.

Everything is gone. Cleared away. Empty, except for the refrigerator wardrobe and the lumpy couch and a long table. I blink, hard, hoping that when I open my eyes the room will be full again, and Flynt will be balanced on his elbows over that long wooden paint-smattered table, sketching some willowy animal-woman with tree branches for arms and a zebra-tuft of hair sprouting from her scalp.

Blink: still empty. I move slowly to the table, run my fingers over the dried paint, wishing his would magically appear to meet mine on the other end.

Maybe he's already left Cleveland—he always said he couldn't stay in one place more than a few months—moved away to Portland or San Francisco like he said he wanted to do. Maybe he's already rising from the ash of a different city, becoming something new.

I'm fighting a rising panic now. I search through my book bag for paper and a pen and the only thing I find is a crumpled receipt from Mighty Mart and it'll have to do. I poise my drying-out Micron 005 between my fingers, flatten the receipt with the side of my hand, and begin to write, tiny pressed-together words.

Dear Flynt,

I'm so sorry. I don't know what else to say. I was confused. About you, and about us.

I think I might know who killed Sapphire now. I'm going back to Tens. I have to speak to the girls again. I know it's not safe, but I have to do this.

It all feels very big and hard to say, but you're the only person I've ever known who makes me feel like I'm better. Like there's hope.

So, in case you ever find this: thank you.

—Queen P

I take a deep breath, fold the note three times, and press it into my hand as I take a last look around, the funeral of light settling into every surface, blanketing Flynt's old home like dirt.

The steps crumble behind me as I ascend. And at the top, before I leave, I'm filled with the *urge* to bow. Six times. Each corner, the floor, the mirrors, the ceiling. *Tap tap tap, banana.* It's loud leaving my mouth. It hits the walls and echoes briefly as I shut the door behind me and leap to the street, bowing again, three times, to the stairs, to the sign, rocking back and forth in the wind, to the big-mouth sky.

I walk to the old birdbath and lay the note into its smooth, curved bottom, beneath a stone. Even if he never goes back to the barbershop—if he's still in Cleveland at all—he might come back here. It's the best shot I've got. I think of his fingers, pressing softly against my stomach, lifting higher, smoothing my skin. I bow again, nine times. A triangle of protection, a plea. Tree branches comb the moonlight. A thought occurs to me: Malatesta's—maybe he'll be there. And, if not, maybe Seraphina, the wig maker, will know where I can find him. Either way—I should go. That place must be full of disguises.

I weave through the streets. Streetlamp light bounces against the pavement, shimmying through the trees, guiding me to the metal hovel, the shack, the drippy black *M*.

The door is already slightly open—I peer inside—no sign of Flynt. My heart sinks a little more, but I *tap tap tap, banana*—three times—and step inside. There's no time to be afraid.

Seraphina and Gretchen are hanging a giant, painted plank of wood on the back wall. "Put this down a second, Gretch," Seraphina is saying, as I step through the doorway. "This isn't the spot—the feng shui's way off."

I clear my throat. Gretchen's hoopskirt swishes as she turns, spotting me. "Hey—Flynt's friend, right?"

I nod. "I'm looking for him."

Seraphina turns, too. "Flynty's MIA at the moment," she informs me. "Haven't seen him in a couple of days."

My heart flips, again; the sinking feeling worsens. I push it away, remembering my mission. "Actually," I say, taking a deep breath, focusing on the nine perfect planks in the ceiling, "there's another reason I came. I . . . I need help with something."

Seraphina wipes her dusty hands against her jeans, covered in blue glitter and gesso. "Sure thing—what's up?"

"You make wigs, right?"

Gretchen grunts. "That's, like, all she does these days. She's *obsessed*."

"Well." I kick at a hardened clump of red paint on the ground. "I was wondering if maybe . . . well, if I could possibly borrow one?"

Seraphina's face lights up. She skips across the room and through a curtain, revealing, for a moment, the storage space—stuffed with paintings, brushes, boxes. She emerges, seconds later, hugging a basket to her chest. It is overflowing with wigs. "I'm trying to get rid of some of these, anyway. Take your pick," she tells me, smiling broadly. "Whatever you want . . . it's yours. Got a costume party or something?"

"More like . . . a performance," I answer. This, at least, is true.

"Need anything else?" Gretchen chimes in. "We pretty much collect costumes like it's our job."

"Anything." I say. Seraphina ducks behind the curtain again and reemerges a second later, dragging an antique trunk spilling with clothes, shoes, bits of fabric and lace. "Everything."

*   *   *   *

Rounding the corner at the end of the block, I pass the small sway-ing man with the hazy violet eyes—the Prophet. I pause, watching him moan and rock, in his own world. I remember how he'd described Bird when I'd asked, that night with Flynt: *a unicorn all the time. And a nightingale when it suited him.* At the time it had seemed like the tangled musings of a crazy man.

I watch his stooped little body swoop left and right, hands raised to the sky as if to pay homage. The Prophet isn't crazy—he was right. Oren's mole, that mystical point in the exact center of his forehead—it really was the *exact* center, we measured it once—made him a *unicorn*; his startling, beautiful whistling, a *nightingale*.

I fumble in my pocket for change, needing to thank him in some small way. Standing right in front of him, I bow six times—blushing furiously the whole time, even though I know he can't see me—before plunking a fistful of change into the hat at his feet.

"Thank you, Penelope," he says.

I draw back, too stunned to say anything. He's smiling at me through half-empty gums, as though he *can* see me. But that's impossible—he's blind. Somehow, he just . . . *knows*, just like he knew about Oren's unicorn mole.

And I'm comforted by it—by the idea that maybe one single person acts as a database for an entire world's knowledge. And he just happens to live in Cleveland.

As I turn away, he calls to me from his light-swathed corner. A few insects beat their wings in silhouette above his head. His voice is high, heart-strung, a moth with holey wings. "He loves you, you know."

My voice starts to catch in my throat; I push it out, past the choking feeling. "Who . . . loves me?"

He doesn't respond, just keeps bobbing, up and down. The light at his back near-blinding, peppered by insects. The grass shivers beyond the pavement. And, suddenly, I understand. I walk back, heart drumming in my chest.

"Tell him to look for the note in the birdbath," I say, stepping closer. He smells faintly of oranges and hums softly to himself, still not responding, still bobbing. "The birdbath," I repeat quietly, two more times to make it three.

After standing there another minute, waiting, I start walking away; stop after six squares, frozen; something's trembling through my entire body and it reaches my toes and, suddenly, I cannot move.

"I love him, too," I announce, to myself, to the Prophet, to the grass. I breathe in the words, fastened now into the night—a rope stretched between us that I'd trace back to Flynt's eyes and bear-eared hat and mouth if I could, fist by fist, wherever he might be.

I continue walking, on a tide of new strength. Moths whisper through the trees, giant flakes of salt across the spray of new leaves.

It's not until I reach the end of the block that the Prophet's belated response wings over to me. "I'll tell him," he says, humming again as soon as the words leave his mouth. My heart spins and beats, wild. Thrilled. Terrified.

CHAPTER 29

I change clothes in the Sunoco bathroom on Harrison Street, a block away from Tens.

Tap tap tap, banana. The bathroom smells like tobacco and body odor; a bucket full of dirty sanitizer liquid sits in the corner, a cloth mop stuffed inside. I breathe through my mouth.

I wriggle into Sapphire's bustier, and when I zip it up, feel her calm and strength holding me in again. The straps fall off my shoulders, I hug my arms into my chest, pull her closer in, draw three concentric circles around my heart with my pointer finger to try and soothe the maniac pounding below the skin. I lift a thick swathe of Malatesta's borrowed dark purple lace from my bag, tie it around my waist, clasp a strand of rhinestones around my neck, tuck the horse pendant into the bustier.

I tug my hair into a tight bun, sliding Seraphina's hand-ventilated wig over my scalp. It itches, hangs in long, wavy blonde strands around my face.

Penciling thick coal black liner around both eyes, I see Oren flash across my face, peek out from my pupils. I remember how he liked to make us brush our teeth in the dark, how giant his pupils would become when the light went out. It always scared me—they'd suck up the green of his irises—black holes, devouring the light.

Blink: he's gone.

It's the forever part that freaks me out most of all. The foreverness of death. I can feel myself teetering between the two worlds—flesh and air; bone and dust.

I remember Mrs. Kim, my eighth-grade Earth Science teacher, telling us: *We never fully die; the matter we assume just changes. We become minerals, layers of sediment and rock after billions of years; food for plants, for sun, for air. If we did not die and our bodies did not melt into the earth, there would be no more life.*

More from Malatesta's trunk: heels—too-tall, red, scraping against the slippery cement floor; black pleather micro-mini; fishnet stockings.

When I'm finished, I'm not me. And I'm not her. I'm someone new—again—a stowaway beneath layers of cream blush and inky mascara and wild-wavy blonde hair. I shiver, bow six times to the chipped toilet—nearly gagging—three more to the mirror.

Juliet—resurrected. Brand-new.

The greasy boy at coat check glances up from his biker magazine as I enter the lobby of Tens, looking furtively around. His eyes go wider; he scratches his head, bites his bottom lip as I pass. In this new body, I don't mind that he's staring. I enjoy it. His eyes trace my body like long fingers. He is thinking about what I might look like underneath. Naked. Of how it would feel to touch me. He leans forward, watching as I stand before the door and *tap tap tap, banana* because I have to. Because there are certain needs that even Juliet cannot shake.

.   *   *   *   *

I coast in, press against the wall until my eyes adjust. Purple light, underwater-velvety dark. The music *bump-bump*s everywhere, a steady pulse. Luckily, the club is packed with people tonight. I rest my bag and coat in the corner, balled into each other.

Flash: bleached-out faces of men staring into the stage lights. They'll die, too, someday. All of them. Their ties will hang limp on a rack in their closets until someone cleans them out and drives them over to the Salvation Army and leaves them in a plastic bag in front of the door.

I need to find the dressing room—to talk to the girls. Now. But when I peer through the darkness, I see that the door guarding the entrance to the break room is blocked: a giant bouncer stands guard, one hand tapping the heart-attack club music beat against his thigh. I adjust my wig, spin on my heels, and walk quickly in the other direction. *It could be him.* The one who threatened me, who wants me killed. Even with my disguise, I probably look suspicious here in the shadows.

I need to think. The VIP area is ahead, and, with no other options, I move toward it, slipping my finger between the cleft in the curtains, peering through. Seeing no one, I insert myself into a dark corner, press myself behind a row of tables lined with glittering ashtrays. I suck in cologne-thick air, hold it in my lungs. I'm not sure what to do next.

I hear voices coming from several of the booths. I can make out infrequent snippets of words and moans—"Ooooohhh"; "Best I ever . . ."; "More if you . . ." Nothing more. Nothing solid.

A minute or two later, the small curly-haired girl I've seen several times before glides out from a booth, bills fanning out from the garter strapped to her thigh. I bow, praying she won't randomly turn around before I finish. Three times. *Three times safe.*

"Hey!" I whisper, just as I finish bowing and she's nearly out of earshot. I step toward her from the dark of my corner. She whips around.

"Yeah?" She shifts her weight to the other foot, bending down to double a rubber band around the money in her garter.

"I'm new," I say. "Brand-new."

She stands up, flipping her hair back. "Oh, hey. I'm Glory." She seems friendly, flush with new money.

"I'm Juliet," I say, needing to bow, again, three times, trying to make it brief, casual, hoping it won't register.

But it does. "Are you okay?" she asks, squinting at me.

My fingers fly to the backs of my legs; I dig them nervously into my tights. "I'm fine. Just a little nervous, I guess. I'm—I'm waiting for a customer."

"Oh," she says. "For a private room? Or a lap dance?"

"Um. Both." I'm not even sure whether my response makes sense. I rush on, "Have you seen . . . Anchor anywhere?" I swallow hard, swivel a heel into the floor.

"Anchor?" She pauses, thinking. I hold my breath. "I don't know who that is."

My heart sinks.

"But I've only worked here for a couple of months," she continues with a shrug. "I don't know everyone yet."

A curtain sways beside me. I angle my head downward so the hair of the wig shadows most of my face. A fat, balding man steps out, smiling at Glory as he passes.

"See you next week, John! Have fun in Jamaica!" She winks as he weaves through the maze of tables and slips from the curtain into the hallway that leads to the rest of the club. The she turns back to face me, hand on bony hip. "Have you asked any of the other girls? They'd know better."

"No. Not yet. I—he said he would be here, and I—I don't want to miss him." I pause, spacing out my words. "It's my first time dancing. And I don't know the other girls yet." I stare at her bare stomach, the small outward pebble of her belly button, her muscular legs capped in purple fringe, glittery-thong girded. I look back at her face. She has small lips and is wearing too much eye shadow.

Glory rips at a hangnail with her teeth, spits it out. "Well, I mean, I'm about to go back out on the floor—I can ask around and let you know, okay?"

I nod, again, again, again. "That would be *amazing*."

She smiles, big. "I'll be back after my stage set, okay? And you shouldn't be nervous around the girls—they're great. Some of them just need a little warming up, ya know?"

I watch her circle back toward the main floor and retreat back into my dark corner to listen, to watch, and to wait.

Anchor. Every single person in this club must have a nickname. Like they know at some point they'll need to become untraceable— like they know at some point, they won't have a choice. *Anchor.* It pumps through my skull to the techno blast coming through the speakers. *Come on come on come on.*

Time expands and contracts around me, birthing images in the dark, out of nowhere: Mom, hugging me before I get on the bus, first day of sixth grade, South Bend, Indiana. *Just go to the bathroom when you need to do those things you do, Lo. Just raise your hand and tell the teacher you need to use the bathroom.* Lightning bugs. Oren and me, trapping them in Mason jars, bodies glowing, yellow light. Sapphire's room. Flynt swept in on a wave. Drum circle. The pounding, the beat. A string of laughter. His arms, stretching to me across the bloodstained carpet. Fingers. Shoulders, skin. His skin. Touching his skin; salt; earth; Sawtooth Oak. Quaking Aspen. Cold, Oren's boots crunching through the blizzard the snow came up to our chests we pretended to swim in it; the graveyard. Walking in a line, heads bowed. Mom. *I'm staying here. I'm not going anywhere.* Dad and me at the swimming pool in Kankakee. Floaties. *I'm right here, Lo. I'm not going to let go, sweetie. I'm right here.*

The past swallows me up until the curtain shifts again, and Glory walks back through, a short, thin man with a gargantuan nose in tow. She directs him inside a curtained-off booth as I step out from the dark to hear the verdict.

"No luck," she says, shaking her head. "I asked around and no one's heard of anyone named Anchor. Maybe he bailed. Just get out there and get another one, girl!" she says, winking at me, slipping fully into her booth and out of sight.

Heart sinking, I begin to bow again, all the way to the ground, touching my toes. Could I have been wrong about how Sapphire knew him? No. The texts made it clear he was a customer of hers. Nine, nine, six. Bow, toe-touch, rise. Repeat. Over and over again—until it hits me: *Call him. Call him again.* He's got to be somewhere. He's got to pick up eventually.

I slip quietly out of the VIP area. Thankfully, my bag and coat are still in the corner where I left them. I hold my breath as I reach the dark hallway behind the booths. Bow, touch, rise; bow, touch, rise; bow, touch, rise. I try to speed through, but my body takes its time. Demands it, has always demanded it.

Click-click. Someone is coming down the hallway toward me. I race back to my corner in the VIP area, crouch low to the ground, cradling the phone next to my ear.

It's ringing. It's ringing. It's ringing.

Someone's cell phone is ringing in the club, too—a tinny tone playing a split second later, in tandem with the ring-back tone in my ear. I end the call, startled. The ring sounding in the club also ends abruptly.

Coincidence—it's got to be—there are any number of people here with any number of cell phones who could be receiving phone calls any minute of any day.

Just to be sure, I dial again. A moment of pause as the signal speeds across some wire somewhere.

But it happens again. The same tinny ring, from *inside* the club.

That wavy, wobbly underwater feeling comes rushing back: dread gnaws at every part of me, tiding up into my throat like a fist—it pushes me through the curtain, out of the VIP section, moves me forward.

Riiiiiing.

Feet away: tall man, gray T-shirt, tan skin, muscles—the back of him—fishing in his pocket for his ringing cell phone. My chest pulses, pulses, pulses as he lifts the phone to his ear. "Hello?"

And the same word, and the same voice, at the same time comes through the phone I'm still holding against my ear. He turns, pushing away a stripper, who has been rubbing his shoulders.

And then I see his face.

His perfect, chiseled, handsome face.

The perfect, chiseled, handsome face of Gordon Jones.

CHAPTER 30

Hands shaking, madly, head spinning, I press the little red button that ends the phone call. For one second, everything goes black. And then it gets clear, X-ray clear, and I realize I have to get out of here. Tell someone. I turn, pulling off my heels as I race back through the curtained VIP area, cutting quickly around the booths through the exit at the other end that leads back into the hallway, into near-darkness, into shadow. *He's here. He's here.*

Gordon Jones: Fantasy Man. Gentleman. Loaded. Murderer.

A little farther—*keep going*—a doorway, and, through the doorway, down a different low-ceilinged hallway: the dressing room. Salvation. *Riiiiiing. Riiiiiing.* I freeze.

It's my cell phone. *Anchor.* The name cuts through the screen.

I answer and hang up. Right away. I didn't think to block the calls. Oh God. He knows.

Riiiiiing. Riiiiiing. Again. It's him. I pick up. Hang up. Turn the phone off, organs punching around inside my body, clenching,

coiling. The back of the club spins around me, the long, dark hallway seems suddenly flipped around, wavy. And I feel paralyzed—
my brain won't work—I can't remember which end I just came
from, which end might lead me directly back to him. I suddenly
feel as though I've been plunged into the icy water of a creek, just
like when I was a kid—frigid water floods around me now. I'm
drowning. I will drown. Oren isn't here to drag me out this time.
Gordon is. Waiting to push me under.

Shaking, I start trying all of the doors—most of them locked—
a whimper working its way out of my throat.

And then I see him.

He's coming from the end of the hall—the same end I came
from, the end connected to the VIP area, following my exact tra-
jectory, pushing toward me—cell phone clutched in hand—face
flushed and twisted. I clap mine into my thigh, hiding it. *He heard.
He knows.*

I whip left and right, searching for an escape route—everything
hot, rushing, electric. I leap toward the opening, mid-hall, that
leads into the center, the pumping heart of the club. The stage.
The balding men in business suits.

But before my body can foist itself forward—where there will
be people, who will see, who will know something is not right—the
urge shoots through me, the stupid all-powerful brain-gripping
force.

And I have to bow, toe-touch, rise; bow, toe-touch, rise; bow,
toe-touch, rise, and just as I finish—about to rise and run and
escape—arms grip me around the waist, squeeze the breath out of
me. A hand lifts to cover my face, nose, mouth, eyes.

"That's a cute trick—your little game of phone tag," he whispers into my ear. His voice is sandy; tiny, salty bits of glass. "You think this is some kind of fucking joke? All right, I'll play. Tag. You're it."

My head feels like it's floating straight off my shoulders, dizzy; my heart keeps stopping and starting, practicing death.

My esophagus gasps, reaching for more air, he's so strong, so strong—

Darkness. Clouds. *Easter baskets.* Mom always took weeks to make our Easter baskets. Ribbon-tied and chocolate-filled and socks, warm socks, I always liked socks and Peeps and she'd sit on my bed Easter morning with it all wicker and cellophane-shiny between her hands and she'd beam, so proud, and . . .

"Didn't think I'd find you, little girl? Didn't think I'd recognize you? Didn't think I'd recognize that necklace? I *bought* it for her. Don't you know I started watching every move you made, ever since I saw you wearing it?" The sharpness of his voice jolts me into consciousness. "I gave her everything, everything she could have ever wanted. And she gave me *nothing*. Shit. How do you think it felt?" His fingers tighten around my face, pull at the skin, rough. "Huh? How do you think that feels? She was mine. . . ." He rips the wig off my head and pulls the silver chain, the dangling horse, from my neck with a fierce tug.

I hear his hand hit the exit bar of a door—I try to kick away—need to *tap tap tap*, need to *banana. Oh God, please please please.* I kick him in the leg, trying to pull an arm free, wailing into his hand, biting the skin of his palm.

"Damnit," he says, releasing his hand briefly before grabbing the back of my neck. "Don't try that shit with me, you dumb bitch." Pain shoots through, blood snakes onto my lip, into my mouth. I gag, choke, as the door opens, air whirring around my bare shoulders, neck, legs. Don't know if the wet down my face is tears or blood. Salt spills through my lips, more blood. It rips through my head: *tap tap tap banana tap tap tap banana tap tap tap banana.*

I want to know if mom will feel it as I die, if Oren will be waiting for me. If he'll be holding a sheet of paper between his hands with my name on it, like at the airport. Or if I'll be all alone, everything shrouded in silence.

A black van pulls into the back alley behind the club. The door opens. Gordon lifts me up by the waist, throws me inside. My head slams against the other door—everything spins, and goes to fuzzy black.

*   *   *   *

I open my eyes. I must have passed out. We're moving, roaring forward. There's a dark sheet of plastic blocking off the back of the car from front. I can't see the driver. He can't see me. Gordon is next to me, watching.

Flash: Flynt, watching me wake up, his hand dancing across his sketch pad. His fingers smoothing the scar above my eye—just before we kissed; that patient, perfect moment. *He doesn't know. He'll never know me again. And I'll never know him. Never know his real name.*

It was my first kiss. It was my last kiss.

"Want to do a dance for me . . . Penelope? Before I put a bullet in your brain? One last time?" I curl myself against the door, as far away from him as I can possibly be, which is still too close. Breath shoots heavily from his nostrils; he wipes some spit from his lips. *He knows my real name. He knows everything.* My brain swivels in my skull; I feel it going soft, preparing to be divided by an inch of quick-moving metal.

"This is your fault," he says, shaking his head, like I'm a student who has failed a math exam. Disappointed. "We told you to stay away. We warned you. And now . . ." He rolls up the cuffs of his dress shirt. There's a dark splotch on his forearm: a tattoo. An anchor tattoo. "Well, now I have no choice. You dumb bitches never give me a choice, do you?"

The watch on his wrist flashes as we pass under a streetlamp. All at once, another piece of the puzzle clicks together. I gasp out: "Your watch—Mario had it at the market with Sapphire's things—" I'm floundering for truth, for clarity, for something to hold on to. "He knew about you and Sapphire. . . ."

Flash: Mario's dyed red hair and bewildered face as he grabbed the watch from my hands at the flea that day. *That one's not for sale.*

"That freaky little bastard started sniffing around in my business. He tried to blackmail me. So I had him killed," Gordon says, voice flat, lifeless. "Unfortunate, but necessary. He was another one who didn't know how to let sleeping dogs lie. Or sleeping sluts, in this case . . ." He half smiles, the neon red of taillights fusing with his face; crazy shadows bloom around his eyes as the car jerks, turning off of the highway, speeding down a narrow ramp, air whooshing around us like a scream.

We jag. Zip. Swerve. The sky is a dark tunnel, no light at the end. I lick the dried blood from my lips. The car *screeek*s into a big open parking lot, jolting forward as it stops.

"Don't try to run, pretty girl. I have a gun in my pocket," he says, smiling—perfect rows of teeth, nothing out of place, no gaps. "And don't bother screaming. No one will hear you."

Teeth. They dance around me, chorus line around my head. Blood. Still on my lips. I lick. Three times. Three times again as he opens the car door with one hand and wraps his fingers tightly around my wrist with the other, pulling me with him, into him, into a stiff dance that makes me want to puke. But I can't— everything is lodged too tightly inside of my body right now, shocked still.

Soon I will go somewhere blank and empty, and I will not be alive. The concept makes no sense. To be alive one second and not alive the next. To be dead. No sense no sense no sense. Nonsense. Nonalive.

I can barely see. Only a few thin bands of light pour out from within the multi-level warehouse in front of us—JONES INDUSTRIAL CHEMICALS SHIPPING # 6.

Keep him talking. Keep him talking. It's the only way, only chance. "The bouncer!" I cry out, into his too-close chest "You had him framed, didn't you?" I try to pull away; he pulls me tighter.

More comes back to me: Vinnie's big red nose. He's sneering at me through the opened curtain of the private booth at Tens. *Mr. Jones, you need another girl?* Gordon grinning, saying: *No, Vin. I've got a girl, thank you.* Then: on the sidewalk near my house, he's there again. Closing his phone. Hopping into a sedan.

"Smart little thing, aren't you? Figuring things out, up and down." His hand slides down my back, squeezes me. "Vinnie has been working for me for a while. I've taken care of him. Now, he gets to pay me back." He laughs, humorlessly. "Getting slapped with a prison sentence is one of the hazards of the job."

"My yearbook pictures . . . it was *you*. The acid . . ." I try to keep the wail out of my voice, but it doesn't work. "You got into my school, you—you knew where my locker was . . ."

"Your locker?" For a second Gordon looks completely confused, and I can tell that he honestly doesn't know what I'm talking about. Then he leans closer, smiling. "You know what? That's your problem. That's been your problem all along. You thought this was a joke. You thought *I* was a joke. Just like she did. You thought I was a goddamn clown, didn't you? I told her. I told her I would never let her go. She didn't believe me. She gave me no choice. . . ." He pulls me even more tightly into him, pushes my face into his chest with the back of his hand until all I can breathe is the too-strong cologne smell of his dress shirt. His mouth is wet against my ear: hissing, foul breath.

"You're—you're right," I tell him, into his chest, trying to squeeze the right words out past the terror. "She shouldn't have left you. She's—she was"—*please listen; please hear me*—"wrong. Anyone who leaves you is—is wrong. I—I'm sorry. Please. Just let me go, and I promise I'll—"

"Shut up, dead girl," he cuts me off, shoving me away from him, and I spin into another man's giant, meaty arms. I smell cigarettes, caked into his skin, his clothes. I gag, he wraps his fist around my throat. I try to scream, but there is no sound.

"How you want this done, G-man?" The words rumble, heavy, loose in the wide-open dark. I recognize his voice. He is the man who threatened me in Tens.

Click. A gun cocks. Muffled voices, my arms pulled tight again—my heart, clicking off, on, off, on; my father and mother, when I'd catch them kissing in the kitchen as he stirred dinner. Sage, thyme, squash, risotto.

"Shut her eyes, Frank."

"Doesn't really matter though, G."

"Just shut them."

More—Oren and me, lying over the vents in winter in our old house in Baltimore—he pulls a blanket over our heads, and we suck in the warm air, feel it blow against our cheeks, the smell that rises from the vents is soft, delicious.

A big, thick, cigarette-smelling hand slides over my eyes, a cold metal lip presses against my temple; his breath vibrates in my ears. My legs quiver and give out. Sapphire reaches for me through the thick air, I feel her wings drawing around me, feel myself beginning to spin and spin, to shrink and change, to rise from my body even as part of me remains glued to the earth and those hands—I still feel them—gripping the flesh part, heavy, tired, terrified while the other part, the soul part, shakes off its weight, rises like mist.

Somewhere far away, I hear Gordon's voice: "It's time."

The air goes still and thick and slow, and every instant of my life—past, present, future—divides, scattering into everything, into nothing.

And in that second, which is like a forever, I'm terrified that

Mrs. Kim, the science teacher, was wrong: that I will not become molecules, become everything; I will disappear and—*click*—Oren will not be waiting because he has disappeared, too, and I will never never never get to see him again because he's gone because we're all gone because we never come back and everything has been a lie and Flynt will never know—never know—never touch— never love—

"Okay, G-man, here we go."

Never know that I love, never know anything, never grow, never smell, kiss, taste—

And then, between the scattering of moments, I hear a sound like screaming, a machine going wild somewhere—closer, closer—other voices, colors—blue, red—the scream right beside me now.

I feel his hands tumble away—like they've been pulled off, Band-Aid quick—and then a different set of hands. Tears roll down my cheeks, sobs shake so hard through my ears I can't hear, I can't see. But these new hands—they lift me up; they pull me in—I don't know how, I don't know who or why. I don't know what is happening.

Suddenly: pine, snow, cloves, grass—the smells of Flynt, everywhere, cloaking me.

Maybe there is something when it all ends. Maybe there is memory, memory of the person you loved, when you lived. Maybe this is the white-light-tunnel deal, and I'm pressing toward it, and it's pressing back, until we become the same thing.

Flynt.

Flynt is holding me, and I still don't understand. I don't

understand if I'm alive, or if I'm dead, or if I'm somewhere in between. I hold my mouth to his shoulder. The sounds around us are tiny, panicked islands, far away—shouting, clicking, slamming, sirens wailing. I try to speak, but my mouth is as blurry as my eyes, and he's saying, "Shh, shh shh," over and over again, and, "Lo. Oh God. Lo, you're okay. You're okay. You're okay." And he's stroking my hair and his fingers feel so good. So real.

I lift my head from his shoulder and look at him. He's sobbing as he looks back at me—we're both sobbing: huge, fat tears staining his face, his beautiful face. "Lo." It's all he can say, again and again. "Lo. Lo. Lo. Oh God."

"Flynt." I choke it out, somehow, and it feels good—the vibration of my voice, saying his name. Our bodies shake together in the dark, in the April chill, in this one stretched-out moment in which every smell, every sound, every single salty tear that rolls into my mouth is so vibrant and perfect that finally, I'm certain of it: "I'm alive," I cry into his chest. He hugs me tighter, shaking.

"You're alive." He smells so good. So good. "You're alive."

CHAPTER 31

"I'll be back in a few," Officer Gardner says. The whir of the Cleveland police station filters through the cracks in the office door, a symphony around us. "Anything else you need? An extra blanket or anything?" Flynt and I shake our heads no and she smiles, clicking the door of her office softly shut behind her. It's funny how being here feels so different now, with Flynt, hot chocolate, and a fleece blanket wrapped around my shoulders.

My mind is still a blur: of blue and red squad car lights blinking against the asphalt, against the blank face of Gordon's warehouse, of cops—shouting commands, clicking guns, handcuffs, lights. Of metal against my temple, of Gordon Jones's shadowy face in the back of the black van, the burst of red around his eyes. *Shut her eyes, Frank.* I keep hearing him say it.

"How—how did you find me?" I whisper.

Flynt pauses, moves his hand to my neck, tracing little circles to the base of my skull. The symmetry comforts me. "I didn't think we *would* find you," he confesses, voice a sway of wind, rain drumming on a roof. "I got your note. I—Lo—I . . . I should have been with you—I should have helped—" He kisses the top of my head—my scalp shivers. "The Prophet. He gave me your message." His voice sticks in his throat. *He knows I love him.* "I went to Tens to find you, but you weren't there anymore. That psychopath must have already gotten you at that point. I found your book bag." He swallows. "I had no idea where to look. I went outside of Tens, and that's where I saw Officer Gardner. She's been on to Jones for a while. I drove with her in the cop car," he says.

Flynt pulls the blanket more tightly around us, hands moving gently to the back of my head, weaving softly through my hair. I reach for one of the mugs of hot chocolate Officer Gardner brought us, blow into it, feel the heat rush into my face, feel his long fingers brush against my scalp, my ears, the soft skin of my temples.

Shut her eyes, Frank.

"Gardner told me she started looking into Sapphire's case because of you," he continues. "She didn't tell me details, just that she'd become convinced Jones was involved. She had to beg the lieutenant to send in officers to his warehouses. Finally got clearance today, even though the case was technically closed. They found things tonight—photos he kept locked away in office files—photos of Sapphire's body, records of text messages he'd sent her. . . . He was completely whacked. A total power junkie. I told her Sapphire had talked to me about him, briefly. I knew some guy at the club was creeping her out, but that's all. She never mentioned names."

I look at his face and notice it's paler than normal, his blue-green-gold eyes angled downward, full of grief. He moves a hand to my back, runs his fingers down it gently. I tighten the blanket around us again. I count his eyelashes, *seven*, *eight*, *nine*. Stop at nine. Nine is enough. Nine fills my vocal cords, pushes words from my lips.

"Sapphire told you about him?"

Flynt nods.

"So . . . she was your friend? This whole time."

He swallows hard. "Yeah. She was," he says, words rushing from his lips. "She became kind of like a sister. A surrogate sister, I lost mine—left her when I left home. I always felt completely awful about abandoning her." He grabs for his mug, holding it in his hands a whole minute before drinking from it.

"I didn't know you had a sister," I say quietly. "How old is she?"

"She was nine, when I left. She's fourteen now." He shakes his head, swallowing hard. "I wrote her letters every week, so I knew my stepdad had started again with his bullshit—drinking and hurting her, and"—his voice breaks and he looks down, at his clenched fists—"I don't know what else. But I knew it was bad. "

Flynt moves closer to me, puts his nose against my right shoulder, kisses it. I turn my head and kiss the other one, and he almost laughs and kisses right again, so I kiss left. And he kisses right. And I kiss left and put my hand out so he won't do it again. Because six is what I need. No more.

"So, what happened to your sister? Couldn't you have told someone, like a cop, or a social worker or something?" I ask.

"My stepdad *is* a cop," he says, his mouth setting into a line. "I knew I needed to get her out of there on my own. I wanted her to leave—to come here—I needed money to send to her so she could start saving up." He shifts a little in his chair, rubs a hand against his scruffy cheek. "And then a friend at Malatesta's introduced me to Mario, who said he'd buy pretty much anything off me for a fair price. So, at first, I was begging or busking for change, or digging through Dumpsters for stuff, but it wasn't enough, so I—I started stealing. Just a little bit. Small stuff, mostly."

"Did anyone know? About any of it?"

He swallows again. "Sapphire. Sapphire knew," he answers. "And a couple of weeks before she was killed, she gave me some of her stuff to sell to Mario. She told me about this necklace she had that she didn't want—said this super-rich guy bought it for her, some customer who was hung up on her. He'd been bothering her, she said."

"That's all? That's all she ever told you about him?" I ask.

"Yeah. It was the only time she ever mentioned him. She told me to sell the necklace because it was probably worth a lot. I got a hundred and fifty bucks for it, but it was probably worth three times that, or more. That's how Sapphire was, you know? Always trying to help out. And she didn't want it. . . . She didn't want anything of his things."

Now, finally, everything is becoming clearer. "She gave you his watch, too, didn't she?"

He nods, looks down at his hands. "He'd gotten drunk at the club and given it to her—tried to pay her for . . . well, for *you know*. She was pissed. I think she wanted to get back at him." He pauses. "I was worried about her. She seemed . . . distracted.

Anxious. I talked to Mario about it when I pawned the watch to him. He knew Sapphire, too—from around the neighborhood and stuff." He shakes his head. "Mario seemed really interested. Wanted to know who the guy was, where Sapphire had met him. I told him it must have been a customer from Tens. I thought he wanted to *help* her." He looks up at me, eyes wide, willing me to understand.

"And instead he wanted to blackmail Gordon," I say slowly, as this last piece of the puzzle clicks into place. "He must have thought he'd hit payday when Sapphire was killed."

Flynt looks pained. "I should have made Sapphire talk to me. But she was secretive, you know? She kept a lot of things to herself."

"I picked up on that," I respond. My heart thumps loudly, a beat resounding through my whole body. "When was the last time you saw her?"

"She called me the day before it happened—the day before she was killed—and told me to come over. And when I got there, she was freaking out, throwing shit around. She accused me of breaking into her house, going through all of her things. I told her she was just paranoid. But I guess . . . I guess she wasn't. It was Gordon, or one of his guys, I guess, looking for any evidence that might link him to her. Notes, stuff like that."

"Gordon probably had Vinnie do it," I say. Pretty good way to set someone up: send them in to ransack the house the day before a murder happens there. Then something else occurs to me. "The day after she was killed," I say, "you were by her house—digging through the Dumpster. What were you really doing there?"

"Truth is, I'd left this lighter at her house on the day of our fight. It was silver, engraved with my initials. It was, like, the *only* valuable possession I had, and I was counting on selling it, on finally having enough to get Anna—my sister—out here. I thought she might have chucked it because she was mad at me. I started getting worried that if it was found, the police would think I was involved. I was worried *you* would think I was involved."

I stare at his fingers, wrapped around the mug in his hands. "I did. For a while, at least. That's why I ran off . . . that day at your place, after we were . . ."

For a moment we sit in silence. Steam curls up from our mugs, twists together, floats toward the ceiling.

"When I went back to the barbershop today," I say, my throat squeezing tight, "I thought you were out of here. For good."

"I almost was," he says, smiling slightly. "I packed all my stuff up and donated it to Malatesta's. I was ready to board a bus, you know, 'go west, young man,' all that shit—but then, I remembered something I'd forgotten to tell you."

"What?"

He pauses. "That I don't want to leave you," he says, simply, lifting his eyes to my face. "That I *can't* leave you." He puts a finger to the scar, right above my eye; I breathe him in. "You make your own rules. You won't compromise. That's amazing, Lo. You're amazing."

"Oh," I say—I want to say it back, want to tell him again and again *I love you*, so badly it hurts—heart growing, rushing with new blood, tingling all over. "Oh" is all I can manage to say, before suddenly Officer Gardner is standing in the doorway, arms loaded with blankets, trying to suppress a smile.

She comes in, lays another thick blanket on the table. "I know you said you didn't need anything, but the heat never really works back here, and you've got to be freezing." She retreats again, and the door shuts.

"You know, she reminds me of you," Flynt says, eyes glittering, moving his hand to mine. "She just charged right up to Tens, without waiting for backup or anything. She wanted to talk to Jones, and she was going to talk to Jones. Thank God. Otherwise we would never have found you." Flynt laughs in disbelief, shakes his head. "You know Jones owed one of the girls forty bucks; she was screaming when we came in about how he'd raced off in the middle of a massage. She was pissed about her money." He squeezes my hand three times. Three. Good. "A patrol radioed in—Jones's car was speeding on Saint Claire Avenue. Gardner guessed he was heading to his warehouse. We—we were almost too late." He puts his hand on my back again, runs a finger lightly down my spine. I shiver, inch closer to him.

"I found Sapphire's SIM card," I say quietly. "That's how I knew it was him, or, knew it was Anchor—that was Sapphire's nickname for him. He was trying to get her to sleep with him, and I don't think she would. I think she—"

"She stood up for herself," Officer Gardner says, completing my thought. Neither of us heard the door open or realized she'd come back with Lieutenant Flack—the tall officer who'd arrived on the scene after I'd found Mario—directly behind her. "Sapphire threatened to publicize his threats if he didn't back off," Officer Gardner continues. "He was edging his way into politics. It would have ruined that, his business, his marriage.

We're pretty sure that's why he killed her. She became a liability."

Flack steps slightly forward, extends his hand to my shoulder: "Penelope, it's good to see you again. It's good to see you *safe*." He removes his hand, and Flynt touches my other shoulder, lightly, and then the shoulder Flack just touched, again. *He knows me.* Knows I need things in threes. A warmth floods my belly.

"Lieutenant Flack gave me the go-ahead to reopen Sapphire's case, even though we'd already made an arrest," Gardner tells us. "He trusted me; I owe him a lot of thanks for that."

Flack rubs his eyes. He looks tired. "I'm glad I did," he says. "Looks like our boy Gordon Jones might be the missing link in two unsolved homicides. Seems Mr. Jones very much insisted on getting his way."

"No wonder she hid the SIM card in the butterfly," I say, as the last piece of the mystery becomes clear. "She must have known he would look for her phone, destroy it to erase the evidence."

"Psycho," Flynt says, pounding a fist hard into his chair. "Ouch."

Officer Gardner meets eyes with Lieutenant Flack; they both laugh. "I'm not going to disagree with you there. Flynt, I'm going to need you to stick around for a bit, okay? I have to ask you some questions. Standard stuff. Nothing to worry about." She turns to me. "Penelope, your father should be here any minute to take you home. Okay?" She comes beside me, puts a hand on my head, removes it gently.

I stiffen, nod. "Okay." I smile weakly. I've been trying not to think about my dad, and how angry he's going to be.

Officer Gardner smiles back, her round cheeks furiously red, shiny; her big dark brown eyes twinkling. "First time meeting the parents?" she asks Flynt. He nods, gulps. "What better time than the present, right?"

She winks, and she and Flack click softly to the door. Flynt's shoulder nuzzles closer to mine beneath the blankets.

A minute passes. The room is very still. The buzzing and whir-ring of phones and voices, the clamor of plastic and metal and hard-soled shoes outside is a staccato symphony far, far away. Flynt takes my hand, tracing his fingers along the lines in my palm. He looks up at me, still tracing.

"You've got a long lifeline," he says, grinning—deep dimples set into his cheeks. "To honor the intentions of the universe, I have to make sure you live, for a very long time." He kisses my hand.

I want to trap his warmth in my palm, spread it through my whole body. I want to feed the dark with light.

But, first, I offer him my other hand. "Two more times," I tell him, resting my head on his shoulder. "It's what the universe wants."

CHAPTER 32

The door opens and I lift my head from Flynt's shoulder, frightened again: Dad's here. He stands in the doorway, a stark, shadowy figure. And then, he runs to me. "Penelope—Lo—" His voice breaks. I don't know what to say, how to explain. I sit, glued to my chair, to Flynt's knees, shaking again. Little-girl shame floods in.

"Daddy—I'm sorry—please don't be mad—" The words leak out, watery, choked.

Then he does something he hasn't done in a long, long time. He swoops down and he gathers me into his arms and he's crying—I can feel his hot tears on my cheeks—and he kisses the top of my head and hugs me tighter. "Lo—I don't care. I'm just so glad you're safe." He pauses, hiccupping. "My little girl. My baby."

I pull softly away from Dad. "Flynt—this is . . . my father." Flynt rises, cautiously, wiping his hands on his pants. "Dad, this is my—Flynt. This is Flynt."

I blush. We both blush.

"Flynt. Hi." Dad collects himself, holds out his hand. Flynt reaches for it—I can tell it's hard for him not to bow, not to lift an invisible hat from his head and speak in funny voices—and they shake, once, firm, and Flynt steps backward to stand beside me. I feel the heat of his skin, through his coat, through my coat, touching me. I feel warm and safe, for the first time in what feels like a very long time.

Officer Gardner strides into the room. She looks to my father. "Mr. Marin," she says, extending her hand to meet his, "I hope you know what an amazing young woman your daughter is."

My father looks directly at me, unwavering. "I do. I do know. Thank you. For everything, Officer."

"You know," Officer Gardner continues, "it was Penelope who really made me keen to this case. Trust me—there were plenty of people making it very, very difficult for her. Most people would have just given up. Most people *did* just give up. I'm sure Lo already knows all about that." She looks briefly to the ground, taking a deep breath, looking back at us. "I have a daughter Sapphire's age. She had her own problems with drugs—now she's doing better, thank God. But when I heard about this case, I started to wonder—what if this were *my* child? Would I push deeper? Would I care more?" Gardner smiles at me. "I think it was meeting Penelope that made me want to do right by Sapphire." She squeezes my shoulder, two times. I squeeze it once more when her hand drops back by her side, and then the other shoulder, three times.

"Sorry," I say, sheepishly, knowing they've all seen, knowing I have to say something.

"Queen P," Flynt says, wide eyes shining, tipping his fuzzy bear ears into my shoulder, "you've got nothing to be sorry about." My belly goes warm; Dad's watching; Officer Gardner is watching. And I don't even care. The four of us stand there, a loose circle, kicking up little flecks of dirt and blanket fuzz against the noses of our shoes. Flynt's long-tongued brown boots; Dad's leather loafers; Gardner's dirt-streaked Reeboks; my scuffy Chucks.

"We should get home, Lo," Dad finally says, his voice raw. "Mom's worried."

I nod, suddenly very, very tired, too tired to be embarrassed, or scared, or nervous—adrenaline settled, smoothed into sleepiness, and turn to Flynt. "Where are you going to go? Back to the barbershop?"

Officer Gardner puts her hand gently on my father's arm, moving him casually to the side. They start their own conversation, too formal, full of pauses.

"Malatesta's, methinks," Flynt says. "If they'll take me back, that is—if they haven't already sold my things for a new tube of ultramarine paint." He wraps his arms around me again, squeezing me into him. "Hey—I'm going to see you really soon, right?"

I stare at the hole in the shoulder of his flannel, move close enough to see his skin beneath. "Yes," I say, to his pine needle, to his clove and his grass and his snow, to his scruffy face. "Yes." And once again: "Yes." He rests his jaw on the top of my head, I feel it move as he speaks, feel the small hairs bristle against my own, and I don't pull away.

"Good. Because I think you owe me at least . . . a date. You know, for saving your life and all."

*   *   *   *

Dad doesn't say much on the ride home, other than asking a few times: "You're sure you don't need to go to the hospital?" to which I reply, each time: "Yes, I'm sure." I don't say much either, but our silence is peaceful. I think we're both thinking the same thing as the road stretches before us, a long black tongue: if they'd come just a minute later, we wouldn't be in this car together right now.

He turns on the radio. I watch him as he drives, look for my features in his face, for what he's given me: dark hair (his now streaked in gray, like Mom's), long forehead (he used to say we needed the extra space for our extra-big brains), pale skin, ruddy from the cold.

And, suddenly, my whole body aches to reverse the awful cycle that was Oren's disappearance, his death—not for me, even, but for Dad. So he'll be happy again. So he'll stop working sixteen-hour days to resurrect a dead city, to bring back someone whose gone-ness is final and resolute. So Mom will come alive again, and the pills will vanish from her nightstand, and we'll dye Easter eggs together and build fires at Christmas.

But I know it's not that easy. Nothing's that easy.

We pull into the driveway and then walk inside together, and the house feels warmer than it usually does, lighter somehow, crisper, more real. I realize once we've gone inside that I didn't *tap tap tap, banana*, and that it didn't matter. I didn't freak out. I'm *not* freaking out.

"I'm going to make some tea, Lo," Dad says. "Would you like some?"

"Yes, please," I say, only once this time. "I'll be right back."
I walk quietly upstairs, press my ear against Mom's door. It's
quiet—no TV, no sobbing. I keep going. Up to my attic room, to
my porthole window and four-poster bed and everything I've
rescued, no longer scattered across the floor where I left them:
the cracked things thrown away, the unbroken things pushed to
the sides, arranged in neat little piles. Dad must have come in
while I was gone—tried to organize, separate, reorder. My chest
swells.

I kneel beside my bed, extracting the rectangular old cigar box,
pulling from within it two letters. Two letters from Oren. Letters
I've kept hidden away, secrets. Short and to the point, they both
say nearly the same thing:

Dear Little Sis,

*I wanted to tell you that I miss you. I've known you since the
day you were born, and it's weird feeling like I don't know you
right now. I don't know how long I'll be gone, only that I had to
go. I was ruining everyone's lives, and I hated that. I don't want
that. Make sure no one messes with my stuff, OK? I love you, Lo.*

Your Big Bro,
Oren

And they end the same way, too: *P.S. Hug Mom and Dad for me.*
Back in the kitchen, Dad pours steaming water into two mugs,
sets them on the kitchen table, folding his hands lightly around
the big, flowery one that Mom, exclusively, used to drink from.

"Chamomile okay, Lo?" he asks. "It's all we have. And that's my fault, I know—I've been . . . so *distracted*. I guess things have been falling through the cracks." He laughs a little, sadly.

I hand him the letters, clutched tightly in my hand. "Chamomile's perfect."

"What are these?" he asks, voice quiet, edged with fear.

"Just read them."

I sit at the table and hold my mug in my hands as he reads, and when I look up again he's smiling, fat tears coursing down his cheeks. And without thinking twice about it—an instinct, a phenomenon powerful as birth, as death—we stand and wrap our arms around each other, and I breathe in his dad smell. It's been so long since I've really been close enough to him to smell it—his leather and peppermint and sap and warmth. It's the safest smell in the world. It's the smell of being carried to your room and sung to sleep in a big, warm bed.

And the house seems to glow around us, to fill and grow lighter than it's been in a very long time and our tired, hopeful hearts thump against our chests and I know that things are going to change. I hug Dad tighter.

Things are already changing.

CHAPTER 33

Being back in school after a near-death experience is impossibly weird. But, weird in a different way than it was, returning after Oren died, when everything seemed coated in this fine, dark ash, shrouded and shadowy. Now everything seems slightly lighter, sharper. Every sound, too—louder, more defined.

Rumor has it that, finally, last week, Jeremy Thoroux asked Keri Ram to prom.

I see Keri just after fourth period. She and Jeremy are standing together. She is in a blissful lean against her locker but straightens up as soon as she spots me.

"Hey, Lo!" she calls out, waving. The words arch toward me, a warm beam—her eyes glow, her cheeks are pink.

Jeremy turns, too. He blushes, gives me a shy wave and a smile, as his hand tightens around Keri's.

I smile back at both of them. They're right; they *fit*. I knew they would fit, just as I know exactly why my remaining stone wolves and stone bears belong beside each other in my room, or how the Chinese gold-fringed peacock rug looks best three inches from the cherrywood printer's drawers. She smiles even bigger, then, and turns back to Jeremy, weaving her arm into his as they walk, doubly redheaded, to last period.

My heart beams in my chest. Maybe I'm not so hopeless after all. Maybe—maybe we'll actually be friends. I picture it: Keri and Jeremy, Flynt and me. Hanging out. Grabbing some pizza. Trash can bowling.

Suddenly—I have an idea.

*   *   *   *

The bus ride to Neverland, just like school, feels new—my body a tangled mass of nerves and excitement and residual fear, the light, pouring broadly through the windows.

It's getting warm out—finally—new smells rising from defrosted plains of grass, from fresh mud and re-budding plants. When I get off the bus I shed my winter jacket, hold it balled up between my arms like a serving dish I'm presenting to this whole cracked, "eternally wasteful nation-home of Neverland." That's what Flynt called it the first time I met him. I still remember that, how he'd spread his arms like a magician offering me a private view into heaven. But that's Flynt—he can go anywhere and make it home, turn garbage into art.

I weave my way through the streets, patchy and raw, passing Flynt's barbershop squat along the way, passing the Prophet at his post, swaying as usual. I fumble in my pocket for change. "Thank you," I tell him, dropping coins into his hat. He doesn't say anything this time, just smiles, keeps singing.

I skirt between the dirty buildings, searching for the graffiti-skulled alleyway, the drippy red *M*, the boy in the bear-eared hat. And, finally, in the distance, I see it—the entranceway to Malatesta's, marked in red *X*s, covered in paint. My heart flips as I approach and walk through to the lean-to, its door wide open to the breeze.

Flynt is squatting on the floor, elbow deep in paint and papier-mâché. Gretchen and the tall musician guy from the Narnia-esque party are here, too, playing twin ukuleles in the back of the space, singing something dissonant, jangly.

He hears my footsteps, raises his head. "Lo!" He scrambles to his feet, wiping his hands on his pants and propelling me back outside and through the streets before I can get a look at his newest work. "Rough draft," he explains. "You'll have to forgive my brutish appearance—wasn't expecting a royal visit today, though . . . I did hope for it." He smiles. "So, how are you, Lady Lo?"

"I'm alive," I answer. "I think that means something."

He grabs my hand and squeezes it in his. Warm. The lines of our palms press. I don't pull away.

"So," I say, "what are you doing tonight?"

"Hmm—well, aside from organizing my army of rats to storm Washington . . . nothing." He turns to me. "Who wants to know?"

"I do," I answer, firmly, "I want—I want to have our date tonight."

He wiggles his eyebrows, laughs. "Couldn't wait any longer, eh?"

"Well, actually, tonight is . . . prom." I squeeze his hand—quickly—three times. "And I want to take you. As my date." I bite my lip and look up at him. "You know, to repay you for saving my life and everything."

He looks surprised, releases my hand and reaches up to grab a spotty green leaf, twirls it between his fingers. "You're sure?"

I'm not sure. Not at all. In fact, the idea sets my stomach curling, but I nod anyway. "Yes, definitely, one hundred percent."

"You're very convincing, Lo," he says, laughing. Then his voice gets serious. "You do realize you're asking me to leave Neverland again, and aside from the occasional life-saving mission, I make a point *never* to do that."

My heart sinks.

"Then again," he continues, turning to me as we approach the busted old birdbath—the point at which Neverland ends and the rest of the world begins—"never say never."

Slowly—timidly, almost—meeting my eyes, taking my hand again in his, he takes one tiny step forward. And then, one more. One more step into the great beyond.

"One small step for man . . . ," he says, lips spreading into a grin.

"One giant leap for mankind," I finish, as we both crack up and he pulls me into his chest and we hug, swaying there for a minute and I feel the muscles of his back beneath his flannel.

"Look at us," Flynt says, his voice growing theatrical, dramatic—releasing the hug to clasp both of my hands—"stuck in the middle, hovering on the line between two worlds."

"I think this is where we belong," I say, as the number 96 bus

comes into sight, rumbling from down the block. Quickly, I tear
a piece of paper from a notebook in my bag, scribbling down my
address. "Pick me up at eight?"

"It's a date," he says as the bus arrives, pulling noisily beside
the curb. He squeezes my hand in his, a long, warm second.
Everything is fireworking inside of me as I board the bus and find
a seat near the back. I stare out at him through the window, still
standing there, saluting to me as the bus pulls away.

*   *   *   *

With less than an hour before Flynt comes to meet me, I pull
Sapphire's bustier from the hanger, run my fingers along its
sparkling black bust, cinched waist, and hold it against me in
the mirror. Something winging through my head says, simply,
yes. One time. And once is enough. I wriggle it over my head and
feel her around me, and again—it's the two of us, crazy-nervous,
dressing for our first prom.

Digging into my closet, I pull out a few hand-me-downs my
mom gave me back when Oren was well, when she was happy.
I've seen old pictures of her wearing them, from high school in
the seventies, when her hair came all the way down her back in
smooth black waves, when she wore giant sunglasses and flowers
tucked behind her ears, when the camera caught her, mid-spin-
blurry, dancing at the edge of the Chesapeake Bay. They're things
I never would have worn before: a soft black linen bell skirt that
ties at the waist, teal teardrop-shaped beads edged along the

hem; red suede heels; a scarf patterned in multicolored daisies
that I wrap, loose, around my shoulders.

I wonder what my father thought when he picked her up for
their prom in his fancy rented tuxedo: if his whole body shook, in
a good way, when he saw her; if he could have imagined that she
would become a dead woman trapped in a breathing, living body;
if he would have still fallen in love with her.

I shiver, slide my feet into my new-old shoes, twist my yellow-
daisy costume ring onto my pointer finger, assess myself in the
mirror. A tingle runs up my spine; for once, I look . . . like me. A
collage of pieces and places and time periods.

I push my bangs back, off my forehead, my scar a deep dia-
mond gash above my eye—assurance that I'll never forget the
day at Butt Creek when Oren saved my life. Not that I ever could.
Every single moment I ever had with him, I have them all—folded
into a million messy drawers in my brain; they belong to me; my
dowry, my heritage.

It sparkles from the corner of my eye—Sapphire's broken
butterfly. I reach for it, grip it in my palm as I stare at myself in
the mirror—no one else's image flitting through—just me this
time. Almost seventeen years old; scarred, but whole.

*   *   *   *

I knock on Mom's bedroom door on the way out. The TV goes
mute, lamp clicks on, bed creaks slightly; her bony frame and
bleached-out face appear in the doorway. "What's wrong?" she
asks, confused, disoriented. She tries to focus her eyes on me,

but they seem to slide from side to side, loose, watery. I wonder if she'll recognize her clothes, on my body, if she'll remember, even for a second, what she was like when she wore them, if she'll come back to me.

"I'm going to prom," I tell her, willing her eyes to go suddenly clear, willing her to smile, huge, willing her to fuss, to run to her jewelry chest and find me the perfect necklace, willing her to pull me to her, to put her hand around the back of my head, to tell me she's so proud of me for trying to live again.

But her eyes remain hazy and she just rocks a bit, trying to catch her balance, as she puts a hand to my face. "Okay," she tells me, trying to smile. "Good."

She walks slowly back to her bed, unmutes the television, clicks the lamp back off again, and slips back beneath the covers.

*   *   *   *

My butt freezes through my skirt on the porch stairs as I sit waiting for Flynt to arrive. Any minute now. Eight. I didn't even think when I suggested it—this most hated of numbers, of times. Of course, of course it will all go wrong—he won't come, I'll be stood up at the prom, shivering in some ridiculous, retro outfit I never should have worn in the first place. Maybe he'll come cruising by in some Dumpster-dived scooter to throw eggs at my head as he passes.

Eight—I brought this on myself.

But, then I see him, rounding the corner of my block in a mint green tuxedo—I notice patched up holes in the elbows and knees

as he gets closer—black-and-white-striped cummerbund; big,
brown tongue-hung boots; bear-eared hat; a bright red feather
stuck out over the left ear. I smooth down my dress and rub my
lips together, whispering his name, softly, three times. "Flynt
Flynt Flynt."

Three times for a chance in hell, for a chance to make this
right. And then I tap softly against the three cold wooden stairs
of my porch; nine, nine, six. *Banana, banana, banana,* finishing
(gratefully) just as he arrives.

He bows grandly. I stand; I curtsy, long black hair gathering
around my face.

"Lo"—he's biting at his lip a little as he rises, watching me
closely, like he did when he sketched me, like I'm the first thing
he's ever seen before, the sun peeking through the darkest of
caves, a basin of water in the desert—"you look beautiful."

The moon cuts through the trees, his eyes twinkling a hundred
different colors as he reaches his hand to me from behind his
back, presenting a bouquet of homemade flowers—bits of metal
and fabric and paper and leaf tied together with wire and string.

"I brought these for you," he continues, grinning. "Happy
prom. That's what you say during prom, right?"

"Right, like the terrible, nerve-wracking holiday it basically
represents," I answer quickly, feeling the nervous words bubbling up into my mouth. "Happy prom to you. These are"—I blush
furiously—"amazing."

I turn back quickly to the house, surprised to see my dad's face,
hovering at the front window, watching us. He smiles and gives a
hesitant half wave and a thumbs-up. I wave back. I smile back.

And then Flynt weaves his mint-green arm through mine, and I tuck his homemade flowers gently into my purse, and we begin our journey into the great unknown: George Washington Carver High's junior prom.

"You're having another Neil Armstrong moment," I tease as we walk through the even, rat-free streets of the suburbs, windows in every identical stone house fully intact, lampposts spread across lawns and concrete in even ten-foot increments, burning blue-orange electric flames. "Coming all the way to Lakewood. That's like, beyond the moon. . . ."

"It's like going all the way to Pluto, Queen P, which, as I'm sure you've heard, isn't even a planet anymore."

"So, you're saying Lakewood doesn't really exist?"

"Yep. That's what I'm saying," Flynt says, gripping my bouquet-less hand in his. "So, if you were to divide your school into subsections of the animal kingdom, or, let's just say into primates, who would be king of apes and why?"

I laugh. "Well, um, based on hairiness alone—"

"Yes," Flynt interrupts, "you can do it that way."

"Well, okay, based on hairiness alone, it would have to be Ganesh Liebowitz—I overheard this guy Kirby in health say that they had gym together and that you really can't see an inch of skin when he undresses for class."

"Wow. Gym class. What even happens in gym class?" Flynt muses. "I can't remember." He pulls a leaf from each of the three black tupelos we pass, only a block away from school now—boxy red brick, sprawl of green lawn, knot of trees lining the walkway to the front entrance visible now. "Do you have to shower after class?" he continues. "What if it's against your religion to shower? What if you don't want the other kids to see your obscenely hairy body because you know, later, they're bound to use it against you in reference to some absurd primate comparison?"

"No," I tell him, "you don't have to shower if you don't want to."

"Whew," he says, running a hand through his dreadlocks.

We reach the driveway that snakes into the back lawn, to the gym entrance lined in twinkling white lights. Flynt's hand squeezes mine—maybe he's as nervous as I am—as we walk up the concrete path.

Other kids file past us as we reach the steps to the gym—nearly all the girls in long, studded gowns and too much eye shadow, hair stiff atop their heads and littered with rhinestones, baby's-breath-and-pink-rose corsages pinned to their pushed-up boobs; every boy in identical penguin-y black tuxedos, patent leather shoes, hair gel, way too much cologne. Everyone too stiff; some people obviously already drunk; some people continuing to touch up their makeup as they walk toward the door, dates awkwardly holding their purses.

It reminds me of Tens—the smells and the show, the promise of sex in the air—and I can't help but giggle.

Camille Allen catches my eye and pauses at the entrance, swaying her pin-straight hair over her shoulder, straightening her pearls. She leans over to Carly and Taylor, whispering, too loudly, "Guess some bitches can't take the hint and not show up where they don't belong."

Carly and Taylor crack up, clutching matching pink handbags

with matching French-manicured hands. Camille continues, "Which would be pretty much anywhere."

Back off, bitch. The words, scrawled across my yearbook picture. On my locker. I gasp, understanding—she wanted me to back off from Keri, from Jeremy, from the precarious balance of popular life. Maybe she thought she was doing Keri a favor.

As she turns away to walk inside, still smirking, I burst out:

"Hey, Camille."

She turns back to me, hand planted on her hip. "What?"

"You're right," I say, feeling the *urge* grip my throat, needing to say it again, and again. "You're right. You're right." I pause, clench my fists, blink six times. "I shouldn't have come. Because some *bitches* actually don't *want* to belong in a place where people like you *do.*" There's tittering laughter from the crowd of people around me. I catch a glimpse of Camille's face as she turns away—nostrils flared, glossy lips set in a straight, hard line—and she and her army advance into the grating blare and glare of Prom World.

The thought of it—my own classmate, threatening me, going to such lengths to terrify me—brings the *urge* back. The need: to *tap tap tap tap tap tap.* People are looking, watching, but I can't control it, can't help myself now. They will all know what I am. They've always known: Penelope Marin, thigh tapper, word repeater, all-around freak.

Just as I'm feeling all my will drain away—my will to be here, to participate, to not *back off*—Flynt's fingers wrap around my own, his thumb rubbing gently along the lines in my palm. "You wanna just skip straight to the after-party?" he asks, trying to keep his voice light. "That's the best part, anyway."

"Yes." Relief breaks through my chest like a wave and suddenly it hits me, what I've just done. I just told off Camille Allen in front of half the junior class. And it felt great. "The after-party is exactly what I need."

*   *   *   *

"Follow me," Flynt says, whisking me off the stairs, weaving us between soccer fields one and two, past the little stream that marks the end of Carver's campus, always clogged with crumpled metal soda cans. It's fully dark now, moon low and yellow behind the silhouetted trees, as we follow the stream a few hundred feet to where it ends, to the beginning of a little bridge across a slightly wider river, this one clear, slick with glassy water and twisting reeds.

He grips my left hand tighter as we step across the wooden planks of the bridge. I can smell the water below us, a warm wind lifting it to us, tiny molecules of wet and grass and the memory of recent sunlight.

The *bump-bump* of prom is still audible in the distance when we reach a small rusty watchtower at the end of the bridge. Its door is slightly ajar. Flynt reaches his arm over my shoulder and pushes the door open farther. I *tap tap tap, banana* softly but not so softly that Flynt won't hear. He already knows about my rituals. Still, I turn to him, cheeks flushed, anxious for a moment. But he just smiles at me and motions me inside.

I gasp as I enter—a woven blanket is spread across the floor, a kerosene lamp burning beside it, reflecting orangey shadows against the grate set up by the little window with a view of the river below. I turn to him, wide-mouthed, unable, for the moment, to speak.

Thankfully, he speaks for me: "I thought this was more our style," he says. His voice is low and soft.

"But how did you . . . find this? And set it up?"

He smiles shyly. "I did a little research. Turns out Gretchen's cousin grew up in Lakewood, and he told me about this place, and how to get here."

"Flynt—you're—"

But he cuts me off before I can say, *absolutely utterly impossibly amazing.* "I have another surprise for you, Queen P."

He turns to the wall, lifting a hulking square object over to me—a canvas.

A painting of a girl.

Smooth, newspaper-mâché skin, tiny twigs painted black for eyelashes, smudged, dark coffee grinds streaming around her face for hair, red flower petals for lips, neck and torso a collection of soft yellow-green leaves and scraps of colorful fabric, in the crook of her pale arm, a cityscape shadow in charcoal. A moon hangs in the background, reflecting against her hair in small, perfect triangles of glass.

It's, without a doubt, the most beautiful thing I've ever seen in my life. My chest begins to rise and fall, heart beating so fast, understanding. "It's me!"

"My major new work." He bites his lip. "Do you like it?"

"It's—it's incredible, Flynt. I—I can't believe you made this for me."

"I made it from the sketch I drew that night, when you fell asleep on my couch. You looked so beautiful. You *look* so beautiful, right now. You—you are so beautiful, Penelope."

I stare back at the girl in the painting, at myself, through Flynt's eyes, and then see something in the lower left corner—a signature—*Aaron Benjamin Greeley.*

"Aaron Benjamin Greeley?" I ask, confused.

Flynt smiles nervously. "Aaron Greeley, at your service." He bows, with a little flourish of his hand.

I think of Sapphire and Oren, then. They never got the chance to tell each other who they really were—she never knew his name, was never able to find him. But *I* can; Flynt—*Aaron*—and I can. We get the chance they never had—to be together, to know each other, good and bad.

All of it.

Flynt kneels beside me on the blanket and our knees touch and our arms touch—tingles run up and down my body—and the sounds of prom—a slow, twinkly song now—reach us from the distance.

"Aaron Benjamin Greeley," I say, my voice catching in my throat, "this night is perfect." Our eyes meet, and we're both smiling. "The best anti-prom ever."

"I still don't know your middle name," he points out.

"It's Riley," I answer. "My mom's maiden name. It was my brother's middle name, too."

"Well, Penelope Riley Marin," he says—marble eyes, soft lips shining in the sheet of moon, flooding through the porthole window; the river gushes below us, the floor smooth beneath us, the air humming, winging warm, grass, wet. "I have to confess, there *is* one regular-prom tradition I was really looking forward to."

Our eyes burn into each other, comets speeding light through the dark.

And then—moving his long, clean fingers around my waist and pulling me closer to his pine, his clove, his grass, his snow, his light—he kisses me.

E N D

ACKNOWLEDGMENTS

There are too many people to thank, I think, and too many ways to thank them. So, know this list is bare-bones, an incomplete account of gratitudes.

Lexa Hillyer and Lauren Oliver: for making everything about this book possible; for patience, generosity, wild brilliance; for thoughtful, to-the-point, incisive edits that helped make every sentence tighter and better; and, for believing in my writing in the first place, for which I am—truly—humbled, grateful.

Stephen Barbara at Foundry Media for helping this book find a home, and Greg Ferguson at Egmont, for being that very kind, very welcoming home.

My parents, Sharon and Donn (who had the third 'n' removed), who taught me how to be a decent person, who have loved and supported me through all variety of phase, whim, wanderlust, who continue to read my weird stories even when they don't get them, and who always told me as a teenager: call us if you've been drinking. It doesn't matter what time it is. We'll pick you up.

All past and present residents of the Hatz: for being my friends, and roommates; for dinner-making, and movie-watching, for all other (enumerable) joy-making activities; for always helping me to understand that things are actually pretty good most of the time, especially when they get weird.

Amanda "Mongie" Powell: Man, Mang-O, you's my Scandal-monger, my muse, you know that?

Ruby Tuesday L-Snyder: for travels to exotic lands, for always listening, for never judging.

And, Steve Waltien: for being my big Spoon, and, really, truly, for loving me. You're really tall, and really funny, and I love you big time, for more reasons than those I just listed.